HULLMETAL GIRLS

HULL METAL GIRLS

EMILY SKRUTSKIE

DELACORTE PRESS

Visit us on the Web! GetUnderlined.com

Educators and librarians, for a variety of teaching tools, visit us at RHTeachersLibrarians.com

Library of Congress Cataloging-in-Publication Data
Name: Skrutskie, Emily, author.
Title: Hullmetal girls / Emily Skrutskie.
Description: First edition. | New York : Delacorte Press, [2018] |
Summary: Aisha Un-Haad, seventeen, and Key Tanaka, eighteen, have risked everything for new lives as mechanically enhanced soldiers, and when an insurrection forces dark secrets to surface, the fate of humanity is in their hands.
Identifiers: LCCN 2017038325 | ISBN 978-1-5247-7019-8 (hc) |
ISBN 978-1-5247-7021-1 (el)
Subjects: | CYAC: Soldiers—Fiction. | Cyborgs—Fiction. |
Insurrection—Fiction. | Science fiction.
Classification: LCC PZ7.1.S584 Hul 2018 | DDC [Fic]—dc23

The text of this book is set in 11-point Apolline.
Interior design by Stephanie Moss

Printed in the United States of America
10 9 8 7 6 5 4 3 2 1
First Edition

To the *Kung Fu Panda 2* soundtrack

CHAPTER 1

AISHA

In the quiet of the early morning, before the *Reliant*'s lights begin to glow, I plan two funerals.

The first is for my little brother. Amar lies in the far corner of the room, a mask over his face to keep him from breathing his affliction into the rest of us. He's mercifully asleep, and part of me hopes he'll stay that way until I leave. With the wasting fever's claws in his tiny body, he needs every moment of rest he can get. His funeral—*if it happens, if the worst happens, if I fail*—will be a proper Ledic ceremony. A temple service, a reading from the scripture, a procession to the airlock. Prayers for his soul's journey following him into the vacuum of space.

The second funeral is my own. All it takes is the scratch of my initials at the bottom of a datapad. There will be no service, no scripture, no procession for me. If I don't survive the procedure, my body will be incinerated before anyone has a chance to pray over it. There's an option to return a portion of the ashes to the *Reliant*, but there are no half measures with a true Ledic burial. I've accepted that I'll never get one.

"Aisha?" I turn to the door, where my aunt Yasmin stands silhouetted by the light in the hall. Her hair is loose from its usual plait, and it makes her even more of a stranger than she already is. "Did you sleep?"

I shake my head, holding up the datapad. Yasmin slips into the dark of the room and pulls it out of my hands. The glow of the screen deepens the wrinkles at the edge of her eyes and swells the dark bags beneath them.

When she reaches the end of the page, she gives me a sharp look. "You're sure?"

I flinch. Of course I'm not sure. Of course I'm scared to pieces. Ever since I showed up on her doorstep mere hours ago, she's been asking variants on the same question. *Aren't there other options? Is this really what Amar needs? You know there's no coming back from this, right?*

My empty stomach keens, and I swallow back the sour taste in my throat. Fasting to conserve money for Amar bled easily enough into fasting for the surgery. Between that and the recent recruiting drive, it almost feels like fate. Providence. A sign I'm meant to walk down this path. None of that is enough to pull the fear out of my heart.

So I'll just have to do it scared. "This is everything you'll need to get the first payments," I say, nodding to the datapad. "And instructions for if . . ."

A glance at the corner of the room finishes the sentence I can't bring myself to end. Silence settles over us, broken only by the slight noises of Amar breathing against the mask and the deeper, ever-present hum of starship machinery.

"Aisha," Yasmin starts.

I sink my face in my hands, my fingers pushing back the edge of my headscarf. "Don't," I breathe. There are no better options, and even if there were, there wouldn't be time to take them. At the rate Amar's illness is progressing, he'll be sent into quarantine aboard the starship *Panacea* before any treatment I can afford will take hold. And if he goes into quarantine, he won't survive it. I can't let Yasmin sway me.

But instead of wheedling, her voice drops low and urgent. "There's something I need your help with. After you're . . ."

This morning is filled with sentences we can't seem to finish. I pull my hands down over my mouth, breathing out my nose into the space between my fingers. Wariness tugs at me, nudging through the quiet terror that's kept me up all night. "What is it?"

In the half-light from the hall, I can't quite read her expression. My aunt purses her lips, her brows lowering. "I need you to—"

A sudden burst of coughing from the corner of the room interrupts us. I push past Yasmin, dropping to my knees at my brother's side as he shudders back into consciousness. "Easy, easy," I whisper, pulling the bottom of my headscarf up over my nose. Love and revulsion wage war inside me, but in the end I know I can't touch him.

Amar blinks slowly. His eyes are slightly gummed at the edges. Furious purple tracks run down his face, the undeniable marks of the disease etched into his skin. "Hurts," he croaks.

Yasmin's hand lands on my shoulder. "The shuttle leaves soon. I'll go get Malikah up to say good-bye."

I nod, trying to keep my breathing shallow as my heart balloons inside my chest. With no sleep and no food in my stomach, I'm struggling to grasp the reality of this moment. *This is happening,* I tell myself. *I've made my choice. I can't back down.*

Yasmin slips out the door, leaving it open so the light floods in.

Amar's eyes roll as he takes in the room—sparse décor, threadbare red drapery, the ceiling cracked in unfamiliar places. "Where are we?" he whimpers.

I clamp my free hand under my arm to keep from reaching out and brushing away the hair plastered to his sweaty forehead. "We went to Yasmin's," I tell him softly. "She's going to look after you now. She'll make sure you get better."

His face screws up with alarm. "You're leaving?"

I make soft shushing noises into the fabric of my headscarf. "I have to go. I . . ." I hesitate, stuck on how I can explain the economics of my choice to a six-year-old without sounding like I'm blaming him for what's about to happen. He's too sick for me to leave him alone anymore, but my janitor's salary isn't enough to pay for his care. "I'm taking care of the money, so you don't have to worry and Malikah doesn't have to work."

I don't specify *how* I'm taking care of things. In his feverish state, it'll only be fuel for nightmares that his weakened body might not be able to handle. It's best for him to rest now, which means it's best I get out of here fast. I bow my head, breathing out a soft prayer as Amar's eyelids droop.

"I'll come back as soon as I can," I promise him. "I'll just . . . I'll just be a little taller."

They take Pascao into the surgery before me, and fifteen minutes later, they're wheeling out his broken, twisted body.

He's the fourth person to die today, but the first I remembered to pray for. Guilt hums through me, and I duck my head as the gurney trundles past and veers down the hall to the incinerator. Pascao

4

gave up his seat for me when I arrived in the overcrowded waiting room. He helped me read the orientation docs, filling in the places where my vocabulary failed and puzzling with me over what things like *purity of integration* and *biostasis* meant. He smiled a lot, and he was volunteering for similar reasons—a family in need, a sense of duty. I tell myself that's why I prayed for him.

I'm lying, though. If those were my reasons, I'd be muttering strains for everyone in this line. With unrest growing in the Fleet and a slew of Fractionist rebels arrested just last week, the General Body has launched a recruitment drive. The waiting room is crowded with desperate people answering the call, and every single person here runs the same risk as Pascao.

But I prayed for the old man because I needed the distraction. It isn't even fair of me to call him "old man." He certainly isn't anywhere near the ideal recruitment age, but he's only in his late forties. *Was* only in his late forties when they tried to strap an exo-rig on him and it snapped him in half. I prayed for him because *I'm* next in line.

But prayer can't do anything for the Godless grip of Scela machinery.

The techs beckon me toward the surgery doors, and bile rises in my throat. I stand, swaying slightly, and for a moment I'm terrified my legs will give out before I can even make it out of the waiting room. *It's for Amar. It's for Malikah. The salary will pay for medicine and food and shelter with Yasmin, and my siblings will never know how cruel the* Reliant *can be to kids with nothing left.*

The thought steadies me. My purpose is unshakable.

Hollow gazes follow me as I set off toward the point of no return. Only the desperate volunteer to become Scela, signing away their bodies and their autonomy to the General Body's command. I used to wonder how desperate someone would have to be to make that pact, knowing that in all likelihood they'd end up twisted and broken like Pascao. That willingness is rare enough that there's barely a prescreening beforehand. A few quick tests when I checked into the ward confirmed that my body was healthy and my muscles could weather the procedure. It could have been even faster—with one look at my hands, roughened from years of working deck janitorial, they'd find everything they needed to know about my mettle.

But the real test is on the other side of the surgery doors. So I leave my desperate fellows behind and let those doors whisper shut at my back as I enter the last place I'll ever be fully human.

The surgery is sparse and stark, pared down to only the essentials and scrubbed unnaturally clean. My gaze fixes on the saddle sitting in the middle of the room, riddled with restraints for every part of my body they could possibly tie down. A red-tinged drain is embedded in the floor beneath it. Even though the room smells horribly of antiseptic, I can still catch a bit of the raw iron scent of blood in the air. I cringe, thinking of Pascao's smiling eyes, of his soul's unmooring in this very seat.

My gaze turns up to find the thing that did it. The exorig gleams in the bright lights, its surface wet with the chemicals used to wipe away any trace of its last victim. The length of its spine curls over on itself like a massive metallic insect. It's suspended over the saddle, and there's something taunting about the low hum of the room's machinery. *Are you the one?* it seems to ask. *Are you the one who'll survive me?*

A technician takes my arm, startling me back into the moment.

He flips my hand palm-up so he can strap on a diagnostic bracelet. The device is lined with microspikes that prick into my skin, sampling my blood, assessing my condition one final time. "You'll have to take that off," he says, nodding to my headscarf.

I reach up for the pins that hold it in place, but my fingers fumble when I try to pull them out. Devoted Ledics cover their hair as the scripture suggests, but I was never really devoted until my parents passed into God's care. I thought that if I was faithful to the letter of the old texts, it would ease their souls' journeys after being ripped so violently from their bodies. Taking it off now feels like an insult to their memory, but I know I don't have a choice. I finally tug the pins free with shaking hands and slowly unravel the fabric until my hair spills out.

I feel lighter. A new shard of guilt plunges into my stomach, joining the tepid mix already brewing there. *I'm doing this for the right reasons,* I remind myself. *Nothing happens without sacrifice.*

"Aisha Un-Haad, seventeen years old, from starship *Reliant,* Seventh District?" The tech's voice is nasal and monotone, as if he's numb to the horror of this room.

I nod. I haven't fully processed that I'm not in Seventh District anymore, that I've shipped all the way from the rear of the Fleet to its head. The smooth hum of this First District ship's machinery is a constant reminder that I'm miles away from the *Reliant* and everything I've ever known. Even the air on this ship is different—crisper, colder, cut with chemicals that sterilize it.

The technician plucks my scarf from my hands and tosses it into a cart pushed up against the wall that I overlooked while I was fixated on the exorig. Beneath it, I catch the glint of a watch, a fine silver chain, a hairband. Scela aren't allowed to keep their personal effects, and the people who leave this room without an exorig won't be needing them either.

A second tech comes up behind me and starts working the back of my smock open. I flinch away from her, and she rolls her eyes. "Girlie, it won't be anything I haven't seen before," she scolds me, then goes back to tugging the ribbon that holds the garment shut. I flush when she succeeds, folding my arms over my chest as soon as she peels the smock off my shoulders and ties it off around my waist. "Honestly, you Ledics," she mutters.

I grit my teeth, swallowing the snappy reply that burns in my throat. She probably thinks I'm some sort of fundamentalist nut-job, even though no fundie would ever corrupt their body the way I'm about to. People outside our faith just like finding excuses to sneer at us.

The male technician steers me over to the saddle, and I uncross my arms reluctantly as I settle into it and lean forward against the bracing board. From the staging area outside the surgery, I heard Pascao's screams. And I heard that perfect, dreaded silence when they stopped. As the technicians wind the restraints around my arms, I press my head into the cradle and squeeze my eyes shut. Ledic faith has no prayers for body modification, so I murmur a section of the Morning Strain instead, pleading with God for peace and success on this day as the bindings winch tighter.

"We can't sedate you for this part," the female technician reminds me. Something in her voice tells me she wishes it were otherwise. I wonder how many times she's watched this process. "Neural integration relies on full consciousness," she continues. "The exo has to get to know you so it can calibrate. Kinda like a handshake. Once that's done, we'll numb you down for the rest."

A clamp settles over my head, and the saddle tilts until I'm staring at that drain in the floor. I wonder how much of me is going to end up flowing through it.

The techs wipe my back down with cloths drenched in some sort of cleaning solution. A chill sinks into my bones, and I shudder. One of the techs pulls my hair forward, twisting it together in a knot and binding it. The low buzz of a razor sculpts a bare path to my brainstem.

I have to keep telling myself that I chose this. That this is a sacrifice, but it will be rewarded. That the survival rate of wasting fever in six-year-old boys is next to nothing without treatment. With a janitor's salary, I could never afford it. With Scela money, I might. I must.

"We're ready to start," the male technician calls, and somewhere above me, machinery whirls to life. The woman crouches by my head and offers up a plastic cylinder. I'm lost for a moment, until I realize I'm supposed to bite down on it. I open my mouth, and she slips it between my teeth.

When my jaw clenches, the tears start.

The exorig above me is dripping. Warm liquid spatters across my back, but it's nothing compared to the hot tears that roll down my nose and disappear into the drain on the floor. My first libations to the rusty hole, and they're nothing but a few drops of salt water. That'll change soon.

"Lower the exo," the man demands.

Pneumatics hiss. The metal spine rolls over my own, adjusting to the length of my back as it aligns. Each of its joints corresponds to a bone. Something heavy settles at my neck, and three needles press insistently at the base of my skull. When I shift against the restraints, they edge into my skin.

"In position," the woman confirms. "All right, girlie. Once you're in, it's not giving you back. You ready?"

It's the kind of question that deserves a derisive snort, but I grunt something vaguely affirmative around the plastic in my teeth.

"Starting neural integration in three . . . two . . . one."

I tense. The exorig clenches around me, the needles drive into my flesh, and for a moment white-hot pain obliterates my mind. It's like someone's poured molten wax along my spine, molten wax that burns through my skin and seeps into my bones. Tracks of wet heat curve around my neck, my ribs, my hips. Every prayer I've ever known leaves me. My vertebrae crack as the exo delves into them and latches itself around my nerves. I bite down on the plastic cylinder until my jaw creaks.

Now my tears aren't the only things leaking into the drain.

The piece at my neck convulses, and I can feel its components rushing toward my brain, reaching out to embrace it. My mind reels as a new consciousness runs headlong into it, one that's robotic and cold and unfeeling. The spine rears up, trying to lift me from the bracing board, and I finally understand how Pascao came out of here in pieces. I fight against it, but the strength of the exo is relentless. Raw Scela power—this machine is the root of it. A scream leaks from my throat, pushing its way past the cylinder in my mouth.

This isn't a handshake. It's a headlock.

Human, human, human, my blood sings for the last time. I plummet toward the point of no return at terminal velocity.

And then something snaps into place. The integration wraps around my brain, and in that moment my mind skews machine, flooded with the understanding of the exorig as part of my body, as the new spine, the better one, the one that will make me the General Body's perfect tool. Its thoughts rush through my brain, overwhelming my own. The metal at my back relaxes, rolling me flat as the restraints slacken, and it's like coming home.

Sheer relief takes over what's left of me, pushing past the pain until my mind is filled with nothing but bliss.

"Neural integration locked," the woman confirms. "We've got one!" At the edge of my vision, I catch a glimpse of the giddy, relieved smile she shares with her colleague.

But the euphoria doesn't last long. The agony comes rushing back in tendrils that creep up my fingers. I can feel the exo fighting it inside me, trying to block it from my brain like a dragon defending its hoard. There's a war for my body and mind between the pain and the new, strange creature that's latched on to my nervous system.

Then one of the techs slides a needle into my neck, and the pain stumbles away in spurts, replaced by a numbness that spreads from my core outward until my whole body feels like it's floating. The exo seems to be the only thing unaffected—I can still feel its pulsing, crackling energy, frustrated that it's gained control over my body only to lose it to a mere drug.

Gentle hands brace my skull, and a buzz starts up behind my ear. I don't feel the razor's passes, but I see the tech carrying away a twisted black knot a few seconds later and dropping it into a bin. Now it doesn't matter that I lost my scarf—there's nothing left to cover up. Something deep in my machine-wrapped mind winces at the thought, but it's barely a twinge against the unyielding peace in the rest of my head.

The techs loosen the bindings and lift me up out of the saddle, carrying me over to the waiting gurney. I'm laid out carefully on my stomach, my head lolling to the side as we start to wheel forward. Not back to the waiting room, like Pascao's twisted remains, but deeper into the suite, out of the first operating room and into a sleek, dark chamber where a surgery tank waits.

One of the techs unties the smock and shucks me out of it, but I don't mind. Might be the drugs. Might be the exo. Might be both. Might be neither. Maybe the pain of the integration has made me realize there are more important things than covering myself up.

Another twinge. The familiar, sickening aftertaste of guilt on my tongue. It washes away on my next breath.

The technicians lift me gingerly off the gurney, position me inside the tank, and start to fill it with a thick, clear gel. I remember reading about this part of the procedure in the orientation docs. The gel's meant to keep most of my blood inside me and help with the massive undertaking of healing my body once the surgeons' knives are done slicing me up and remaking me. The parts of me I'm sure are *me* are ambivalent about it.

The exo is thrilled. It can't wait for my new body, a body that will match the Scela power that the neural integration begs for. It whispers to me in time with my heartbeat, a steady hiss of *I'm alive, I'm alive, I'm alive.* And as the gel folds over me and one of the techs pushes a breathing tube past my unfeeling lips, I whisper back, *I will be the General Body's weapon. I've paid my price, and I will be paid in turn. I will save Amar. I will save Malikah.*

When the surgeons come in, when the steady hands start the work of my unmaking, I let that hope curdle inside my chest, let it distance me from the sight of my body being flayed and broken and reshaped. My flesh peels back. My bones are sawed and spaced and lengthened. Endoscopes burrow through me, paving metal highways along my skeleton, weaving matrices of nanofibers through my muscles, sewing new circuitry into my nerves. Ports blossom from my skin, promising a place in my anatomy for the metal rig that will make me nigh unstoppable. The surgeons work with careful precision, all too aware of what they're crafting, leaning over me with something like holy reverence in their eyes.

Bit by bit, I become more than human.

Bit by bit, I am made Scela.

CHAPTER 2

KEY

I wake. Or maybe the voice inside my head does. Something hauls me back into hazy consciousness, my awareness dampened by enough drugs to drop a horse. The world glows outside my eyelids, but I keep them shut. No bright lights. Not yet.

My brain feels like a second mind has thrown down bags inside it and made itself at home. A mechanical hum rattles my bones. I can't remember if it belongs there.

"Miss Tanaka?" The voice is older. Male. Walking on eggshells.

I snort, because it's hilarious. *Miss* Tanaka—what part of me deserves anything remotely close to the word *Miss*? Maybe the old Key Tanaka. The First District sweetheart. Not what she's become.

Apparently the snort is answer enough, because the guy keeps talking. "You're coming out of Scela conversion surgery."

No shit.

Well—

On the one hand, that's definitely what's happened to my body, and it explains a little of what's going on in my head. But there's still something *off* about all this, and an ache prickles at my temples as I try to grasp what that *off*ness is.

"You're going to find movement very difficult during the first few hours of consciousness." I try to give him an earned gesture, but it only confirms what he's saying—I can't lift a single finger. "This is perfectly normal. It's all part of your neural integration getting to know you. The exo is a conduit of will, and it has to get used to processing *your* will specifically, as it relates to your body. We'll be monitoring you very closely for the next two weeks, and we'll make sure you know if anything is wrong."

I decide to risk cracking an eye open, which seems to be within my body's abilities. The guy leaning over me doesn't look quite like what I expected. My eye struggles to focus as I try to give him a once-over. He seems to be in his late thirties, and he has the look of someone who grew up in one of the frontend districts. Polished, poised, put together—with the notable exception of the tattoos covering his arms where they aren't sheathed by the sleeves of his lab coat. Not artwork, but text. Like he's been taking notes on his skin. I squint, trying to make out the words against his dark complexion, but my vision is still hazy.

He bends down, pries back my eyelid with a finger, and shines a light on my pupil. I make a strangled, startled noise, but I can't force my mouth around the unkind words I want to spit at him.

"Calm down," he soothes. Like the words *calm down* have ever had their intended effect on anybody.

I try to relax anyway. Better not get on his bad side while my muscles are still useless. He turns to make a note on his datapad with a jolting, uneven step, and my gaze drops down to his legs. His right one is cased in a brace that starts at his hip and ends at his ankle. When he turns back around, he catches the line of my sight. "Don't get any ideas," he warns, smiling in a way that makes him look boyish. "A particularly rowdy, newly converted Scela did that. He panicked, and I got a shattered femur for my troubles. Promise me you won't give me a matched set, okay?"

Guess that explains the bedside manner. My mouth finally feels like cooperating, and I take a deep breath, ready to tell him exactly where he can shove his easy charisma.

But then the *thing* on my back wakes. Its vengeance slams down on my brainstem like a hydraulic press. For a moment I lose my body, lose any sense of the person Key Tanaka is supposed to be— I'm nothing. Machinery in the hands of the exo. And then it's over, and my lips mumble nothing but a quiet, hoarse "Okay."

Something's definitely wrong with my mouth, but it goes beyond the exo wrenching my control of it away. My teeth don't set the way they used to. I run my sluggish tongue over the wrongness. The ridges of my molars feel too sharp, their edges too smooth. I don't know what to make of the change.

The doctor doesn't seem to notice my discomfort. "Name's Dr. Ikande. But please, call me Isaac," he says. "I'm head of Medical on the *Dread*, so you'll see me around a fair bit." His mention of the ship triggers my memory at last. I'm on the starship *Dread*, First District, and before that I was on—

The exo burns a warning into my nervous system that swats me back into the present. I want to lash out, fight back, do *something*, but I don't even know how to go about confronting this strange beast woven into my nervous system.

"I'm Key," I announce, mostly because the exo seems to think it'd be polite. I'm surprised to find that the choice to speak is mine and mine alone. From the way it's been shoving me around, I thought that the exo was calling the shots. But its forceful suggestions are just suggestions. Only I can tell my mouth to move.

"You're doing great so far, Key. Around now, you're going to start getting some sensation back in your toes. See if you can wiggle them."

I can. The exo basically does it for me. Nothing about the slight motion twitching the bottom of the sheets feels the way toe wiggling used to feel. It's like the orders to control my body have to get processed through the machinery strapped to my back before they get sent all the way down my nerves. I guess this is what Isaac meant by "conduit of will."

I feel my muscles flex. Feel the gentle tug of sheets over my skin. There's something a little terrifying about it. Wiggling my toes didn't use to feel like it might snap my bones.

"Very good," Isaac says. It sounds like the sort of thing that should be condescending but isn't when it comes out of a mouth that's probably done this a hundred times or more. "Fingers?"

It's easier now that I know what to expect. I test my control, twitching my index, middle, ring, and pinky fingers on each hand. Then I try out the gesture I wanted to flash earlier, plowing past the exo's buzz of protest.

Isaac smirks, but he seems unfazed. Judging by the brace on his leg, he's dealt with worse from recently converted Scela. "Looks like you're on track. When you feel comfortable, start experimenting with your arms." He sits back on a stool, his fingers flicking over his datapad. He tips the screen for me to see, and I watch the readouts jump and jolt with every impulse I feed my new muscles. "During post-op, we monitor your head directly—makes it easy to ensure that the new connections are working," Isaac says, turning the charts back toward himself. "Plus it helps us stack you up against the other new Scela."

The notion digs into me like a spur, and I clench my fists hard, pulses of sensation throbbing up into my wrists. The commands my nerves send flow through the exo, but my hands are starting to feel more *mine*. Next come my elbows. I lift my forearms off the bed but falter before I can get them more than an inch in the air. I grit my mismatched teeth and try again.

For the first time, I can see my body. As I raise my arms into view, I take in what the conversion has done to me. My forearms are striped with bright red lines where my flesh has been resealed around the enhancements woven into my muscles. Ridges of metal run parallel to my lengthened bones. Ports stick out around my joints, begging for the attachments that will let me use the full potential of my Scela power. My flesh bulges in awkward places, betraying the machinery beneath my carved-up skin.

The more I look, the more wrong it feels. My mind goes flimsy as buried thoughts hack their way toward the surface. I process the sight of my body, I think of what I know, and the exo helps me ground myself in the facts.

I know who I am. I know my name is Key Tanaka. That I'm eighteen years old, most of those years spent on the starship *Antilles,* First District. I know this puts me at the top of the Fleet's pecking order, and I know how much I enjoy that. I remember zero-G galas, beautiful dresses, a life of the best things our wandering ways could offer.

I remember our Fleet's mission. The seven tiers of ships, three hundred years of history at our backs, searching for a planet to call home.

I remember my parents. Cold, distant, but never unkind beyond reason.

I know myself. I know who I was before my mind got crossed with a machine.

But I can't, for the life of me, remember why I did this.

The thought feels like missing a step—there's no memory to catch me, and by the time the exo's *strongly* suggesting I think about something else, I'm already too far gone. I don't have any memories of before the surgery. No memories of the conversion itself. No justification for why I'm lying in a ward bed. What brought me here? I close my eyes, trying to block out the new feelings itching up my legs, grasping for the reasons I ended up this way. *Why* did I do this?

I come up empty. There's nothing there. No explanation for the metal and fiber laced into my biology.

I can't remember why I became Scela.

Isaac notices I've stopped testing my limbs. "Something wrong?" he asks, his demeanor still pleasant.

What do I tell him? *Do* I tell him? "I don't remember . . . ," I start.

"That can happen sometimes," he says. His eyes are already back on his datapad. "The drugs we use post-integration have to be powerful enough to subdue both you and the exo."

"But I can't remember the start of my surgery," I counter, my voice growing stronger. "I don't even remember deciding to take the metal."

"It's unusual, but not unheard of. The orientation docs they gave you gloss over that part, unfortunately." The exo urges me to notice the hint of terseness in his voice. A lie? A deflection, at minimum. Something's off. And I don't remember any *docs* anyway.

I push myself upward far too fast, my hyperpowered muscles nearly catapulting me from the bed as I wrap my arms around my head. I'm vaguely aware of Isaac shrinking back, no doubt worried he's risking another snapped bone. "Easy, easy. Deep breaths, Key," he suggests.

But all I can really focus on is the unnatural—*natural,* the exo insists—protrusions around my head, the bracing supports sprouting from my shoulders that keep it upright despite the massive weight situated at the back of my skull. I run my fingers over the ports embedded in my chin, in my cheekbones, all places for larger equipment. Equipment that will turn me into a monster—*a tool*—for the General Body to wield at will.

The drugs have cleared from my blood. The frantic nudges from the *thing* on my back aren't enough to keep my panic pinned down. My breathing doubles, triples in speed, and Isaac hits a button on his datapad that dims the lights as he retreats to the other end of the room, pressing his back against the door.

"Key," he warns. "I can knock you out through the monitoring software, but that's something I'd really rather not do when your integration is so new. Try to focus on relaxing your muscles—it's not good to stress them like this so early. You can shred them if you winch them too tight too fast."

He has a soothing voice. I wish it did something for me. There's too much chaos, too much noise, too many blank spaces in who I am. The scream builds in my lungs, rattling out between my teeth as I dig my fingernails into the flesh of my forearms. The exo tries valiantly to talk me down, but I fight its noise, straining against the strings that control my muscles. If I had the strength for it, I'd rip the damn machine right off my back. I don't want it in me. I don't want the presence in my mind, urging my fingers to loosen. I don't want this thing to keep me from destroying it. I'll take it out with me if I have to.

My muscles lock, and suddenly I feel more than just the darkness of the room creeping over my vision. My eyes roll, finding Isaac furiously swiping at his datapad.

"I'm sorry. I'm so sorry," he says.

My vision fades, the holes in me growing until they consume me. Until I'm nothing but an empty girl, more holes than substance, and somehow in my last second of consciousness, before the darkness overtakes me, I feel . . .

I feel right.

CHAPTER 3
AISHA

I'm six days into my life as a Scela and flat on the floor of my recovery room.

Please, I beg God, beg my exo, beg myself. *Please just let . . . let me . . .* I'm not even sure what I'm asking for. Ever since I woke up in this unfamiliar body, I've been floundering for control. Yesterday I thought I made solid progress—I took my first steps.

Today it feels like it would be a miracle if I could even lift a finger. I'm trapped in a five-hundred-pound, seven-foot-tall rag doll, seething through my teeth as I roll my face over the cool linoleum. Getting off the floor feels as unlikely as the Fleet finding a habitable world, and being ready to start basic by the end of the two-week observation seems mathematically impossible.

I'd settle for just quiet and stillness, but my body won't even let me have that. As a human, I could forget about my breathing and my heartbeat. But as a Scela, I'm constantly assaulted with the facts of my existence. I can't tune out the exo—in some ways, the exo *is* me. Its thought process is woven so tightly into my own that sometimes I can't tell us apart.

I press my palm down on the floor, mutter a strain of scripture, and suddenly it's starkly clear that the exo is *not* me and never will be. Religion, I've quickly discovered, is an alien concept to the machine on my back. It can see the logic of having something to believe in, but the notion of faith escapes it entirely. It wants concrete facts. Clear causality.

It doesn't want *me*. And I can't escape that—not when it's sewn through my biology in a way that can never be undone.

But if I can't get my feet under me, I'm useless as a Scela, and then my sacrifice will have been for nothing. At ten years old, Malikah will have to take up the burden I've been carrying since fifteen, and no ten-year-old should have to carry a family on her back. No fifteen-year-old should have to, either, but Seventh District isn't the kind of place that has anything left to spare when your life unravels in the span of an afternoon.

Yasmin wasn't an option back then. Growing up, I felt like I only knew my aunt in the ways she contrasted my mother. She was severe and standoffish to my mother's bright warmth, atheistic to her unshakable faith, cautious to her cheerful flirtatiousness. They'd always kept their distance from each other, but just a few weeks before the riots that changed everything, Yasmin had come by. I watched from a crack in the door as my mother and her sister spoke in hurried whispers that slowly became louder until my mother was shoving Yasmin away, warning her to never come near our family again. I never found out what they fought about. All I knew was that after that day, my mother made each of us swear on the temple to never talk to Yasmin again. From then on, my aunt was a stranger, a ghost, a memory.

When we lost our parents less than a month later, I did everything in my power to keep us away from our aunt's door. There were times when I almost caved. When the money was thin, when the orphanage Yasmin runs loomed over me on my walk to work. Every time, my vow to my mother burned in my veins. I had sworn. I had sworn on the *temple*.

But on the night those purple tracks showed up on Amar's forehead, I finally gave up. I went to her door with Malikah on my heels and Amar swaddled in a sheet, cradled in my arms. I begged and bargained, my oath crumbling to dust, and I promised God I would do everything in my power to justify breaking it. And the next morning, I was on a shuttle to the *Dread,* begging for absolution with a hand pressed against its hullmetal.

My sacrifice has to be rewarded. I summon every drop of willpower in me and urge my arms to push against the floor. Instead, my muscles snap taut, straining against every new fiber and wire and support strut woven through them. I clamp my teeth together and let out a snarl that sputters into a low, frustrated groan.

This can't be happening. I didn't survive the integration and conversion just to be reduced to a useless, fuming beast. I try to calm my mind with a prayer, but the exo's thoughts spiral through my own. *It's not hullmetal you're praying against, it's a linoleum floor, and anyway, prayer against hullmetal is derived from the old engineers' practice of listening at the ships' walls to identify mechanical failures. God isn't going to push you up off this—*

"Stop," I hiss out loud. "Stop it, stop, stop, st—"

The recovery room's door swings open, and Isaac sweeps in, crouching unsteadily at my side as two of his juniors follow in his wake. "Good morning, Aisha," he says. His voice is calm, but both of the assistants behind him maintain a wary distance.

"Hi," I reply flatly.

"The call button is there for a reason."

I frown at the little red trigger that's been taped to my wrist. I shouldn't need it. I was *walking* yesterday. "Doesn't . . . make any sense," I grind out.

"Recovery isn't always a linear process," Isaac says. He shifts to stretch out his braced leg, leaning forward to balance on his knee. "You had a really good day yesterday, and that's great, but you have to get used to working with the exo if you want to keep improving. Remember, we talked through this. You're giving orders *to* the exo, and the exo—"

"—tells my body what to do. I know. I *know*. But then I try, and . . ." I heave again, floundering for the right way to "order" the exo. I was never the kind of person who *gave* orders when I was human, so it's no wonder I'm lost on how to do it as a Scela. Something clicks just enough that I'm able to get myself propped up on my elbows, but I can't hold on to it and end up stuck, my head drooping forward between my shoulder blades in a way that pulls uncomfortably at the support struts balancing its massive weight on my shoulders. And *that* just reminds me of all the other metal laced through my biology, of the exorig clamped onto my spine, of the way a wicked ridge now rises out of my split, shaved skull—

"*Aisha,*" Isaac warns, and I realize I've started seething again. "I don't want to hook you back into the monitor, but if you keep stressing yourself like this—"

"Sir?" A third assistant pokes his head through the door. "Sorry, but the glitchy one's acting out again, and—"

Isaac scrambles to his feet, pushing up his glasses to rub at his eyes. "Spirits, this batch, I swear. Help her back into bed," he orders the other two juniors, before limping out of the room without another word.

The juniors move to grab my arms, but I let out a deep, savage

25

snarl that sends them skittering back and earns me a little ping of approval from the exo. "Sorry," I whisper. "Please, just … I want to do this on my own."

One hesitates. The other sets her hand on his shoulder. "One more shot," she says, a tremulous note of encouragement in her voice.

I let out a long, slow breath, thankful that at least *that's* still as easy as … well, breathing. My eyes drop shut, and I turn my thoughts toward the exo on my back. I can feel the machine scrutinizing me, weighing and measuring, trying to decide if I add up to a worthy vessel.

I think about what I want to do. About giving orders. When I was a janitor on the *Reliant*'s intership deck, I did nothing but *follow* the instructions I was given. Authority was never a part of the job description.

But I wasn't just a janitor. I was the oldest child, too.

I think of every time Amar threw a tantrum. Every time Malikah tried to stay up reading into the darkest hours of the night. Every time I had to act as a substitute parent, wrangling my brother's rambunctious energy and my sister's unstoppable mind. It didn't feel natural at first, but I worked up to it.

The exo seems bemused by my thought process. *You think controlling a Scela body is like chasing down a six-year-old? Like telling a girl to get dressed for temple?*

I don't bother to counter it. Instead, I breathe deeply, hold those memories in the part of my head that's still *mine*, and *push*.

My torso lifts smoothly off the ground. I pull my knees underneath me, then push again, trying my best to ignore the awkward length of my limbs and the twinge of artificial muscles still settling into place. With a heave that feels monumental enough to knock a starship out of its tier, I rise to my feet.

A grin breaks over my face, uncontrollably wide thanks to the augmentations. I can do this. I can command my body, be the perfect tool I was sculpted into, earn my place in the Scela ranks. I can carry the weight of the exo on my back—it's nothing compared to what I've borne already.

I may not be a useful Scela yet. But I will be *damned* if I'm not a useful sister.

The door swings open with a rush of warm air from the corridor. At first I ignore it. It's just Isaac, here to run more tests and tell me again that *No, the* Dread *is kept under a communications lockdown and there's no way to contact your family.*

Except that it isn't. It's my fourteenth day as Scela, the last in the recovery ward. My exo does the initial processing, scooping the audio from my ears and urging me to notice that the footfalls are far heavier than those of anyone who's entered this room in the past few days. I roll over and find myself face to face with a towering Scela woman. For a moment, panic drenches me, a knee-jerk reaction to spotting a Scela. My human remnants go live with fear that I'm about to be evicted, that they've come to take my siblings away. But the exo calms me. With a soft nudge, it reminds me that I'm Scela too. This woman is my kind. We belong to the same world.

But we're not the same—not even close. Everything about her screams easy confidence with her hyperpowered body. She wears the metal of the full rig, each port in her skin melded to pistons and armor that turn her into a walking tank. Her platinum-blond hair is cleaved in half by the exo's ridge protruding from the top of her skull. The rest of it is tied back in a braid that weaves around her enhancements. This woman looks like she could tear a starship in half.

I feel like an infant next to her, and the fuzz on my skull isn't helping.

"Marshal Gwen Jesuit, head of basic," she says, extending a hand for me to shake. I stand and take it, surprised at how my grip matches hers. After two weeks of Isaac's and his assistants' cautious distance, two weeks away from my siblings for the first time in my life, I'm starved for contact. A handshake shouldn't be overwhelming, but it hits me somewhere deep in my chest. The exo scoffs, herding me away from the sensation.

In her other hand is a bundle of clothes. "Brought you your training gear. Report to Gym Deck in ten minutes." Processing her request, the exo starts a little countdown. She foists the bundle into my hands and turns for the door.

"I don't know where that—" I start, but before I get a chance to finish, Marshal Jesuit knocks her knuckles into the side of her exo.

"Ship's layout is all up here. Let it do the thinking."

A wary prickling runs up my spine, but the exo is quick to soothe it, reminding me that this is exactly what I signed up for when I became a living weapon. The second Marshal Jesuit closes the door, I shuck out of my loose smock and sweats.

The jumpsuit she's given me seems intimidatingly complicated. The garment is covered with vents that line up with my ports, and the shoulders are a mess of straps that, as far as I can tell, are supposed to go *under* the support struts that balance the exo's weight. The exo itself nudges me in the right direction, suggesting just how

I should move my fingers to finagle the clasps. It takes three of my countdown's minutes to make sure I've got everything on right.

Then I try the door. At last, it opens when I turn the handle, and for once the thoughts between the exo and me slip into perfect harmony as a quiet thrill overtakes me.

I want to *run*. My muscle control has locked in, and with joy crackling through my nerves, there's nothing holding me back. I bare my teeth in a grin and take off down the hall, blowing past Isaac as he limps out of what looks to be his office. "Careful!" he shouts after me. "I don't want to waste my evening rebuilding any part of your anatomy."

I wave over my shoulder as I barrel around the corner.

A quick consultation of the ship's schematics in my exo reveals that Gym Deck is right around the corner from Medical. A few more turns and I'm there, with three minutes to spare. When I enter Gym Deck itself, the part of my brain that's still from a Seventh District ship immediately freezes. The *Reliant* had a habitat dome, a vaulted ceiling painted in an approximation of sky that looms over the buildings beneath, but I've never been in a *room* this open before. There's no attempt to hide the ceiling behind cloudy murals—it's just a crisscrossed tangle of beams dotted with blinding industrial lamps. Even with my exo whispering in my head, the unnatural space sends something primal inside me reeling for comfort, for enclosure, for cover.

I'm jolted out of my shock by a Scela girl brushing past me. She's about my age, dressed in a jumpsuit like mine, her head similarly shaved and her resealing skin similarly fresh. But unlike me, she doesn't seem to be all that impressed by the size of the room. Her dark eyes sweep over a group of Scela running in a pack at the far end of the deck. She pauses with momentary interest when she spots a group doing combat drills, then finally fixes her gaze on me.

"Aisha Un-Haad," I say, offering my hand, trying not to be overeager about it.

She doesn't take it. Straightening her back, she says, "Key Tanaka."

The exo works to suppress a tinge of embarrassment rising in me as I drop my hand. Key has a haughty tilt to her chin that can only come from a First District upbringing. I thought that kind of thing wouldn't matter once we'd been wrapped in Scela metal. The exo reassures me it doesn't, but it means very little in the face of Key's dismissal. This girl immediately saw through me, saw my backendedness, and saw that it wasn't worth it to shake my hand.

I try a different approach, my voice shakier than before. "Is this . . . How long have you been Scela?"

Key's lips part like she's about to answer the question, but a look of momentary confusion flickers across her features before any words make it out. "Probably about as long as you have," she says at last, though my exo reads what's written over her face. *She doesn't know,* it whispers, then clamps down on the shudder threatening to work its way up my spine. My exo started keeping a careful internal clock the moment it was integrated. Is a Scela's relationship with their exo not a uniform experience? Or is there something wrong with the way the exo's been threaded into my mind?

A shard of panic slices through me, but before my exo has a chance to respond, another young Scela wanders through the Gym Deck doors. He flashes a mischievous smile when he sees us, then jogs over and sticks out his hand. "Woojin Lih," he says.

Key ignores him, but I step forward and shake his hand before

30

the moment has a chance to get awkward, my skin warming sooth-ingly at the feel of his palm against mine. "Aisha Un-Haad."

His grin goes sly, and my exo points out how *human* it looks. We aren't supposed to be human anymore, but something about this boy is dancing circles around the machine strapped to his back.

It's almost repulsive, I realize. Humanness in the metal-laced boy in front of me is nothing short of unsettling, and it's not just the exo thinking that.

My wary processing is interrupted when Marshal Jesuit calls out, "Good, you three made it on time." We whirl to find her at the door with another young Scela at her side, a girl with rich brown skin. "This is Praava Ganes. She'll be the fourth member of your squad."

Praava tips her hand, her smile broad, exaggerated by the lack of fine control her enhanced muscles have over her face. Her eyes are unaffected, focused, and calculating, just the way they're meant to be. *A perfect Scela smile,* my exo thinks with approval. I grin back.

"You four are the latest Scela to make it through integration and conversion," the marshal continues.

My smile snaps shut, and I swallow, thinking of how many people passed the screening, how many people sat in that wait-ing room outside the surgery with me. Twenty? Thirty? I barely remember their faces—I was too lost in my own fear.

All those people. Four of us. I offer a quick whisper of prayer for their souls' journeys.

"Today marks the beginning of your basic training. Due to the recent uptick of Fractionist activity in the Fleet, we'll be on an ac-celerated schedule—the General Body needs good Scela in the field now more than ever. Over the course of the next month, I'll be evaluating your performance as a squad against the current Scela ranks. At the end of those twenty-eight days, you'll graduate as a functional Scela unit and begin your specialization training. What tier you specialize in will depend on your performance in basic."

My exo keeps my face neutral as a vicious tumult takes over what's left of my organic mind. There are seven tiers of Scela pay, with duties ranging from the lowest patrol to the Scela elite, who hunt down enemies of stability in the Fleet. A middling Scela salary is enough to get Amar basic care, but if we end up with a good assignment, there's an even better chance he'll survive his illness. If we end up on patrol duty . . . well, it will take some budgeting.

Maybe the Fractionist movement will help us out on that front. For the most part, they've been little more than irritants. Their demands to split up the Fleet and spread out our search for the next good world were just background noise in the form of propaganda casts that briefly overtook the channels. Easy to tune out. But occasionally their actions turn dangerous—dangerous enough to put our ships in jeopardy. Dangerous enough that the General Body wants them stopped. And just a couple weeks ago, a Scela task force arrested a Fractionist cell in one of the First District ships, proving that the movement's roots and resources were more abundant than previously thought. It got the General Body spooked, and the announcement of a Scela recruitment drive was fast to follow.

They certainly aren't looking for more people on the patrol level—they need Scela who can help root out the Fractionists. But that means the pressure's on us to fulfill that need.

The marshal glances between us. "From here on out, you'll be spending six days a week linked together in an exosystem. It can be disorienting at first."

"What does that mean, exosys—" Woojin starts.

He doesn't get to finish. Marshal Jesuit narrows her eyes, and something snaps in my head. My awareness explodes, ballooning outward as three new pieces of consciousness smash headlong into mine. Our exos weave together, our identities meeting and merging and diverging over and over again. We mix like water, plunging into *sameness*, our sources indistinct. Then like oil and water, each of us pushing the others away. Then like thread, braiding into something stronger.

I'm in each of their heads, feeling Woojin—he prefers to be called Wooj—reel back in alarm, feeling Praava's confusion, feeling Key's simmering disgust. I know little details about them as well as I know myself, from the scar on Wooj's palm to Praava's XY chromosomes.

You wanted contact, the exo cackles against my brainstem.

The connection twists deeper. I feel their stories sink into me like I've been hearing them all my life. Their histories, their memories—I'm halfway to living them.

I'm Wooj with nowhere else to go, sleeping in the piping between the hull walls of the starship *Orpheus,* Sixth District. I feel a life's worth of nervous energy humming through me, the residuals of years spent running illicit jobs, smuggling goods across the ship. My own heart aches for his desperate scramble to get off the *Orpheus,* to move up in the Fleet, to make something out of nothing. And then there's the hollow, sunken feeling from three weeks ago, when he was caught the day after his eighteenth birthday and forced to choose between a jail tank and becoming a weapon of the General Body.

Praava's mind is a comforting space, haunted by a flavor of love I know so well. But hers isn't a split infinity like my own—it's focused on one entity in particular: her older sister. A brilliant doctor, the family's gem, working on the starship *Aeschylus,* Fourth District.

I slip into her life, living in the shadow of my sister's greatness, believing in that greatness so wholeheartedly that when a grant fell through, I decided to offer up my body at its altar. My salary goes to funding her research on the wasting fever, knowing in my heart that one day my older sister is going to save the whole damn Fleet. My body, my path, my own life—it's nothing against that.

And I know that Key is from First District, the very head of the Fleet, and . . . well, not much else about Key. The information I'm getting from her feels odd and disjointed compared to the others. It's like she has . . . *holes*. There are no images, no specifics, only the immediacy of her thoughts. She's washed out by panic as she takes in three new minds and sees that none of them are like hers. With a smoothness that betrays its familiarity, I feel her exo clamp down on her alarm until it dissolves into the cool disdain she wore when she introduced herself. Key goes willingly, her contempt for us backenders radiating through the system in place of any concrete memories.

We're all young, born within a year of each other, which the exo assures me is normal. The prime age for Scela integration lies somewhere in the late teens, when the body is grown enough to take the metal and the mind isn't too entrenched to welcome the exo. It's the reason the General Body knocked the age of legal adulthood down to sixteen a few decades after the Fleet launched. As I think of Pascao and all the other older people who knew the risk, tried anyway, and got snapped in half before they ever got a chance to become what I am, a sick feeling twists my stomach. The others share my sympathy—even Key.

The longer we mix in the system, the more our selves rise to the surface, until finally we're out of our heads and back in our bodies. I find that I'm crouching, my hands on my knees, taking long, deep breaths that swell my chest against its metal reinforcing. Wooj is flat on his back, and Praava kneels beside him. Key's the only one of us still standing tall. We can all feel the sheer stubbornness keeping her legs locked and her spine ramrod straight.

Marshal Jesuit claps her hands together. "Looks like you're settling into the exosystem." Eyeing Wooj sitting up on the ground, she continues, "This is the vehicle for ensuring the distribution of orders and enabling the cohesion of a Scela unit. You may be able to bend hullmetal, but this connection is a Scela's true strength. Does your system feel balanced?"

Our system feels confusing and chaotic, but our exos understand the gist of her question. None of us is overpowering the others, though Wooj's connection feels a little unsteady. We nod.

"Good," the marshal breathes. "No Big Bobs. Great way to start."

We raise our eyebrows in unison, and she smirks.

"Big Bob is one of the scariest Scela we have. Not physically, of course—guy's scrawny as a toothpick, looks like a damn joke walking around in his full rig. But Big Bob and his exo get along a little *too* well. You all have probably seen him before. He's the one in the recruiting videos."

I remember the video. It was on loop in the office just outside the waiting room. The man lies calmly, quietly in the saddle as the needles sink into the back of his skull and the exo spine clamps down on his bones. Nothing about it meshes with the memory of my own integration, and my experience quickly twines with the others'. Praava saw it when she volunteered. Wooj doesn't remember. Either he wasn't paying attention when they showed it to him, or he wasn't shown it at all, and the resentment seething through our system tells me it's the latter. Key isn't sure whether she's seen the video or not, but she's rooting around inside herself for something to match the memories. She presses down the panic again, trying to focus on the marshal's next words.

"Turns out Bob has a natural talent for interfacing with his exo. Wields willpower almost as well as the Chancellor herself. So the first time we jacked him into an exosystem, he was able to seize control over his squadmates. Basically turned them into drones to do whatever he wanted. Not what those poor bastards signed up for. Took a while for his instructor to pick up on it, too."

"What happened to Big Bob?" Praava asks.

Marshal Jesuit smiles, Scela-wide. "He's one of our most valuable assets. But he works in a squad of Scela who can stand on equal footing with his abilities. Balance is critical when you're working with minds in concert," she says, looking each of us in the eye.

"Hold on, hold on," Wooj blurts. "So one of us could have seized control of everyone in the system?"

The marshal's smile drops, and a shift blows through the exosystem like a gust of wind on an Old Earth cast. A buzz starts up on the back of our necks. Wooj tries to reach back and touch his exo—tries, but the impulse never makes it from his brain into the machine on his back. We're frozen in place, trapped by a foreign will rattling through us.

"This," Marshal Jesuit says quietly, "is willpower. This is how direct orders will be delivered to you from your superiors, both Scela and human. It's also how you can control other Scela, should the need arise. There are systems of permissions in place that allow you to combat it with your own willpower, dependent on rank. Your exo can also circumvent an order in some circumstances for your own sake—again, contingent on how far up the chain of command your orders' source is. In a squad's exosystem, it's every

Scela for themselves. But if you find yourself under orders from a General Body member or the Chancellor herself, you *will* carry out those orders. This is the pact you signed, the autonomy you forfeited in your integration. Respect it. Is that clear?"

The buzz lifts, and all four of us nod in unison. We're still swept up in the shock of the exosystem, trying to balance being inside four heads at once, and this new information is almost enough to overload us entirely. But despite that, our bodies are settling into a shaky equilibrium, our heartbeats thudding in uncomfortable synchrony. We draw breath as one.

"Enough dallying," Marshal Jesuit snaps, her voice suddenly harsh and authoritative, though a smile edges back into it. "Give me twenty laps around the deck perimeter. Welcome to basic."

CHAPTER 4

KEY

I wake to the soft buzz of an order, with the ghost of a dream dissolving around me.

It's the same one that's been haunting me throughout my recovery, and my memory of it is as frustratingly vague as ever. I sit in darkness, illuminated by blinding lights. Somewhere past their glow, a golden boy watches me with cameras for eyes, unblinking lenses devouring me as the lights get brighter and brighter. No other details make the leap to my waking mind, and my exo gently encourages me to keep it to myself. No reason for the other three people in my head to get a glimpse of just how fucked up my head seems to be.

Our room is nothing special—sparse, undecorated, holding only four beds and a dresser full of one-size-fits-all Scela clothing. Last night, Wooj and Praava claimed the top two bunks instantly, while Aisha and I simultaneously offered to take the lower ones. It's a little eerie how conflict-free settling sleeping arrangements was, but it's one of the few things made simpler by the exosystem.

Waking up in the system, however, is a mess. The gentle buzz that startled us awake fades, and my squadmates' *noise* rises to fill its place. We've had an entire day to settle into the way our minds weave together, but the morning makes it brand-new all over again. As I roll out of my bunk, I drown in the chatter. Aisha's already wondering if there's a way she can contact her aunt and siblings, even though it's been explained to her over and over during recovery that the *Dread*'s communications are locked down. Praava fills our shared headspace with a keen, confused longing for the mornings when her sister dragged her out of bed by her ankles. And Woojin can't seem to keep his mouth closed for more than ten seconds, much less rein in his thoughts—he's already prattling on both internally and externally about what we've got on the schedule today.

Which, granted, *is* exciting. I can't deny that, and even if I tried, my exo would vehemently disagree. But it's not enough to distract me from the fact that my memories are still missing. I'm nowhere near figuring out why I took the metal. Barely anyone from First District volunteers for Scela conversion—there are plenty of better lives to live in the frontend. Plenty of choices that don't involve the risk of being killed by an untamed exo. The Scela from First District who give up their bodies to serve are supposedly noble. Or at least they're supposed to be a better class of Scela than the desperate and the backend felons who make up the brunt of the General Body's fighting force.

I must be noble.

I *have* to be better.

So I keep my thoughts corralled and follow the rest of my squad obediently as we dress and swing through the mess for bowls of a protein-packed, stewlike substance that's simply— and unhelpfully—labeled "breakfast." A massive display takes up one wall of the cafeteria, covered with a complicated-looking, ever-shifting web of information. Focusing on one area, I see that each node represents a Scela, and the glowing threads are their exo-system linkages tying them together into squads. Occasionally the linkages shift or break as people drop in or out, as systems combine or dissolve, as the structures mutate to accommodate the Fleet's needs.

With only one day of training under our belts, we must not have earned a place on it yet. My exo informs me that each squad's position on the display marks their rank, and their coloring indicates their tier of pay. The blinding white stripes of the Scela elite at the far left of the screen hold my gaze as I drain my bowl. Something close to hunger awakens in my empty spaces.

When the marshal shows up to collect us, all four of our exos snap alert with anticipation. She leads us through the *Dread*'s wide hallways, past other squads of Scela who move together like pack animals on an Old Earth cast. Compared to them, we're blunted, awkward, gangly little creatures, our heads still bristly and our hides still marked with the unmistakable red striping of a fresh conversion.

I bite down on the urge to sneer at them when their gazes flick our way. *Better,* I remind myself. *Be better.*

"This is Assembly Deck," Marshal Jesuit announces as we reach the terminus of the hall and step out into a massive bay. Our footsteps fall in sync as we file behind her. When all of us are focused on an objective—like following the marshal's orders—our connection feels smoother, but already I can feel Woojin getting distracted by the back of Praava's exo.

As I keep my eyes fixed on the marshal, the rest of the squad starts to space out. The clamor is overwhelming—engines firing, dockworkers shouting, the heavy rumble of Scela footfalls. The metal beneath our feet vibrates with the energy of the place. The others take in the shuttles parked in their docking slots along the far edge of the deck and the bays where hundreds of full Scela rigs rest. A flutter of numbers pours into the exosystem from Praava as she calculates how many rigs are in use. Roughly seventy percent, she concludes.

Woojin wonders if it's because of the Fractionists, and I let out a low, exasperated growl. The Fractionists are *nothing*. Just a bunch of backenders bent on chaos, insisting on splitting off from the Fleet as if that will get us any closer to finding a livable planet. They're desperate and bitter about being from lower districts, and so they do their damnedest to rip the Fleet apart. But their movement's dying off, and with so many Scela in action, it won't be long until they're stamped out for good.

"These bays are yours," Marshal Jesuit says as we approach, gesturing to a row of four rigs. Just seeing them feels like they're calling out to our exos, and for a moment I'm wrapped in the dream of wearing one, the sensation of sheer electric power rushing over my skin. My exo's delight snaps through the system, rebounding off the others, and I'm nearly knocked senseless by the ricochet of four overexcited computerized entities bouncing around between us.

The bays are built out of scaffolding and metal mesh, each of the full rig's pieces strapped into their outlets. I move to the one I know is mine, guided by the exo. It wants the chestpiece first, so I grab it from the center, jerking it roughly from its plugs. It settles onto my shoulders like it was sculpted just for me and melds against my ports, clicking into place as the exo adopts it.

My vision goes fuzzy as the new body part attaches, my augmented nervous system reaching out to embrace the piece as one of its own. A data structure blossoms within the exo, a tree with a single node that branches out into leaves of information. The most prominent leaf quietly informs me that the piece is one hundred percent charged. The chestpiece winches snugly around my midsection, and just like that, it's part of me.

The rest of the rig goes on easier, once I'm past the strangeness of snapping on new body parts. I align plugs with the ports that dot my skin, and each new piece makes me feel a little more complete, a little more grounded in myself. New nodes attach to the tree, uploading a report of each piece's status. Unlike the muscle enhancements, there's no learning curve for the rig. The exo knows exactly how to move each piece, and it coaxes my brain into working in tandem every time I pick up a new part.

My body becomes an elegant assemblage of metal. The curves of the exo meld into the harsh lines of the rig. The pieces hum with energy, and everything feels *mine*. Feels *right*.

Then the headpiece slams down.

I stagger backward as darkness plunges over me, the exo doing its best to mute the sensation of spikes pricking into the ports that dot my jawline. My mind melts into it, and my vision flares back in brilliant digital color as the headpiece's cameras take over. A HUD flickers to life, though I can't tell if it's a construction of the exo or an actual feature in the headpiece. There's no way to tell which inputs are from my eyes and which are an addition wrought by the exo's intermingling. The thundering pulse of my heart echoes in my ears, trapped there by the protective plating that encases my skull.

Suddenly I'm the sole denizen of my mind and body, and it knocks me sideways. Beneath the headpiece, my vision goes black. *Don't panic. Don't let them see you panic. Don't give in to it.* Some of those thoughts are the exo's. Most are mine.

I catch myself on the grated metal of the bay, shaking my head as I adjust to my new field of view. An electric buzz settles into my skull, comforting and cradling, and I feel my heartbeat slow. *This is right.* This is what a Scela is meant to be. A living weapon, a replacement for the ancient guns that blew holes in the hulls of ships we lost so long ago that their names are no longer taught. We're more elegant weapons. More civilized. Less clumsy or random. We're built with the strength to hold this Fleet together.

For the first time in two weeks, I'm proud of what I am.

As I adjust to the power glowing through me, I find the dividing line between myself and the others. The full rig's metal sharpens it, grounding us in our bodies, making the exosystem a choice. My exo nudges me forward, and I slip into the collective, already bracing myself.

In the next bay, Woojin's rigged up and on his knees. His exo's alarm spirals into the system as it tries to get him back, but he only rolls forward, pressing his shielded head against the deck floor. A low groan shudders out from between his teeth.

"Lih!" Marshal Jesuit barks, thundering toward him. I follow in her wake, the exo guiding me into a flock as Aisha and Praava settle into formation at her side, both of them assembled in their rigs. A ping of delight warms through me as I notice Aisha's having a hard time keeping her right armpiece attached, and it only doubles when she senses my mirth radiating through the exosystem.

Woojin clasps his gloved hands behind his head, the metal wailing as he squeezes his fingers together.

"Something wrong with your exo, Lih?" Marshal Jesuit's voice snaps like a whip, but there's a note of genuine concern in there that I don't have to be linked to her to detect.

Through both the exosystem and the helmet's hypersensitive

audio sensors, we hear his panting breaths. I swear I can smell the sweat curdling off him. Woojin's integration is eerie in a way I can't quite put a finger on. His exo's control is somehow *loose,* and his mannerisms skew uncomfortably human. But the full rig has reversed all that—his exo's grip is ironclad and his mind is lost in its hold, reducing him to a hyperventilating puddle on the Assembly Deck floor.

The marshal drops to one knee beside him. "Work with it," she coaxes. "Don't glitch out on your first day in rig, kid."

"Not—a—*kid,*" Woojin gasps.

"No? Then stand up. Show me what you're made of."

His fingers unlock, his arms falling limp at his sides. For a moment, all he does is shake. Then, as if the weight of the Fleet rests on his shoulders, Woojin shoves himself to his feet. The motion is so smooth and swift that it catches Marshal Jesuit off guard. She jerks back Scela-fast, her rig crackling with energy.

Woojin stands tall. But there's something fundamentally different about him, both inside and outside. His thoughts have gone quieter than we've ever known them, his end of the exosystem wrapped in an uncanny calm. It almost feels like the rig is puppeting him instead of the other way around. My exo urges me not to worry about it, which only makes me worry about it more. I don't want *my* body taken over by the full rig.

Marshal Jesuit stares at Woojin, her brow furrowed. "Isaac warned me you sustained some heavier than usual neurological damage during the integration. He said it might translate to difficulty differentiating your will from the exo's guidance. It's already hard enough for new Scela to figure out who owns what impulse, but for you . . . there's a chance you might never fully grasp it."

Praava, Aisha, and I recoil. In the system, it feels like his exo has

written over his mind, and he projects nothing but smooth accep-
tance back at us. This is a truth of what the integration has done to
him, and it's a truth we'll have to work around if our squad's going
to succeed.

But it's not a truth I can accept. I press deeper into his side of
the system, absorbing the way his body's been broken and the way
it's been reconstructed. Something's not quite right. Something
that can never be put right again. I see the way his rig is compensat-
ing, taking over, pushing him into submission just to keep his legs
working properly. My exo assures me that it's fine. The exo's sup-
plements should work better than his own spine as long as Woojin
has the sense to stay out of his own body's way.

Somehow I doubt that's how this plays out.

Dread rumbles in the pit of my stomach. Something's wrong
with Woojin. Is something wrong with me? Is it some kind of neurological damage that's smashed my memories to pieces?

Marshal Jesuit clears her throat, jolting me back into my own
head. "This is one of the most important parts of basic. As a squad,
you have to function as a unit, even though your abilities may vary.
And those above you—the people who give your most critical
orders—to them, you're tools and weapons. You'll be expected to
perform every command they give, and they won't hear excuses,
no matter how reasonable. That means you have to figure out how
you work and how you work *together*. How to get results, no matter
what. And how to take care of each other, because no humans—not
even Isaac and his team—are ever going to really understand the
way you function. Got it?"

We nod in unison.

"Good. Now get yourselves together and head back to Gym
Deck, the lot of you," she barks.

It's fucked from the start.

Woojin trips over his own feet two steps into our assigned ten laps around Gym Deck. Praava catches him by the collar before he hits the ground, but the damage is already done. The system skews out of balance as our synchrony breaks.

Aisha and I pull ahead of them, and the exosystem goes fuzzy with worries that leak out of Aisha's consciousness, too powerful to be contained by her rig. *We can't fail. For my family. Amar. Malikah. It has to be enough.*

Maybe if I put distance between the two of us, it'll shut up the thoughts she's slugging into my brain. I grit my teeth—they still don't feel right—and try to lengthen my stride. The bulk of the rig's metal may feel natural to the exo, but my brain isn't used to having cameras for eyes, much less legs that could kick through hullmetal. My steps are lumbering, and behind me, the others aren't faring much better.

Except for Praava. When she lets go of Woojin, she takes off down the track, closing the distance between us with graceful, thundering steps that make her metal seem fluid. She wears the full rig like a second skin. As she gains on me and Aisha, I force myself into her headspace to see how she's doing it. It throws her off, my mind slamming into hers, and she accidentally checks Aisha with her shoulder.

Get off me, Praava snaps, shoving me back into my own head. We round the bend, all three of us jockeying for a position on the inside of edge of the track.

Guys, wait up, Woojin thinks behind us. His steps are uneven, like one of his legs doesn't work quite right. In the system, we feel his exo's sputtering attempts to keep his body under control, like trying to make a fist around a live eel.

We all know the rules. It doesn't matter that I've done nothing wrong. It doesn't matter that Praava's a natural. Our squad only advances as a unit, and Woojin is lagging far behind us. We have to work together, or we're going to end up on the wrong end of the rankings board.

We shorten our strides and wait for him to make the turn.

Once he closes, the four of us set off at a more moderate pace, letting our bodies fall in sync. Each of us has our own camera feed, our own web of data from the exos' attachments to the rig pieces, and our own thoughts about this chaotic *thing* we've been thrown into. Balancing it while running is a tall order, especially on our first day.

But with each step, we get a little better. I feel the thrill of success warming through me, and something about it lines up with the empty spaces in me. The sensation is familiar. From the drills we've been running over the past few days, but also—I'm realizing, I'm *remembering*—from the years I spent clawing for the top of my class in the *Antilles*'s academies. That was *me*. That was something true about the life I lived before all this. I let a savage smile loose as I spur the squad faster. If this is my reward for success, I want more. I want *everything*.

And just when I think I'm starting to get the hang of having four hyperpowered bodies jumbled in my brain, Marshal Jesuit flicks a thought into our exosystem from the far end of the deck.

Look up. We have an observer.

Our cameras spin, zeroing in on a higher platform that looms over the rest of Gym Deck. A figure stands there, swathed in an ivory cloak. I adjust my cameras, but even though I can't bring her face into focus underneath the hood, I know exactly who she is.

Chancellor Vel.

A shiver of reverence runs through my exo at the sight of the Fleet's leader. The head of the General Body. The champion ushering humanity through the stars. I know I've seen her in person from time to time at events on the *Antilles*—a vague memory, not concrete enough to celebrate, but one that nonetheless bubbles up from before I was stripped down and rebuilt into a machine meant to serve her. My resolve swells even more. *I'm going to be the best damn Scela the Fleet has ever seen.*

And that's the moment Woojin trips again.

We unravel all at once, the moment exploding in the crash of rig on rig. All four of us go down this time, caught in the panic that seizes the exosystem. I can't distinguish impact from impact— what's me hitting the ground, what's me hitting one of the others, and what's one of the others being hit. It's like the system is fresh, our minds indistinct once more.

Only when Aisha boils over do we come back to ourselves as individuals. Her thoughts go sharp with rage about how our squad's going to end up with a dead-end patrol assignment thanks to Woojin. Because of him, she shrieks internally, she gave her body away for *nothing*. Her sister will work herself ragged in the hell of the *Reliant's* textile plant, and her brother's plague will consume him. Praava's mind snaps to her own sister—the dangerous, critical research she's doing, the thin funding her salary is supposed to bolster, the chance that her sister might not save the Fleet after all. I'm drowning in their thoughts. Like my empty spaces are making extra room just for me to swallow them up.

Woojin is mercifully silent. He's the first back on his feet, swaying on his unstable legs. It's his cameras that flick up to the observation deck and confirm it. The Chancellor's turned her back on us.

She's seen enough.

As the *Dread*'s lights fade toward deep night levels, we strip out of the rigs, muted both outside and in.

With every piece that snaps off my body, I feel *lesser*. I feel powerless. Or maybe it's the exo that's doing the feeling—the blending between me and the machine leaves me uncertain of which intentions I can claim as my own. But whatever's mine, it's coming back stronger as the percentage of my body composed of metal dwindles. By the time I disengage the last armpiece and set it in its charging ports, I feel downright human, my machine parts inconsequential, my holes cavernous, and today's faults and failings all too tangible.

The marshal was merciless after our disaster in front of the Chancellor, but not in the way I expected. She didn't yell. Didn't scream. Didn't do anything we deserved. She just kept the orders coming. Kept us running in circles until it felt like our flesh was about to liquefy around our enhancements. Kept us scaling the climbing wall until our fingertips were rubbed raw inside our gloves. The brief breaks we took for lunch and dinner felt like barely anything at all—just enough time for the ache to sink into our muscles before the marshal had us marching back to Gym Deck. All four of us avoided looking at the board in the mess. Marshal Jesuit hasn't said outright where our performance today puts us, but we have no doubt it's right of the ranking board's center.

Her disappointment has settled like a weight on top of the

exo's. I should find it infuriating, but after today's ordeal, I'm too tired for that.

A nudge from my exo tells me we have a schedule to keep, urging me out of the bay. Praava and Aisha fall in step with me, and Woojin lurches behind us. We make our way back down the darkened halls to our shared room.

There's resentment in the air between us. Everybody thinks everybody else hasn't been pulling their weight, and no one wants to take the blame for the way things went sour today. I hit my stride as ordered, but I'm stuck with a fucking felon and two desperate backenders. *They* were the ones holding us back. Woojin's glitchy integration. Praava's worries. And above all of it, Aisha's constant, obnoxious fear. They're the ones who will be responsible if this squad makes anything less than the elite ranks.

The empty spaces in me feel deeper with the little joy that progress gave me now absent. Today's events have left me hungry. Starving for anything that will put my mind at peace. The steady hum against my skull reassures me as I sink back into the cradling foam mattress—I *will* feel complete. I *will* feel whole again.

But only if we come out on top.

CHAPTER 5

AISHA

I snap awake from our usual dreamless sleep on the Fleet's 301st Launch Day, near-human jitters rattling through my nervous system on the heels of our alarm-order's buzz. It's the Fleet's biggest and most celebrated holiday, but that's not what has me humming with anticipation.

Today's our first day in the field. Our first real chance to redeem ourselves after the long, slow disaster the past five days of training have been.

Our morning accelerates recklessly. The *Dread* is the most lively and cheerful I've ever seen it. We dress, scarf down breakfast, and every Scela cleared for active duty packs onto the shuttle decks, waiting for their assignments.

Our squad gets directed to a shuttle bound for the starship *Porthos,* a First District ship that flies adjacent to the *Dread* in the Fleet formation. The marshal splits us into two teams—me with Praava, Key with Wooj. "As a squad, your exosystem makes you part of a unified experience," she explains. "But as individuals, your perceptions are inherently different. Running in a pack and

51

other actions in unison feel natural, but in the course of your duties, you'll have assignments that will require you to each tackle separate goals without getting distracted by the others or co-opted by their will. Today is about easing you into those situations."

So when the shuttle docks on the *Porthos*'s intership deck, we're hit with instructions and a layout. We disembark in orderly lines and file off the deck and into the ship's habitat. Praava and I peel away at the same moment Wooj and Key split off in the opposite direction. Together, the two of us take up our posts on a walkway overlooking the ship's main thoroughfare, feeling the other two mirroring us in the system from its other side.

And then, as far as I can tell, we stand around and wait for something to go wrong.

The street between us seethes with activity, people flocking to the Launch Day festivities in droves. Steam rises from the vendor booths, and the ventilation systems groan overhead as they try to process the extra strain.

It's a First District ship. It can probably handle it.

It's strange to think that the arrangement of the Fleet into seven tiers was mechanical in origin. Ships were grouped according to their functions and maintenance requirements so that in the event of an emergency, the right servicepeople wouldn't have to launch across the Fleet to get where they were needed.

In the three hundred—three hundred and *one*—years since, the districts have evolved into something halfway between states and castes. First District leads our formation, carrying the General Body seat, the most prestigious education centers, the pride of humanity in the sleekest of starships. The middling tiers of ships follow, each of them arranged in careful balance. And my own Seventh

District makes up the rear, with its manufacturing cores coloring everything we do.

My exo urges me to settle, and I breathe in deep through my nose. *Don't pick a fight*, it reminds me. *You're here to stop trouble, not make it.*

The exo doesn't see things the way I do, and everything about today is making that divide worse. Its voice is a constant contradiction, meeting my righteous fury with its cold, Godless animal instinct. It's a machine built to enforce stasis, and every second I spend with its thoughts running parallel to mine makes me feel like more of a fanatic.

The full rig is supposed to help with that. Key and Praava feel like it helps—I feel their contentment radiating through the system every time they snap the pieces on. Wooj's rig deadens him, like his body is being passed over to the exo to handle. But mine—mine makes the gap between what my body was—*is*—*is supposed to be*—and what it is—*was*—*always has been*—overwhelmingly profound.

Fortunately, we're not rigged up today. The orders passed through the *Dread* this morning specified that we're meant to promote a sense of peace and security among the festivities, and full rigs generate the wrong sort of impression. Instead, we've been suited up in dress uniforms that must be worth an entire month of deck janitorial salary, placed in strategic stations, and told not to move, an order our exos enforce very literally.

The will behind our instructions is stronger than any we've encountered so far. Its uncomfortable buzz hums against the back of my neck, a constant symptom of an order strong enough to take our bodies away from us. It doesn't *feel* natural—it makes my skin crawl.

Fidgeting is human, the exo croons, its unyielding, hullmetal-sturdy grip locking my muscles in place. I scowl—it's kind enough to let me have control of my facial muscles. Or maybe it knows I'll panic if I feel completely locked in.

Below our station, the festival is moving into full swing. Loud music pumps from the main stage, families swarm the streets, and the *Porthos*'s General Body representative moves through the crowd with his retinue, shaking hands and making promises about the policy he'll enforce with his seat. His partner and counterpart, the ship's governor, must be out there somewhere too, making similar promises about the way she and her cabinet will oversee the *Porthos.*

The walkways of this ship are lined with greenery—there's enough space available on the *Porthos* that plants can take a little of it. They wind around trellises that arc over the crowd, swaying slightly in the breeze from the ventilation. I watch with a hint of fascination and a hint of what Key would call "backend bitterness." The *Dread* barely counts as First District—it's a warship, not a city. So here, for the first time, I see the finery.

It's not really that different from the *Reliant.* The blueprint is similar—a city laid out under a habitat dome, orderly streets and buildings, the metal sky above painted the same soft blue. But it's *more.* More spacious. More polished. *Better,* a cruel part of me admits.

The people around us are dressed in colorful silks, and the stalls sell *real* food, not the synthetic stuff we get in the backend. The rich, savory smell of true meat wafts over us before the ventilation can swallow it up, and if it weren't for my Scela biology, I'd be salivating. In the distance, I feel Key's disdain. *It's just street food,* she scoffs, but she can't hide her own envy. Anything sold on these streets would be better than the slop served in the *Dread*'s mess.

My eyes catch on the fluttering silks trailing after two girls. They dart through the crowd, clutching spun-sugar wands, and my exo prickles as a swell of nostalgia hits me. My heart thunders in time with the heavy bass beat. Last year's Launch Day was our three hundredth, and each ship's representative went all out to commemorate the occasion. I'd never seen the *Reliant* so bright, so cheerful, so clean.

I'd just gotten off from a shift helping with that cleaning on the intership deck, and I didn't bother going home to change. My stained coveralls stood out in the crowd, but I didn't care. Amar and Malikah met me in the main thoroughfare, under the vaulted sky of the ship's largest open space. I'd told them no treats before temple. Their faces were sticky anyway.

I scooped my little brother up on my shoulders, took my sister's hand, and told them they could beg forgiveness at the service. Throughout the hour, I kept expecting them to zone out, as they often did at temple. But the air around us was electric with three centuries of celebration, and for once Amar didn't tug the hem of his shirt loose and Malikah didn't play with the tassels on her headscarf and I felt like I was *managing*. Like maybe after everything that had happened, things were finally working out.

I'd started crying then. Now I'll never cry again, thanks to my new biology.

I'd pulled both of them close to me in the pew. Now I'm districts away from the *Reliant*, from my siblings, from everything I've fought so hard to protect.

I'd thought the worst was over.

My heart rebels, pumping so hard that it feels like it's hammering against the metal reinforcements that structure my ribs. I feel the exo slipping around my brainstem, encouraging my lungs to steady, but every nudge just makes it more apparent that my body isn't what it used to be.

I was human. *You're better now,* the exo insists. In a way, it's true—being Scela is stronger. Faster. Control, control, control.

My eyes burn, like the tears should be coming. They *should* be coming. Why does my Scela body have to rob me of something that makes so much sense? I try to lift a hand to my face, but the orders we've been given keep my limbs locked up, even as my own will urges the exo to slip their grip. For its part, the exo is trying to help—it's always looking out for our well-being. It knows it would be better for me to be able to move. It wants that for me. I'm grateful.

I'm *not* grateful. I want it out. I want my body back the way it was—*wasn't*—*shouldn't have been.* I can never have that, and the very idea feels so enormous that it finally shatters the orders' will and allows me to slump back against the wall behind me, burying my face in my hands as the hum behind my skull dissipates.

So much for making a good impression on our first day out in public.

Aisha. Praava's presence swells in my head as she hits me with her full attention. I feel her eyes on me, taking in the way my body has broken free and collapsed. A fierce internal battle rages inside her, and at the end of it, her exo frees up one arm. She reaches over, then pauses.

Her thoughts swirl through me, half formed. *Do you . . . Would it be okay if I . . . Okay, this is stupid.* Praava lets out a thin sigh, barely detectable. *When I was too young for hormones, I used to get a little . . . like this, and it always helped when my sister rubbed my back.*

The exo's spine covers the parts her sister used to trace. There's no sensation there anymore, just segmented metal. I feel the difference, and the loss hits her. I watch her face it, feel her accept it and tuck it away with a thousand other experiences.

Try, I plead.

She slips her hand under the drapery of my uniform shoulder, the loose fabric meant to smooth out the harsh lines formed by the exo's headpiece and bulk. Her fingers instinctively go for the spine, but she hesitates. It feels wrong, somehow, to touch another Scela's metal. Praava ducks the wrongness with a compromise, running her thumb in a careful circle around the ridge of my shoulder blade, over the lines where my skin's been resealed.

The touch is comforting, faint as it is. But when my sensation hits Praava's head, she returns fire with memories that flood my mind as if we're newly linked again.

Ratna. Her sister's name is Ratna, and Ratna would sit on the edge of Praava's bed, comb her fingers through her hair, rub her back, talk to her in low, quiet tones, promising a better future. I've felt Praava's certainty that Ratna will save the Fleet, but only now in the immediacy of her memories do I *understand* how it was planted, grown, cultivated.

In her memories, Praava's dysphoria melts. And even when it sometimes doesn't, even when it racks her still, her sister's there to help her ride it out. And she's here with me now, and even though these things aren't the same, not even close, there's something parallel that lines up between our minds.

My breathing slows. The burn fades behind my eyes. I let my exo guide me back into parade rest, with a few extra degrees granted to the angle of my neck so that for a moment, all I do is stare down at this body—this *wondrous* body, the exo tries helpfully, but I shunt the thought aside. No adjectives. This body is a body. This body is a fact. This body is *mine.*

Praava pulls her hand back, tucking her memories away from the system. She slips into our mandated position again, and a brief glimmer of pride glows through her thoughts before she can clamp down on it. Not pride in me, but pride in herself, in being something close to what her sister is. Her teeth flash out in a too-brief Scela grin.

My focus finally shifts out to the Launch Day festivities. I let the ship back in around me. Watch the people moving, hear the music, drink in the smell of that wonderful food.

See a pattern moving through the crowd.

Start to panic.

CHAPTER 6

KEY

"Okay, what about this?" Woojin muses, fingers drumming against his palms. "Sick parent. Sick parents—that'd be even stronger. Wasting fever, maybe, or really anything else. Ring any bells?"

My lip curls. "We're civilized up in the frontend—we have health care. They wouldn't need *this* to be looked after."

Down below, the festival's building to a fever pitch. The thoroughfare is packed to capacity, and the windows along the street spill the noises of smaller gatherings out above the main celebration. It pales in comparison to the spectacle of the *Antilles*'s three hundredth Launch Day—I remember that much. And the bit about my parents is definitely true too.

I think.

With the *Dread*'s communications locked down, I haven't been able to contact them. I'm not desperate enough to keep begging for a chance to send out a message like Aisha, but surely my parents must know why I took the metal.

If they know I took the metal in the first place.

"What if you did it on a dare? Or with a friend—both of you

tried to see whether you could take the conversion, and you were the only one who walked away?"

"Fucking dark, Lih," I snarl. "And no. Pretty sure I'm not *that* stupid. Spirits alive, where do you get this shit?"

He shrugs. I'm not exactly sure how he shrugs, given how firmly the orders have locked down my own body, but Woojin plays fast and loose with the rules that govern the rest of us when he's not in his rig. "What about . . . ," he drawls, and in the system I feel him reeling in the next idea.

He's been at it for what feels like hours. I don't know how to make him stop. I already tried ignoring him, but the silent treatment doesn't really work when he's in my head. With my body locked in place by the orders buzzing at my neck, there's no way for me to physically shut Woojin up. At this point, I'm just waiting for him to wear himself out. At least his prattle is drowning out whatever's got Aisha throwing a fit on the other end of the exosystem.

Woojin opens his mouth again. I can already anticipate what he's about to say, and there's no way I'm going to let him vocalize the suggestion. "Is there a boy—"

"Stop," I hiss, blasting the sentiment through the exosystem at the same time. The combination of the two is enough to shock him into silence. "It's pretty clear that I don't remember, and I'm never going to. All I know is that I'm *here.*"

My head goes quiet, and it takes me too long to realize that it's my exo throwing up walls. Not to protect me from Woojin's nattering—no, it's not that merciful. It's clamping me down to keep me away from the others. Shuttered in my own head, just to keep me from lashing out.

Next to me, Woojin's gone abruptly still. Locked from his thoughts, I'm forced to wait for whatever he's going to blurt next.

"It's not so bad," he says at last, reaching up to pinch a leaf from the vine arcing over our station. "I mean, I've felt the holes in you—I know you're dealing with a different monster. But when I took the metal, it wasn't for any grand reason. Not like, y'know, those two. It doesn't have to be for a grand reason."

"You took the metal because you're a fucking criminal," I mutter. I'd settle for just a *reason,* even if it's not all that grand, and something tells me that I'm not the only one. When he isn't being pinned down by a full rig, Woojin's thoughts are awash in existential confusion. The guy's spent his whole life clawing just to live another day, and he barely knows how to function outside of survival mode.

"It's going to be okay," he says gently.

Part of me knows he's being kind. Most of me knows I don't deserve it. And all of me is certain it's the most ridiculous thing he could ever say in this situation. It's not okay. It's not going to be okay until I recover my memories. Until I understand why I did this to myself. Until I get *answers.* I'm about to tear down the exo's barriers and *make* Woojin understand exactly why it's not okay when they fall away abruptly, leaving me unsteady in my own head.

Something's happening. Aisha's alarm slams into us from the far end of the thoroughfare. Whatever weirdness consumed her, she's gotten over it now—or at least she's got it locked down enough that she's no longer spilling her issues into the exosystem. *There's coordinated movement in the crowd.*

Blood in the water, the exos sing between us. Woojin drops his leaf. Our restless energy snaps into awareness, bridging the things we see, the things we hear. We're one being in four bodies, four sets of eyes and ears, four brains, four exos working in tandem.

The crowd below us rearranges into statistics, and our mechanical minds pick out the errors in the dataset. Not many of them, but they're there. People who suddenly have an objective. A vector. A rendezvous.

Somehow I already know exactly what I'm looking at.

Not good. We have to do something. My exo agrees on both points. It's a wide-open opportunity. Intervene. Save the day. Make up for embarrassing ourselves in front of the Chancellor. Pull ourselves leftward on the rankings board. Unlock that *right* feeling and the memories attached to it. I can feel my former self on the other side of a curtain, just waiting to step in.

As I take my first steps forward, the Fractionist protest takes shape beneath me.

Their numbers are weak—the strength of the movement comes from the backend, not the frontend. But they don't need many for what they're after. They converge on the General Body representative in the middle of the crowd. His retinue collapses around him, fencing him in, but it's not enough. The protestors came prepared. Fractionists unfurl banners scrawled with their slogans, hoisting them up on telescoping poles.

WHERE IS THE PLANET THAT WAS PROMISED?
HUMANITY WILL DIE IN THE STARS.
SPLIT THE FLEET. SPLIT THE FLEET. SPLIT THE FLEET.

The buzz on my neck shifts in pitch as circumstance mutates our orders. *Stand still and observe* evaporates into *Protect the representative.* I leap down from our perch and plunge into the crowd, Woojin quick on my heels. He ducks through the food stalls with practiced grace, his muscles alive with memories of Sixth District smash-and-grab runs. I don't have his grace or his time to waste.

I'm chasing my former self, and that calls for brute speed and every bit of strength in my limbs.

A satisfied snarl rasps out of my throat as people dive out of my way. No matter what your political stance, when seven feet of enhanced muscle and metal comes barreling toward you, you'd better move your ass.

In my academy training, I remember reading about citizen rights back when humanity had a planet to live on. Freedom to assemble used to be one of those. It didn't last in space. With people in such close quarters. With the engineering of a starship dependent on people staying put. Chaos has to be shut down.

Has to be shut down *fast*.

The chanting starts. My exo dims the audio—it doesn't want me getting confused. *End this, before it gets out of hand.* Woojin is two steps behind me. Aisha and Praava close on us from the far end. We're flocking into a herding pattern, like wolves on an Old Earth cast. *Hunt,* the blood roars in my veins.

Stop, a new voice commands, and my exo locks up, bringing me staggering to a standstill just twenty feet away from the knot of demonstrators. I catch the panicked stare of the representative, and purpose thunders down my spine. But the word we've been given is laced with the hullmetal will of the marshal's orders humming against the back of my neck. *You four have zero training on how to handle humans. You're a danger to innocent civilians if you go charging in like that, and I'm not giving you any points for it. Let the regular patrol rein the Fractionists in.*

I rage, seething for a chance to prove myself, a chance that's lying right in front of me. But the marshal's will bats my own to the side and clamps down hard, and I'm left feeling less like a wolf, more like a pup. I don't know how to slip her grip, and none of the other three seem willing to try. My lips fall back down over my teeth.

I square my shoulders as the mature Scela surge forward around us. The protest falters, the less-committed abandoning their banners and scattering into the retreating crowd. The holdouts stand tall, trying to fill the gaps in their formation, but it's too late. Scela strength rips their slogans in half. The Fractionists' chants go silent or turn to begging. The representative ducks to safety, swiftly escorted away by his cowering retinue.

Back to your stations, the marshal orders. My exo growls. It wanted the fight, the test, the chance, just as much as I did. But her willpower's too forceful to disobey, and I find myself reluctantly trudging back the way I came, my eyes unfocused as the nervous stares of the citizens follow us back to our posts.

It sinks in. This is the reality of patrol duty—being trapped in our heads while we wait around for something interesting to happen. The occasional flurry of action, followed quickly by an order to stand aside once the cavalry arrives. And then back to standing still, stuck in the quagmire of the exosystem and the void of my own mind.

This can't be the rest of my life. For a moment there, I forgot about my missing pieces. For a moment, nothing was missing in the first place—with the Fractionists ahead and orders driving my muscles to action, I had everything I needed. I don't know why I became Scela, but it certainly wasn't to stand by like this. I'm meant for more—I have to be.

Overhead, loudspeakers crackle on, and every screen in the vicinity turns to the stark image of the General Body seal. For a moment, I think it's a reaction to the protest, but then Chancellor Vel's face appears, smiling benevolently, and I remember: The annual address. The reason we're here.

"Citizens of the Fleet," the Chancellor says. She stands in her stateroom aboard the starship *Pantheon,* framed in rich mahogany and backgrounded by a sweeping galactic mural. My exo tries to discern any minute twitches of her facial expression to shed light on what she's feeling, but I can't get a read on her. If she knows what's unfolding on the *Porthos,* she doesn't show it.

"I come before you on this, the three hundred and *first* anniversary of our Fleet's launch. Today we celebrate how far we've traveled in the time since we left humanity's ruined cradle and our hope for a day when we might set our roots once more. Last year, I spoke at length. Today, I have but a few words for you."

Some of the captured Fractionists have started shouting over the Chancellor's voice, hurling insults and petty taunts at the screens as if she can hear. Others—ones the Scela are far quicker to muzzle—try to agitate the crowd around them as they're hastily hauled away.

"Our ancestors left us with no choice but to wander. It was the life we were born into when the resources of the Old Solar System could no longer sustain our race. The task we have been born into, the task these great ships around us were built for, is not an easy one. And it certainly isn't one that can be accomplished on our own.

"It's through our *unity* that the Fleet sails on. Our unity is what we celebrate on Launch Day. And it's our unity that will bring humanity to the world we've been searching for. I wish each and every one of you peace and blessings, and a happy Launch Day to all." The Chancellor gives the camera a beatific nod, and the feed cuts to black.

The concourse rings with the echoes of her last words. As I settle back into my parade rest stance, I realize that my heartbeat's holding steady at twice its usual rate. I push a question at the exo. *Why the fuck am I still so worked up?*

But naturally it's still not telling me anything.

CHAPTER 7

AISHA

The morning after Launch Day, we wake not to the buzz of an order but to Marshal Jesuit shoving into our exosystem. I get five words into the Morning Strain before her presence swells in our heads, stalwart and impossible to ignore.

Today is your first day off. Un-Haad, your request for leave has been granted. Report to Assembly for immediate departure. Tanaka, you'll be escorting her. Lih and Ganes, you're free to spend the day however you wish aboard the Dread. *Your exosystem will disengage in ten seconds.*

A muffled curse rings out from Key's bunk.

The marshal pops out as suddenly as she came, leaving the four of us blinking in uncanny synchrony. A few heartbeats later, our collective mind snaps four ways, and for the first time in days, I'm in no one's head but my own. The sensation is so unfamiliar that I get lost in it for a moment, transfixed by my own individuality.

Then the marshal's words come back, and my thoughts narrow sharply.

Amar. Malikah.

I'm just a shuttle ride away.

Three minutes later, by my exo's count, I'm sprinting down to Assembly with Key on my heels. I feel lighter without the weight of her judgment pressing into me constantly, but the exo warns me not to get too comfortable. More often than not, having Key Tanaka in my head is going to be a fact of my existence.

I'm so caught up in the idea of seeing my siblings again that when I skid into Assembly, I nearly run headlong into Marshal Jesuit. "Slow down, Un-Haad," she says, catching me by the back of my exo. I resist the urge to squirm at the way the sensation jerks through every piece of machinery rooted in my body. "Your shuttle is waiting at the end of the bay. You'll have three hours on the *Reliant,* and then you'll be shipped back to the *Dread.* Understood?"

I nod, a snap of my chin. We have the day off—most everyone in the Fleet does on the day after Launch Day—but the marshal clearly isn't included. Something had her up early this morning, and it's a matter that needs her in her armor. She wears the full rig, her headpiece cocked back and her hair in a complicated plait that runs parallel to her exo spine. It's hard to tell, but I think she's exhausted. She catches the suspicious sweep of my eyes. "I'm delivering your first progress report to the General Body this morning. They ... prefer to see Scela in full rig." She shrugs, but my exo notes a hint of discomfort in her voice.

With a more pointed nod, the marshal dismisses us, and we jog down Assembly, passing rows of shuttles that include—

Even with the uncontrollable urge to run for my siblings driving me, I stagger to a halt, transfixed. As a former deck janitor, I know spacecraft wear and tear as intimately as scripture. I know how dirt accumulates on the shuttles that ferry people between starships and across the tiers of the Fleet. But I've never seen damage of this sort in person.

These ships have heat shields. These ships have *burned*. These ships have been to planet surfaces, scouting for our promised home.

My eyes sweep down the swell of their Faster Than Light drives, fear and thrill warring inside me at the thought of traveling that fast. In my lifetime, the Fleet's starships have never accelerated past the brink of light speed. We've been coasting on the same trajectory for years, and it's been decades since the last time we elected to fire those drives. But these shuttles do it routinely. Over feeble protests from my exo, a prayer rises on my lips for the holy work they do. It's humanity's grandest purpose in the sight of God, finding a habitable world. Three hundred and one years of searching has been a test of faith, and my prayer takes a selfish twist as I conclude my strain with a plea for that search to end in my lifetime.

I steal a guilty glance back at Key, all but hearing her condescension in my head, but she's gawking at the shuttles too, her expression confused and almost vulnerable. She catches my eye and scowls. "Move," she grunts.

I move.

"Morning, ladies!" a friendly voice calls from farther across the deck. I turn and find a human beckoning us over to a smaller passenger shuttle. He wears the gray uniform of the *Dread*'s dockworkers, but the stiff, drab fabric does little to diminish his warm brown skin or his glowing grin. "You two must be the ones shipping to the backend today," he says.

Key's lip curls into a sneer, and I can't tell whether it's for the overly cheerful boy in front of us or the prospect of descending past the First District. I've been in her head enough to know she must be boiling with disdain about this excursion, and I'm especially glad that I won't have to share her thoughts when we land on my birthship.

"Ride's ready to go," the dockworker says, rapping his knuckles against the hull. "Name's Zaire—I'll be getting you two ready to launch."

"Thanks," I tell him earnestly, and Key sniffs haughtily at my side.

"Let's hurry it up!" a harsh voice calls from the front, and I'm surprised to see a Scela pilot leaning out of the door to the cockpit, spinning a set of key fobs lazily around her thumb. "We're wasting starlight just sitting here."

"*Nani,*" Zaire begs. "Don't harass the fuzzheads."

The Scela woman scowls, her expression rough and exaggerated against Zaire's subtle human quirks. Her hair is loose and wild, much of it woven around her shoulder pieces in a way that looks both unintentional and painful. "I got business I could be doing," she mutters.

"Ooh, *business,*" Zaire says, wiggling his hips. "What dreamboat are you gonna find on the *Reliant*?"

Nani smirks, a forceful look on her restructured face. "One with deeper pockets than you."

Key scoffs, and I wish I were linked to her, just so I could shove her without these two noticing.

Zaire ignores her disdain. "C'mon," he says, beckoning. "You'll be riding in the back."

My stomach drops as the door to the passenger hold folds open. Three weeks ago, I took my first shuttle ride, along with three other Scela conversion candidates shipping from the *Reliant.* If my stomach hadn't been empty for the anticipated surgery, it would have been by the time we docked with the *Dread.*

Repeating the experience when we shipped to the *Porthos*

yesterday wasn't terrible—but it was such a short trip. A brief jaunt in the void, with too much going on around me to get properly anxious. Now my exo's crooning in the back of my head, promising me that it will keep me from hurling, but even so, I feel the panic creeping up my spine as we mount the stairs and slide into the seats.

"Word of advice," Zaire mutters as he snaps the restraints around us. "Don't ever let Nani into that system thing you've got going on. She's been in the middle of some kinky stuff, and she won't hesitate to use it against you if you piss her off. Makes me glad I don't have it," he says, tapping the side of his head.

My stomach turns. Key bares her teeth at him, and he jumps.

"All right, no need to get nasty," Zaire laughs. "Enjoy the backend, you two." He pats the ridge of her exo, then leaps away before she can take a swipe at him and skips down the stairs. The shuttle's hatch swings shut behind him, and I'm left with nothing but silence and Key Tanaka fuming next to me.

Then the shuttle lurches forward. Instinctively I slap my hand backward, pressing my fingers into the hullmetal behind us. The exo urges me to keep my prayers internal, but the wiring in my brain can't override my fear.

"We aren't even in the void yet," Key groans.

The shuttle's wheels bump over the Assembly Deck floor as dock crews drag us to the launch tube. It barely matters. We aren't in the void yet, but we will be any second. The prayers come faster.

Something whirs. Something clunks. I add a second hand to the hullmetal.

The wall starts shaking behind me. A roar builds in pitch, then vanishes like a snuffed candle, the vacuum dampening it to the low rumble that vibrates through the shuttle. Acceleration sinks me into my seat, my restraints going loose around my shoulders. My exo forces me to unclench my jaw before it shatters my teeth.

The change sweeps over us like a wave, the gravity below our feet evaporating as the shuttle glides out of the launch tube and clear from the *Dread*'s gravitational field. I lift against the restraints, and the taste of bile leaks into the back of my throat despite the exo's best efforts. My prayers go quiet as my focus shifts to keeping my nausea in check.

"Thank God," Key mutters beside me.

"These things are outrageously safe, you know," Key says, breaking the silence of the journey as we clamber out of the shuttle. She raps her knuckles twice against the ship's hull, then wrinkles her nose as the smell of the *Reliant*'s only intership deck hits her.

We stalk down the stairs and across the deck—stalk, because there's no word more appropriate for the gait of an unrigged Scela. With our enhancements powering our muscles, our strides lengthen, bearing our bodies feather-light in a way that draws the eye of every human in the vicinity. I wonder if anyone will recognize me, then quickly dismiss the idea. They'd remember a girl with a headscarf, a girl who lived in constant fear of the universe consuming everything she loved.

They wouldn't see her in this monster of flesh and metal.

But even if the *Reliant* has forgotten me, I haven't forgotten this deck. The smell of engine grease and burned-off fuel carries memories of sweat and rust, days when my life was reduced to cleaning solvents and the ache of my shoulders. Deck janitorial kept my siblings in school and out of the steaming hell of the *Reliant*'s dyeworks, and on top of that, the rough physical work was probably what made me strong enough to take the integration and conversion in the first place.

The exo wants me to be thankful.

I want to rip it from my back.

"Spirits alive, calm down," Key says, as if she's read my thoughts. My lips peel back from my teeth. Ever since I became Scela, I've been a mess of contradictory impulses, and Key's been no better. She doesn't get to judge me when I can't keep whatever's left of my humanity in check.

The people on the deck would be hard-pressed to see *any* humanity left in us, especially given that Scela don't get shipped out to the *Reliant* often. There isn't much of value on a Seventh District ship, after all. Glimpses of them were always limited to casts from the front of the Fleet and the rare occasions when a crime would bring a small pack of them prowling through the market streets. They never blend in, and we certainly don't now. Even if we slowed down, hunched over, shortened our strides, limited the pulse of our muscles. Even if we hooded our heads to hide the wicked ridges that rise from our skulls and the bulk of the metal that structures our shoulders. Even if we didn't move in sync.

There's always something that gives away a predator in your midst.

I lead the way off the deck, through the gateway that connects it to the main body of the *Reliant*'s habitat. As we step out into the open, an ache hits my chest. Now that I've seen the *Porthos*'s immaculate streets, I can't help but compare them to the *Reliant*'s dingy, slightly crooked landscape. The sight of the habitat dome above us is crowded by the apartments that have stacked higher and higher over the years as the ship's population overflowed the edges of its carrying capacity. The streets feel even more claustrophobic in my new body, and I find myself tucking my elbows carefully against my sides as we wade forward into the crowded market.

My birthship's warm, familiar air sinks into my skin, and I breathe deep. Decorations are still up from the Launch Day celebration, and the streets have the turned-over, post-festival look. Despite the press of the crowd, the humans around us shy away, giving us a two-foot berth. *Fear,* I think, just as the exo insists, *Respect.*

"... just *kids,*" we hear from behind us. Key's head snaps around.

I yank her back by her support struts. "Leave it," I growl. I'm not giving her a chance to cause a scene before I get to see my siblings.

Key mutters under her breath—something about the breeding in backend districts—and the exo has to keep me from punching her right then and there. No one explained why *she* had to be the one to escort me home, and I'm desperately wishing either of my other two squadmates were at my side today. They'd have some compassion. They aren't as classist as Key Tanaka.

I keep moving forward before my human impulses get the better of me. But even that proves impossible, because out of the corner of my eye, I spy a familiar dome, and every atom in me gives thanks that Key isn't listening in on my thoughts right now. To get to Yasmin's, we have to walk right past the entrance to the *Reliant*'s Ledic temple.

I clench my hands into fists, tamping down the urge to divert, to walk through that doorway, drop onto one of the kneelers, and plead for just a little more grace. Just a little more of God's strength to get me through this. The old hurts rise in me, but I remember the feeling of Praava's hand on my back and let the exo help me keep my body steady. I feel stretched thin by the time that's passed since the last temple service I attended, but there's nothing I can do about that today. Not with Key and her infuriating judgment on my tail for no apparent reason.

Yasmin's orphanage is situated just off the main square, under the vaulted sky's highest point. Approaching the side door to the part of the building that houses her apartment doesn't feel real in this body. It feels like I've been gone for much longer than three weeks. My exo tries to soothe me, urging the thunder of my heart to slow as I step up to the door and press the buzzer.

The door swings open, and I notice three things in rapid succession.

First, the look of horror in my ten-year-old sister's eyes as she takes in what I've become.

Second, the shine of her hair, no longer wrapped under a Ledic scarf.

And third, her hands.

Malikah's hands are dyed blood-red.

Rage flushes through me, unchecked by the exo. I step forward, allowing my frame to fill the doorway as Malikah shrinks back. "You weren't supposed to be working in the dyeworks. *Why does she have you in the dyeworks?*" I ask, my teeth bared. My little sister's fear registers, but my exo urges on my fury before I can react.

There's something even more wrong with this picture. The stain on her hands is too vibrant. Too ingrained. To work up to a stain like that, Yasmin would have had to move Malikah down to the vats the minute I walked out the door. My gaze moves from her hands to her eyes. She squints up at me, her spine straightening even as silent tears track down her face. Her expression is somewhere halfway between terror and delight, so painfully human that it makes me wish I'd never done this to myself.

"Aunt Yasmin said you . . . you might not . . ."

"Malikah," I say, lowering my voice to an even growl. "I'm here. I'm fine. And you were supposed to get my signing bonus and salary. *This* shouldn't have happened." I glance over my shoulder at Key, but she shrugs. She's never worried about money before— why should she start now?

I turn back to Malikah, whose gaze is stuck on the ridge embedded in my skull. When I start to get down on one knee, she flinches away from me. "I'm sorry," I tell her, holding out both of my hands. She takes them, but I feel her tense when her fingers skip over the ridges of metal and resealed skin. I trace the brilliant dye that marks her forearms. "This will wear off in a few days," I say, trying to ignore how frail she feels, how a single mistake could pulverize her in my grip. "We'll make sure the money comes."

"Not your fault," she mumbles, before throwing her arms around my neck.

I don't dare hug back, not with Scela power in my muscles. The most I can do is set one hand on the small of her back and rest my head as gently as I can manage on her shoulder. For a moment, I let the past day, the past week unravel around me until I'm human again, home again, on the starship I've belonged to my whole life. And in that moment, it's all worth it.

Then my exo yanks me back, mentally and physically. It knows I can't linger in a near-human headspace, even if I'm getting better at managing the reality of my new body. I snap to my feet like a puppet on strings, nearly knocking Malikah backward. As my awareness of the machine in my head sharpens, I feel my blood grow hot.

My body. My sacrifice. My purpose.

"Where's Yasmin?" I ask through my teeth.

Fear creeps back into Malikah's expression. She lifts a shaking hand, pointing down the hall that connects the apartment to the orphanage next door.

I start down it without another word. I can feel my exo honing the violence inside me to a bladed edge, shivering with anticipation. As I tear the door open and turn the corner, Key's footsteps reluctantly give chase.

The narrow hall opens into a dimly lit, grungy cafeteria. It must be lunchtime—dozens of red-handed children chatter at the tables. But my eyes settle on the woman who towers above them at the other end of the room, bent over to answer a question that's being shouted in her ear.

The noise fades. I feel the weight of the children's eyes fall on me as the whole room stills.

Yasmin straightens, looking as if she's seen a ghost.

But her eyes aren't on me. They're fixed somewhere over my shoulder. My exo picks up the quick flutter of my aunt's lips, barely more than a strangled whisper—*angel,* she mouths, then swallows the words.

I don't know what that means, and I don't care to find out. I stalk forward.

"Why does my little sister have red hands?" I snarl. The exo tugs at my shoulders, rolls my neck, pulls me up to as tall as I can stand. There's something so awfully, wonderfully *right* about it, like I'm stretching my muscles for the first time after a long sleep.

Scela power overwhelms me, and the only human thought that passes through my exo is a quick note that I wasn't taller than my aunt three weeks ago.

"N-now, Aisha," Yasmin stammers, nearly tripping as she staggers back.

As if words are enough to calm me. She's crossed a line that can never be uncrossed. "Explain," I demand.

"Your money didn't come. We had to do something—there wasn't enough to pay for—"

"I told you to keep her out of the dyeworks. Have her on janitorial, have her fucking dancing in the streets for coins!" The curse isn't mine—there's something in my wrath that snatches it out of Key's lexicon and hurls it from my lips.

"There's always work in the dyeworks," Yasmin mutters.

I lunge forward, grabbing her roughly by the front of her shirt. My exo blinks a half-hearted reminder that I haven't been trained to handle humans yet, but its glee at my unfettered rage warms through me all the same. I lean in until the edge of my ridge knifes into her forehead. "You know *exactly* why there's always work there," I growl.

Key's hand comes down on my shoulder, snapping me back. "Holy shit," she hisses. The ringing in my ears clears, and I hear faint whimpers from the kids cowering at their tables. Reluctantly I release Yasmin, blinking, and she sways, clutching the end of her plait as she stumbles away from me.

I glance back and confirm my worst fear. Malikah stands at the edge of the cafeteria, leaning slightly against the door frame. Those silent tears aren't silent anymore—she has a hand over her mouth to rein in her sobs, and in her eyes, I see every inch of the monster that I've become.

It lights a fire in me, a little ember compared to what just ignited a minute ago, but enough to square my shoulders again as I roll my gaze back to fix on Yasmin.

Key's fingers tighten on my shoulder. It strikes me as ridiculous that Key, furious and petulant Key, is the one holding me back, and I almost laugh.

"Yasmin," I say finally, trying for Malikah's sake to keep my voice even and calm. "Where is Amar?"

She tells me.

Key expects me to snap when I hear Yasmin's answer—I feel her press her feet more firmly into the floor, dropping her weight just in case she has to pry me off my aunt again. But there's no fury that roars through me this time, no flare of violence unleashed.

There's only dullness.

The dry, warm air of the *Reliant.* The red-handed children around me. The losses I've endured already. The inevitable things in a Seventh District life. I shrug off Key, bow my head, and walk back through the ranks of trembling orphans, down the narrow hall, through Yasmin's dingy apartment, and into the kitchen. I collapse into the rickety chair at the breakfast table, ignoring how it protests under my new weight. Elbows on the table. Head in my hands. Her words sinking in until they're as deep as the metal on my bones.

My brother has been quarantined on the plague ship.

When the wasting fever first broke out, the Fleet's medical ships tried to handle it individually, each devoting a ward to treating the victims. But soon it became clear that the epidemic was burning through the Fleet. The General Body chose to sacrifice a single ship for the good of the many, and the *Panacea* fell to the rear of the Fleet, behind even the Seventh District ships.

It trails us, a city of the dying.

"We scraped enough together to get him on the third tier," Yasmin says from over my shoulder.

I hitch my head, intending a slight nod, but the exo exaggerates the gesture. Out in the hall, there's the sound of the front door closing. Key, it seems, has had enough of our lower-class dramatics and decided to wait outside.

"How much would it cost to get him to the first?" I ask, my voice cracking under the strain of asking a question I already know the answer to.

"It would be everything. Your entire salary—no more left over for Malikah's upkeep."

Like almost everything in the Fleet, the *Panacea* has tiers. Five of them, in this case. The upper levels for those who can afford proper care. The lower levels for those willing to be fodder for the experimental treatments that the labs are constantly synthesizing. Putting Amar in the middle gives him a shot, but he's already so small and weak, and . . .

I swallow, pushing away the images of my little brother's face scarred with purple tracks, the feel of dead skin under my powerless hands. "Is that why you—"

I have to fight back against the simmering anger threatening to boil inside me. Key's gone—nothing could hold me back if I gave in. I pour my will against the exo like a prayer, trying to shape it into the kind of order the machine on my back will listen to. *Please, God, don't let me deck my sister's only caretaker.*

Yasmin slides a hand onto my shoulder—a bold move, the exo notes with a grudging twinge of respect. "We had to do something to make the first payments with your money not coming in. Look, the kids in my care all work for their upkeep. I used to, when I first came here. It's not as horrible as you make it out to be."

She wouldn't know. When she and my mother were orphaned, Yasmin managed to secure work assisting the orphanage's former owner. But my mother, young and small as she was, had to earn her keep with red-dyed hands. While Yasmin coordinated schedules and balanced finances, my mother toiled in the factory until the stain sank so deep that it never washed out for the rest of her days. Toiled until a lasting cough took root in her seared lungs. Toiled through sickness and broken bones, through inhuman hours, through accidents that claimed some of the other children working at her side.

And now Malikah's hands bear the same mark.

"Aisha, I'm on your side," Yasmin says, low and persuasive, the voice she must use to coax favors out of the children. "You're so insistent on doing this yourself, but I want what's best for all three of you, and we both know you're taking too much of the load."

I think of our horrific training sessions after the Chancellor's visit. The record-low times we clocked, despite the full rig's power. The way Wooj plummeted off the climbing wall when his exo lost control of his body again. The paralyzing hatred that pours out of Key Tanaka's every thought. The contents of the report Marshal Jesuit was on her way to deliver this morning. Our chances of making anything past patrol are slim.

Maybe it's the reality I have to accept: I can't carry my family by myself.

When I glance up, Yasmin is hovering. *Waiting to strike,* my exo warns. The machine doesn't understand our history, doesn't understand the way blood forges loyalty. All it's seen is a woman who betrayed my trust, who knew my will and went against it—and if there's anything an exo hates, it's disobedience.

Maybe I'd be wise to listen to my exo's instincts.

Then Yasmin sinks into the chair next to me. The machine on my back homes in on the moment she stops holding herself together and lets her true exhaustion show. "Aisha, I understand," Yasmin says. "Really, I do. You want fairness. You want justice. You want the sacrifices you've made to balance out. You Un-Haad girls are obsessed with order and rightness. Your mother was the same way, and not a day goes by that I don't regret the wedge it drove between us."

The exo prickles against my spine. I hold my breath.

"Before you left, I tried to talk to you about something that I hoped you could do for me. A way to settle your debts. As Scela, you have access to information that's outside the reach of an average citizen. Outside the reach of *humans,* really. Information"—Yasmin pauses, inhaling deeply—"that could be useful in the hands of certain groups. Groups fighting for . . . fairness, shall we say?"

My exo panics more than I do. Notions of the laws surrounding treason, the way my bodily autonomy has been signed over to the General Body, the way the exo *has* to obey certain orders stir in the mechanical side of my mind. But in the rest, there's just quiet certainty as the pieces snap into place. The way Yasmin lives alone, runs an orphanage, and seems to do little else. The way my mother cut her out in the span of an afternoon. The way she never even offered to help us until the day I turned up on her doorstep, announcing I was going to turn Scela.

I know what she's asking. I know what she *is.* And I can't believe I haven't realized before. I look my aunt straight in the eye and say, "You want me to be a spy for the Fractionists."

Yasmin nods. With a jolt, I grasp that this isn't a game of manipulation and power—not the way my exo wants it to be, not the simple, animal method it understands. For Yasmin, this is a matter of life and death. My mother must have shielded us from her the moment she found out, trying to protect us from the family revolutionary.

And now Yasmin's just hauled me headlong into it. She tried to talk me out of taking the metal at first, no doubt spooked at the idea of a General Body weapon in the immediate family. But once it was clear that I was going through with my conversion, she wove a net, and now there's no way I can escape. My aunt knows exactly what she's doing. That the Scela recruitment drive was triggered by a series of raids that captured key Fractionist cells on frontend ships. That their movement is weakening day by day. And now Amar and Malikah are in her hands, not mine. If Yasmin goes down for her ties to the rebellion, my siblings will have no one left to take care of them.

Their safety depends on me keeping her secret.

I feel myself teetering on the edge of rage. I've walked right into her trap. I could snap at her again, scream in her face for forcing me to harbor this truth. But doing that wouldn't put me any closer to getting Amar and Malikah away from the danger I've led them into. The only way out is through.

So I close my eyes, feeling the metal and wires and circuitry wrapped into my biology. Accepting the truth of it, the way Praava showed me. Understanding. The exo looks out for my best interests. It keeps me steady, helps me harness my will and focus it into this enhanced body. It will keep my secrets, and it will help me keep my secrets for as long as it's able.

I throw out an intention, trying to hone it down to something simple, a subroutine I can keep running even when my mind is elsewhere. *Keep this part of my thoughts from the exosystem.* I remember the barriers Key's exo threw up between us yesterday during my meltdown on the *Porthos* and try to shape my will into something similar. A little wall. Something so small that no one will notice until they trip over it.

When I'm sure it's steady, when I'm sure I've built my protection up to the best of my ability, I let my eyes slide open again. "What information?" I ask, and Yasmin bares her teeth.

"We've been struggling to get a Fractionist cell running aboard the *Dread,* especially with the recent crackdowns in First District. We have a few people who are willing, but there's only so much humans can do on a ship full of Scela. For a *Dread* cell to be effective, we need information only *you* could get. Numbers, patrols, timetables, and the like. Nothing that would require anything close to *snooping*—all I ask for is your observations."

Sure, that's all she asks for now, the exo notes, and I can't help but agree with its suspicion. I've seen the look in her eyes before, in fellow janitors trying to get me to cover extra shifts on the intership deck. It starts with a small request—just a few hours tacked on to the end of one of mine. But it grows and grows, and since I never get less desperate, it never stops. I've been taken advantage of enough times before to know that Yasmin will only ask for more. One favor will lead to another. And then another and another. Being in her debt is a dangerous thing.

But worse is the prospect of a Fleet without my brother.

I see Yasmin's game. Or at least, I think I do. I remember she tried to ask me something right before I left the *Reliant.* Did she stop herself in an effort to spare me the mental strain? Did she think it would be too much to ask, knowing what I was about to go through? Or did she realize how much it would play to her advantage to wait until after my conversion, after she had sent Malikah to the dyeworks, after Amar's illness took a turn for the worse? Because now her leverage is guaranteed. Now she *knows* she has me.

My fury seethes, but it's accompanied by a curl of ambition that almost veers recklessly into hope. If I can spy for her *and* we make a good assignment—

I sigh, rolling my shoulders in a way I hope makes me look bigger. "What's to promise that you'll keep my siblings safe if I do this for you? The very second I was out from under this roof, you had my sister doing the one thing I begged you to keep her away from."

Yasmin opens her mouth, but I'm not giving her a chance to defend herself. Not yet.

"I know the fact that we're family has a very loose hold on what you're willing and not willing to do."

A nod.

"And now I know I can't trust you."

"Trust is nothing in the face of need. And we need each other, Aisha," Yasmin says. "I can take care of your siblings. You can save the Fractionists before the General Body wipes us out entirely. I've given my whole life to this cause, and you've done something similar for yours," she says, nodding to my body.

A twinge of rejection rattles through me, uncomfortably close to the feeling that triggered my meltdown yesterday. So maybe my aunt understands me a little more than I'd like. And maybe I relate to her a little more than is comfortable. And maybe it won't be so bad, owing her. As long as Amar gets his treatment. As long as Malikah stays out of the dyeworks.

But I've never been great with optimism, and this dingy kitchen doesn't seem like the place to start. "I need a guarantee. Something stronger than your word."

Yasmin holds out her hands. "Aisha, you know I can't give you anything stronger than that. Look, this is why I've given my life over. Everything that ever mattered to me, my own sister included,

I lost because I *believe* in what Fractionism will do. This is the greater fate of humanity at stake—we weren't meant to be ruled by the General Body's tyranny. We deserve a choice in the heading of our starships. It's our only chance of finding a planet, our only chance of bringing this Fleet to the berth we've been seeking for three hundred years. Tell me you wouldn't do anything to achieve that too."

I scowl, the exo deepening the expression until my face aches. I can walk away now. Leave my sister in Yasmin's care and my brother at the mercy of the *Panacea*'s midtier doctors. There's no threat, no leverage I can use that doesn't put them in harm's way. Briefly I entertain—and the exo can't help but encourage—the idea of turning her over for a hefty reward from the General Body, but even that wouldn't be enough to keep my siblings safe forever. I need Yasmin more than she needs me.

My aunt draws a deep breath, her eyes closing. "I've lived far too long. My parents—your grandparents—died in their mid-twenties. Factory accidents, the both of them. Your parents were lucky to have as much time as they did. Every day I find myself holding people at arm's length because I know an early end is just around the corner. For me, for the children in this orphanage, for everyone. It's a fact of our district. A fact of the backend. And it *shouldn't be*."

Her voice catches before she can say anything else. Yasmin draws a deep breath and bows her head. I take in the apartment around us—the battered walls, the distant noises of children in the dormitories adjacent. I understand the weight on my aunt's shoulders. She owes her life to this place. It raised her, gave her purpose, and now it's dragging its claws through her.

I know I can't trust Yasmin entirely. But I trust the General Body even less. I've felt the unfairness that deepens the lines in

Yasmin's face. I live with Key's constant disdain for the backend echoing in my skull, and maybe there's something in me that thrills at the thought of sticking it to the system she believes in, the system that's already robbed us of so much.

Maybe my sacrifice wasn't in the surgery—a simple tradeoff, body for cash, one of the oldest human transactions. Maybe this is it here. To shoulder this danger, to do something not just for my family's sake, but for the sake of humanity—that's how I'll earn my siblings' safety. Fractionists believe that splitting the Fleet will bring us closer to finding the next good world. What if they're on to something?

I rise from the table, drawing myself up to my full height as if a string pulls me from the ridge of my exo. Yasmin stands with me, her eyes hooded and wary. I lock my gaze with hers. "If my sister goes back to the dyeworks, I'm burning your life to the ground."

"Understood."

"Then you've got yourself a deal," I say, extending my hand. A wicked thing goes wild in me when she takes it. Both the exo and I enjoy the way her expression shifts as my grip winches just a little too tight.

I don't know what it says about me, that I like the feel of her bones under my metal, but for a moment I *love* being Scela.

CHAPTER 8

KEY

I'm trying to ignore how long this is taking. My exo ticks off the minutes we've been on the *Reliant* in an irritating little count, but I distract myself from the subprocess by making a careful study of the enhancements on my forearms, peeling back my sleeve so I can prod at the metal and ports. Yasmin's stoop is mercifully tucked away from the bustle of the main street, but the reek of this place is inescapable, and I don't want to know how much of it my ass is going to retain once I stand up.

I still don't know why I was assigned to this trip, and the sheer *pointlessness* of me sitting here is making my prodding a little too aggressive. A warning flashes as I pull at a port on my wrist. Forget why I'm on this ship—I don't even know why I'm in this body.

My brain is stuck in a loop, attempting to dredge up the dream I had last night. All I can remember is a street much better than this one, a rip in the leg of the dress I was wearing, and the golden, camera-eyed boy watching me like he always does. With a computer in my head, you'd think my recollection would be perfect, but maybe the exo doesn't play nice with the subconscious.

Or maybe I have memory problems. I mean, I *definitely* have memory problems.

I huff, pulling at a band of metal striping my face so hard that I feel something *unstick* inside my cheek. A dull pain flushes through me, followed by a wave of embarrassment that my exo wholeheartedly encourages. I glance back at the door, but there's still no sign of Aisha wearing out her family's welcome.

I don't let myself get jealous, and the exo is happy to beat back that particular urge. My request for leave was clearly denied. I wanted to go back to the *Antilles* and see my mother and father. Wanted to ask them to fill in my missing pieces, explain how I ended up in Scela metal. But apparently Aisha's need to see her family was the more urgent concern in the eyes of the higher-ups. So no clean, elegant corridors for me. I've been shunted off to the backend. Apparently just to sit around and keep Aisha from beating up her aunt.

I guess if I'm going to find any answers, I'll have to do it myself. Keep throwing myself against the holes, exceed expectations as a Scela, and hope that it's enough to unlock the memories I've lost.

I tip my head back, staring up at the ceiling of the ship's habitat. The buildings on this street crowd into each other, looking dangerously unstable and slightly menacing. Now I'm not sure if the sensation of being watched is an aftertaste of the dream or a real thing. I don't know how people in the backend live like this. Everyone's listening. Privacy's unheard of. Even the air feels thicker.

When Aisha emerges at last, something's changed about her. Her lips are pursed, her brows set in a determined line. The anger that nearly had her decking Yasmin in front of a bunch of kids has cooled, but something still gnaws at her.

Unsurprisingly.

Her sister's at her side, and I can't help but stare at the barbaric dye on her hands. I've never seen workers' marks up close like this, and I feel a morbid fascination take over through my exo's disgust. She has her little red fingers wound around a port on Aisha's forearm. My exo mirrors the ghost of the sensation even without a connection to Aisha's mind.

"And it was *huge,*" the little girl chirps, clearly halfway through a story she's keen on finishing. "And the rep was right there, and I got to shake her hand, and I told her that one day I'm going to be a representative too."

Aisha nods, her facial muscles strained as she smiles Scela-wide. Her eyes still look lost in thought, and there's an extra element of tension that I'm sure comes from imagining the contrast between her sister's red hands and the representative's undoubtedly spotless ones.

My exo keeps nudging me with the countdown until our report time, and I'm sure Aisha's is doing the same. She's dawdled long enough, eating up every spare minute of the marshal's generous three hours.

"Un-Haad," I warn, just in case she's not getting the message.

Aisha crouches low next to Malikah, holding out her hands and turning her palms upward. I flinch as the little girl's red fingers skim over the metal. I have to look away. My enhanced hearing feeds me the soft words that pass between them anyway, and I stuff down a twinge of jealousy, telling myself they aren't worth it.

"I'll come back," Aisha promises. "Soon as I can."

The exo's disdain runs parallel to my own. We both know she's blatantly lying. She has no idea if the words she's saying are ones she can follow through on—she's not the one who decides when she gets to visit. With a sinking feeling, I realize I'm dreading the moment her mind reconnects to mine. I'll be forced to share the weight of this day. This moment and its fallout. The longer she wallows in it, the worse it'll be. I turn my back and start off down the street, knowing her exo will pull her in my wake.

I never want to come back to this ugly, forsaken place.

On the ride back, Aisha stews quietly. Maybe it's over her sister. Maybe it's over her brother. Maybe it's her aunt, or maybe something else entirely. Whatever it is, she's rattled enough that she didn't utter a single line of prayer when the shuttle launched.

Her aunt certainly rattled me—something about that woman put my exo on edge, and I didn't care for the way she flinched at the sight of me. I could do without humanity's horror, especially coming from the horror of the backend.

"What happened in there?" I finally ask. Not that I'm interested, but *some* noise is better than the empty rumble of the shuttle.

Aisha doesn't bite. Her gaze turns to the rear port, and I follow it. We watch the *Reliant* fall away, fading into its position in the District formation. Just over the ship's left wing, a shadow lurks farther back. The *Panacea*.

Aisha finally presses her hand against the hull, muttering prayers for her brother. Only a handful of people from Seventh District make it off that ship, and all of them must have been on the upper tiers.

There's an impulse inside me to comfort her. I don't know if it comes from the scrapings of my humanity or from the Scela urge to see Aisha as my comrade, my squadmate, part of a greater whole. All I know is that I can't do it. I can't tell her it's going to be all right—because I don't believe that. I'm not sure if I've ever believed that. And unlike Aisha, I won't waste words that could be worthless later.

I do what I can. The bare minimum. I watch the rear port with her until the *Panacea* is out of sight.

By the time we unload on the *Dread,* a notification from the ship's systems tells us to report to the mess for lunch. Wordlessly, we follow the impulse it feeds us, winding through the narrow, darkened hallways until we spill into the low-ceilinged cafeteria.

I'd forgotten my hunger, or maybe my exo repressed it, but in the presence of a simmering cauldron of chunky stew, it lets my stomach rumble. Aisha and I load up massive bowls—far too heavy for any human to carry—and find a spot along a bench in the back row of the cafeteria, underneath the rankings board. I spare it a quick glance, though with no training this morning, there's nothing that would have boosted our position farther left or dragged us farther right than the last time I checked in. After our shaky start, our standing has been improving steadily. But it's not enough for the gnawing ache inside me that won't settle for anything less than the white stripes of the elite.

There's no time for lunchtime chatter. Scela wiring makes us efficient about everything, including eating—we have to be to consume the amount of food it takes to power our bodies. We tip our bowls back and chug. If the weird, protein-packed concoction has a flavor, my exo keeps my brain from registering it. The cooks aboard the *Dread* have only three meals in their repertoire—breakfast, lunch, and dinner. Some of the older Scela swear they can taste the difference.

I try to remember the last thing I ate that was delicious, but I only end up stumbling into the big gap in my memory, like I've just run up against the edge of a precipice.

Now I think the stew has a taste. I think it's sour.

I'm just starting to wonder where Woojin and Praava are when a siren wails. Lights flash along a strip on the wall, and the ship's broadcast snaps into me as if I've been loaded directly into a *Dread*-wide exosystem.

ALL AVAILABLE UNITS REPORT TO ASSEMBLY DECK FOR IMMEDIATE DEPLOYMENT TO STARSHIP AESCHYLUS, *FOURTH DISTRICT.*

The cafeteria dissolves into the closest thing to chaos that we're capable of. Scela wolf down the last of their stew and make for the door, filing in orderly lines, guided by the tug of their exos.

Aisha glances at me, lowering her bowl. "They can't mean us, right?" she says, her fingers tightening. "The marshal said—"

What the marshal said is irrelevant, because all of a sudden the marshal's in our heads. *Sorry, kids. Your day off has been cut short. The situation aboard the* Aeschylus *is ripe for another field test, and after today's report, the Chancellor has given orders to push your training forward.* A note of skepticism needles through our exosystem in the wake of her announcement. Seems like the marshal isn't convinced that we should be out in the field so soon. What *situation* is going down on the *Aeschylus* that she doesn't think we could handle? A perfect little storm of resentment rises in me, ready to counter her.

But Marshal Jesuit doesn't give voice to her doubt, doesn't push it into the realm of solid thought. *Suit up immediately and meet me on Assembly,* she concludes, and I snap back into the mess's bustle, breathing like a hand's been clenched on my throat. I tip back my bowl, sucking down the dregs of my stew before the impulse rattling down my spine jerks me to my feet.

We race down to Assembly to join the frantic pack of Scela preparing to deploy. I skid into my bay, the exo humming with energy as it practically begs for the parts that will complete my body. I snatch the chestpiece from its mounts. Getting the rig on is far easier now, and as the data tree blossoms in my mind, I bask in the sensation of being whole.

Then something clicks in my head, robbing me of that wonderful feeling as three other minds slam into mine. The relinking of the exosystem leaves me paralyzed, clutching the metal grating. I close my eyes, half of me trying to sort through the jumble of thoughts, the other half trying to block them out entirely.

But something's *wrong* with the exosystem, and it's not even coming from Aisha. It takes a moment for me to process what's different, what the strange sensation creeping across my brain is. Then I start to clue in on the signs. Aisha's exo smacking away her blush response. Woojin and Praava holding back a strange cocktail of laughter and embarrassment.

Why? Aisha groans internally, squeezing her eyes shut as if that'll do any good.

Woojin breaks first, a cackle slipping from his lips, loud enough that the nearest Scela whip their heads around. Praava glances across to his bay, and suddenly the exosystem swells with the memory of her hands tracing down his enhancements, of his unnaturally warm body pressed flush against hers, of ports clacking awkwardly together and sweat and flesh and—

I instinctively shake my head, trying to clear away the images, the sensations, the *sex*. I've never regretted the exosystem more. *Why have you done this?* I ask flatly. *Don't you dare tell me that you two—that there are* feelings *involved.*

We were curious, Praava says, scoffing. *Wanted to see what it'd be like.*

And you put no thought into the fact that the four of us basically share a brain? Aisha asks. She clenches her fingers, and I catch a flash of worry from her before she tucks it back inside herself.

Woojin smirks. *Aisha, we share a brain. Do I really seem like the kind of guy who puts thought into anything?*

I want to bury my head in my hands.

It's not that bad, c'mon, Praava urges.

It's not only bad. It's ridiculous. I don't even know what I signed up for, but I definitely didn't sign up for this.

Do you think— Aisha starts, then frowns. *Do you think we should maybe discuss this? How this whole thing is going to work? Because if this affects us as a squad, clearly we should have discussed this before.*

Oh, so I'm gonna need permission from a Ledic prude before I—

Woojin doesn't get a chance to finish that thought. Aisha's reaction sears through the exosystem, her will coming down on Woojin like a sharpened blade. All four of us feel the rattling buzz that overtakes the back of his neck and yanks his speech away before he can say anything more.

His eyes go wide. The breath stops in his lungs.

Aisha loves it—the feeling of having a life in her hands. Warnings flash through the exosystem, even though her exo seems to enjoy it just as much as she does. *Let's start with this,* Aisha growls. *Take any cues from my religion about how I see sex again and permission won't be—*

Praava slices through Aisha's hold on Woojin's mind, and for the second time today, I pull Aisha back before things get ugly, mentally shoving her away into her own mind. Woojin gasps in relief, his memory flickering to a similar moment—I get a flash of a Sixth District gangster pinning him against a wall with an elbow on his throat before he suppresses the image. *Point taken,* he says once his head clears.

Can we all just stay in our own heads and discuss this? Can we have a rational discussion, like rational mechanically enhanced people? Praava mutters.

That's asking a lot, I groan.

I'm aroace, Aisha declares. *So you won't get this problem from me.*

Woojin rolls his eyes. *I'm pansexual, and it* isn't *a problem. That's not what's holding this squad back, and you all know it.* He dares us to say otherwise, but we know better.

I'm hetero, Praava says, just to round it out.

They nudge me.

And I recoil in a way I don't fully understand. It's a simple question. It's a question I should have an answer for already. And yet—

There are chasms in who I am that I haven't even begun to explore. Holes that go deeper than the memories I'm missing. I think of my dreams, of the camera-eyed boy—did I *like* the way he watched me? Did I like *him,* or just the feeling of being watched? *It's just a dream,* my exo insists, but the more it tries to shepherd me away from the edge of my empty spaces, the more I want to dive. Something is getting more and more solid inside me, something that begins and ends with a golden boy and an unblinking lens.

But I can't—

I try—

Fuck this.

Key? Praava asks across the system. I feel her brace herself to leap into my head and see what's eating me, but Aisha and Woojin hold her back. Surprised, I thank them. If all four of us are going to share heads, we can't be allowed to wrench secrets away from each other. Some things we should be able to keep to ourselves.

It's only when we fall back into our own headspaces that we notice a fifth presence in the system. Across the deck, Marshal Jesuit raises an eyebrow at us. *Well, you all handled that way better than most recruits,* she observes, and even her thoughts are having a hard time holding back laughter. *This is my favorite part of any fresh batch.*

Does this happen . . . a lot? I ask.

Every damn time, she says, and strains to keep her chuckling internal. *There's always at least two fuzzheads who want to see what it'll be like with these bodies. Weirdos.*

Woojin crumples.

Oh, now you're embarrassed? Praava cackles.

And just like that the mood switches, the unsettling question of . . . whatever the hell that was brushed aside as the others start to grin. I play along, letting the edge of my smile out, but there's nothing genuine in it. I need answers. I need to know why I'm missing so much.

The marshal shakes her head. *Enough of that. We've got a job to do. Report to shuttle—*

Her words get sliced in half by an incoming transmission. The herald of the *Dread* system swells in our heads, blasting, *THREAT OF HARD VACUUM DETECTED. EQUIP BREACH SUITS.*

CHAPTER 9

AISHA

A flurry of emotions passes through the squad, and for a moment our identities blur as we're folded into the tumult. We're nothing but fear, anxiety, excitement—until Marshal Jesuit swells her presence and brings us back to ground. *Suits are on the racks in your bays. Trust that your exos know what to do,* she says.

I grab the breach suit from its hanger on the scaffolding and wrestle the skintight garment over my ridges and augmentations. It's cumbersome, near impossible to get on straight, and my rapidly accelerating pulse isn't helping.

I've barely had time to process what happened on the *Reliant*. But the rest of the chaos in our exosystem—Wooj and Praava, Key shutting down, the threat of breach—is a blessing, and as I get my thoughts in order, I make sure to thank God for it. The exo maintains those gentle barriers between myself and the others, screening each thought that flows out of me. Its urge for self-preservation has brought it down squarely on my side of this, and it's doing its best to make sure no one gets wind of the treason I've agreed to.

The headpiece slams down, my HUD flares up, and metal

creeps down my neck, interlocking with the breach suit's edges and forming a seal. My breathing echoes in my ears as my vision adjusts to the cameras.

Whatever's happening on the *Aeschylus,* there's a risk a hull could blow, venting the ship's air. Though my human remnants curdle with fear at the thought, the exo soothes them, its cool logic reminding me that my breach suit is airtight and insulated to protect me from the void. I reach out into the exosystem to find that my squad is boiling with nervous energy but ready to deploy.

There's too much going on for me to be anxious about packing into the shuttle. A constant stream of data pours into our exos, lecturing us on combat forms that my enhanced muscles have never put into practice. On my left, Key gulps down the download, her mind whirling with thoughts of greatness, of finally proving herself, of putting all this new knowledge to the test. Across the bay, the data's doing little to put aside Praava's worries. Her thoughts jumble between the download, her birthship in danger, her sister and parents, and the hell there'll be to pay if anything happens to them. And Wooj is utterly overwhelmed—between the full rig and the years of knowledge and facts being slammed into his brain, he's practically catatonic in his seat.

A hint of derision rises out of Key, pointed at Wooj and, for no clear reason, at me too. Already she's bracing herself for one of us to mess up and sink the squad's position on the rankings board before we've even set foot on the *Aeschylus.* I shove her headspace, which earns me a snarl from my left and a mental swat that makes my HUD flare blindingly white.

Marshal Jesuit's attention whips around. She knocks us back into our own heads, her scrutiny settling like a weight on my shoulders. *What happened on the* Reliant? she asks. I can't see her from where I'm strapped in, but she must be up front with the higher-ranking officers.

Everything's fine, I tell her. I'm lying, and I'm fairly sure she knows I'm lying, but hopefully Marshal Jesuit believes I'm lying because it's what I need to tell myself. Not because I've struck a deal with the very movement I was recruited to combat.

I press a hand back against the hullmetal and pray for strength. The Scela on my right openly stares, his headpiece still cocked back and his expression unreadable.

"What's it to you?" I snap, letting the exo pour its harsh edges into my voice.

"You really think that's going to do any good?"

Though my exo hums warnings about respecting Scela who clearly outrank me, my lips curl from my teeth, a hostile snarl brewing at the back of my throat.

"I used to be like you—before I was like this," he says, knocking his knuckles against his exo ridge. "Went to temple every week. Kept my hair covered whenever I grew it long. Prayed my Morning and Evening Strains." He slaps his hand back against the hullmetal in a gesture that conveys equal parts familiarity and bitterness. "Did everything right. And sure, I made it off the *Kronos* in one piece before it melted. But the rest of my family didn't."

My gut drops, as if the shuttle has already launched into the void. "I'm so sorry," I tell him, my hand flinching off the ship's hull, but the Scela's already turned away, snapping his headpiece down to cover his face.

I wasn't really old enough to comprehend the *Kronos* disaster when it happened. I remember casts announcing that Fractionists had overrun a starship control room and tried to free it from the General Body's directives. They fired the FTL drives without giving them time to warm up, and the resulting meltdown reduced the *Kronos* to a warped glob of hullmetal before most of the citizens had time to evacuate. I could never grasp loss on that scale—I'm still not sure I can.

But I understand what this man lost perfectly. Though I've managed to keep my faith, I know how it must have cost him his. And now we've both landed in the same place, on the same shuttle, bound for another ship that could end up the same way.

I hadn't been thinking about the *Kronos* when I shook hands with Yasmin. All I cared about was protecting my siblings. But now I'm mired in doubt. Historically, the Fractionists have tended to value their movement's progress more than the Fleet's people. It's part of the reason the General Body sees them as the most dangerous threat we face. As long as it puts them closer to their goals, the Fractionists will do whatever it takes, and people have suffered for it. Anything to break the General Body's hold on the Fleet's destiny and take it into their own hands. I don't know if I believe those sacrifices are worth it. I haven't had time to process any of this.

What exactly have I thrown myself into the middle of?

I press my head back against the restraints as a familiar human face moves down the line, checking that each of us is securely locked into our seats. "Hey, Zaire!" one of the older Scela shouts, and the dockworker turns his head. "Save a spot at the table for me tonight."

"You that keen on losing your money?" Zaire shoots back, grinning wide—human wide, uncomfortably wide, too much of his eyes in the gesture—as his nimble fingers fly over another harness.

"I'll beat you this time," the Scela says.

"Sure, keep telling yourself that. I won't complain." He replies, reaching Key in line. "Hey, newbie, how's it going?"

She doesn't reply. In the exosystem, something leaks out of her, sour and . . . a little pleased? Her face stays locked in stoic contempt, but I can feel her exo pressing down an urge to smile.

"All right, got a grouchy robot over here. How about you?" Zaire asks as he moves onto me. "Looking good, fuzzhead."

I mumble a gruff "thank you," my thoughts flickering self-consciously to the scarf I should be wearing.

Zaire skips down the rest of the line, finishing his restraint checks. He turns back to the cargo bay with an impish grin on his face. "Y'all are a real pleasure. Have a nice flight!" He tips us a salute, then jumps off the rear hatch, slamming it behind him. Through the tiny window embedded in the hatch, I can just make out the shapes of more dockworkers retreating from the ship's aft. A second later, a shudder rolls through the hullmetal behind me.

I don't care about the dirty looks I'll get—my hand is back on the hull, every prayer I know spilling from my lips. The exo keeps trying to shut me down, and I keep pushing it back, because no amount of wiring in my brain is going to make me hate flying any less.

We're deploying into an unknown situation, one where the very *air* stands a chance of vanishing around us, and the Chancellor will be watching, I'm sure. I need everything God can give me.

I grit my teeth as the shuttle rushes out the launch tube and into the cradle of zero G. My exo does its best, but the afterthought of stew bubbles up in my mouth no matter how hard I try to swallow it back. Murmurs rise from the ranks as a cargo bay full of Scela lift against their restraints. I'm surrounded by drifting, hyperpowered limbs, our metal gone feather-light without gravity to enforce its mass.

As if that sensation weren't strange enough, a click in my head sweeps me into an exosystem—not the pool of my squadmates I've become accustomed to, but the torrent of every mind in the shuttle. My breath comes in confused hitches as my brain struggles to equalize against the currents of thoughts. Familiar threads wind through it—snatches of Wooj, of Praava, of Key, flocking instinctively toward the ground the marshal holds for herself in the chaos.

Un-Haad. A solid line of thought wraps around me like an anchor, digging in with the weight of my name. *With me.* The marshal's lungs are my own, and I follow their push and pull until my breathing slows and I settle back into myself.

A broadcast plunges through the exosystem, warming brightly as it overrides our earpieces and pumps audio out of them. *Just minutes ago, a Fractionist demonstration began on the starship* Aeschylus. *They've managed to shut down a large portion of the ship's research quarter.* My exo informs me that it's Grand Commander Ilych, chief among Scela, speaking.

In the turmoil of the massive exosystem, I pick out Praava's fear sharpening to a point, so familiar that I feel for a moment like we're one and the same. In the shadow of the marshal's mind, she loops her sister's name until underneath the voice of the commander there's a constant buzz of *Ratna Ratna Ratna Ratna Ratna Ratna Ratna* humming through the current.

Reports show that the protestors are armed with stunsticks. One hit from their weapons has the potential to short out an exorig. We'll be working to disarm and restrain them, with a larger goal of restoring order on the ship.

I leak worry into the exosystem, despite my best efforts to hide it. A download can help, but it's nowhere near true combat training. Can we really handle armed protestors? The Chancellor must think so, though the doubt radiating out of the marshal is difficult to ignore.

The grand commander drones on anyway. *A threat of hull breach has been made. In the event of a breach, our priority will switch to securing the citizens in their designated emergency seals.*

She'll be fine, Wooj reassures Praava as a wave of crippling fear surges out of her. *She's smart, right?*

Smartest person I know.

So she'll be smart enough to get far away from the protests and into a sealed zone.

Unless they breach that zone too, Key shoots back, and Praava twitches in her rig.

I hate to admit it, but Key's on to something. Ratna is a doctor, so she'll most likely be in the research quarter, the nexus of the protests. If Fractionists there are threatening to breach the hull, the emergency systems will quarantine the rest of the ship and let that quarter vent.

But why are the Fractionists targeting the *Aeschylus*? And why now? With the rest of the squad overtaken by Praava's panic and the grand commander's orders, I dare to let my own worries bleed into my thoughts. My bargain with Yasmin was about supplying information, but I don't have enough information of my own. Would she expect me to help these Fractionists? Will she know if I don't?

The shuttle pitches suddenly as we slip into our approach. Praava's worry crescendos. The front of the ship jolts as we run up against our docking struts, and alarms sound through the bay, warning that the airlocks are about to seal. We unsnap our restraints the instant the rear door springs open, our exos pushing us to our feet in unison. As we disembark, another download drills into our exos, this time filling us with the ship's layout until we know every bolt of it.

Something's stirring in Praava. Her frustration spikes outward— she should be soaking in the scent of her birthship, and instead all she has is the processed air inside her suit.

The marshal reaches out and plucks us out of the larger exosystem like kittens lifted by the nape. *Steady,* she warns, shepherding the squad back into our usual configuration. *We'll be a part of the rear guard, watching the backs of the more seasoned Scela. We're still waiting on orders.*

But waiting won't do. Waiting is a suffocating vacuum, boiling us from all sides. Ratna's out there, and we *have to get to her.*

And before the four of us can come to grips with what's happening, we're running. The tidal wave of Praava's urgency pummels into the backs of our necks, sweeping us down the corridor even as the marshal shouts for us to stop and the other commanding officers cry out in alarm. But none of the other Scela come after us—their exos must keep them in place.

Our exos are panicking. They've never had to deal with something like this, and the machines are completely at a loss. Their control over our bodies cedes to Praava's sheer force of will. She doesn't need the exos to navigate this ship. She knows the back hallways and ladders that will get us to the research quarter without running into a single soul. This is her home, her birthship, her place in the Fleet, no matter how much the exos try to insist that her loyalty belongs to the *Dread.*

And we're all along for the ride.

Key's the first to come close to breaking her hold. She rears her head back, her thoughts a jumbled mess as she tries to extract herself from the quagmire of Praava's emotions. *What the fu—* she gets out before she's smothered again.

Distantly, I feel the tug of Marshal Jesuit in pursuit, but Praava's fast to dismiss that fact. She can catch up once we're sure Ratna's okay.

Wooj is gone. His mind's already so subdued, so loosely attached to his body with the full rig on. Praava fills him, gives him guidance, keeps his legs moving as we crest another set of ladders and pour out into a service tunnel that runs just beneath the bounds of the quarter's hull.

We may be driven by love for Ratna, but our bodies are still weak, still unused to the full rigs that encase us, and Marshal Jesuit is closing fast. As we draw up beneath a manhole that will take us to the quarter's main streets, my rig's cameras catch her distant form charging after us. Praava lunges up at the manhole cover. Her enhanced legs power the jump so forcefully that she smashes right through. Our cameras' apertures whirl as they adjust to the sudden wash of light that pours down from above. She yanks Wooj up after her, and Key follows a moment later.

Don't you dare, Un-Haad, the marshal rumbles, her voice cutting through the roar of Praava's thoughts.

But I can't stop. Even if I wanted to stop, I couldn't—the urge in our system is too primal, too fundamental, too familiar, too overwhelmingly human. My body is just a tool under Praava's command. I take a running leap and catch the edge of the manhole, then swing myself up into the light.

And freeze at last.

Praava's run us right into the main thoroughfare of the research quarter.

Right into the middle of the Fractionist protests. And almost immediately, the four of us realize the mistake we've made.

The demonstrators on the *Porthos* were a concentrated group, a small, single-minded gang focused on gaining the attention of the ship's representative. They went down in mere minutes. This is not that.

This is a mob.

The streets are crowded with people, some of whom got knocked aside by our frantic ascent to the surface and are only now crawling to their feet. The rest of them are slow to grasp what's happened—they stare, blinking, trying to wrap their poor human brains around the way we've just rocketed into their midst. The bulbous lenses of a camera crew's rig turn on us.

Then a roar comes from farther down the street. All heads swing that way, even ours, and my heart sinks as my cameras zoom in on the commotion. The Scela deployment has arrived. They wade through the crowd, swinging stunsticks of their own as they beat back the frightened mass of people.

Driving them straight toward us.

"They're cutting us off!" someone behind Wooj screams. The sharp crackle of an unsheathed stunstick draws my attention, and I duck just as the weapon swoops over my head. My exo uses the distraction to try to break free of Praava's hold. It pours instructions on how to disarm my attacker into my head, but before they can settle, the heavy hum of Praava's will slams into the back of my neck—she's just spotted the building her sister works in. Protestors are crowded around it, and the urge to carve a path through the mass of people to get to Ratna builds.

The stunstick comes down again, the exo screams in my ear,

and I manage to dodge to the side. A buzz runs through my right forearm—the weapon missed me by inches.

"We're not here to—" Key tries to yell, but the rest of us quiet her as we press our backs together, the crowd backing up around us. Of course we're here to hurt them. We're Scela, and they're Fractionists. Praava urges us toward the building, but before we can take a step, three more protestors draw stunsticks and advance on us.

There's too much noise in the exosystem. Too much confusion. I know I'm supposed to fight, I know my body's been loaded with instructions on how to engage, but with Praava's control wrenched tight on my brainstem, I can't match that knowledge to my body's function. None of us can. The buzz of electricity in the air sends fear roiling through the exosystem from all four of us.

The closest man lifts his stunstick.

When I was a little kid, I once saw a cast of a thunderstorm on Old Earth. I used to imagine being there, on a planet, feeling God's power in the forces of chaos around me. First the flash of lightning, then the roar of thunder. Natural and inevitable.

The stunstick cuts through the air. Lightning.

And then the thunder. It comes in the form of Marshal Gwen Jesuit hitting the ground with a massive *thud* as she leaps between us and our attackers. She strikes, fluid and devastating. In one motion she locks her hand around the man's arm and wrenches it back. The Fractionist barely has time to gasp his surprise before the weapon is out of his hand and into hers. She swings it over her shoulder without looking and parries an incoming blow from a woman.

She's faster than anything I've ever seen before, power rolling off her in waves as her enhancements flash in the bright day lights. She dodges another attacker, letting his own momentum send him toppling over his feet as she snatches his weapon out of his hands, turns it over in the air once, then drives its dull point into his back. He goes limp. With two stunsticks in her grasp, she becomes a whirlwind that sends the crowd scrambling out of her way as she drops anyone who dares lift a hand toward us.

The four of us cower, pressed together, doing our best to stay clear of her fury. Even the buzz of Praava's will fades as her mind goes quiet with awe. This is it—the weapon we're supposed to be, the true meaning of Scela power. Through our weak link to the marshal's exosystem, we can feel the pureness of her integration, the way her mind and exo work in tandem to turn her into a perfect blade.

She cuts a path around us, beating back the crowd until we're ringed by unconscious bodies, some still twitching from the stunsticks' touch. When she finally comes to rest, we're left with a thirty-foot berth. The marshal flicks the controls on the stunsticks' grip, and a collective sigh of relief breathes through our system as the crackle and snap of electricity in the air dissipates.

Marshal Jesuit turns to face us, and all four of us instantly decide that we'd rather take the Fractionists. Her linkage to our exosystem cranks up to its full power, restored by her proximity, and the weight of her anger crashes down on us. *What is it about you four?* she snarls, and a strange, numbing feeling washes over my mind. It takes me a moment to realize she's ripping up our exosystem, isolating us in our own bodies to protect us from Praava. *I've never had a squad go charging headlong into danger like that. And it's not even the first time you've done it. And you're barely a week into basic.*

I picture the board in the cafeteria. I picture our squad falling rightward, below patrol, off the edge. Shame and anger clash in the pit of my stomach.

Praava flinches as the marshal grabs her by the exo, just in case she tries to bolt again. Marshal Jesuit's will buzzes hard on the back of our necks, sending us scurrying into an alleyway before the protest can converge on us. With her guarding the entrance, a sense of calm settles over us.

"What . . . what happened?" Wooj asks, swaying slightly.

"Emotion is the bane of the exosystem," Marshal Jesuit says. "It's raw and powerful, *will* incarnate—it can take you over, and if your mind is linked to others, it gets messy. You're still learning the exo, which made it very easy for *this one*"—she smacks Praava on the shoulder with one of her deactivated stunsticks—"to take over the system when she felt something so strongly."

"I'm sorry," Praava mumbles.

Something light and motherly flickers out of Marshal Jesuit, but she quickly clamps down on it. "You four ran off before getting your weapons. Now we're in the middle of an active clash, and I only have two stunsticks." She shakes her head, a laugh bubbling through the system. From the mouth of the alley, we spot some of the humans she dropped stirring back into consciousness. Marshal Jesuit strides back out into the open, crouching next to the closest one. "We need to keep these people from getting trampled," she says, laying her hand on the twitching woman's back. "Pick up what you can carry. Praava, I'm watching you. The rest of you can have this back."

She waves her hand, more for dramatic flair than anything else, and our exosystem linkage restores in a rush. It's almost a relief, having Key and Wooj's thoughts back alongside my own, now that we're clear of Praava's dominance. Our exos greet each other like old friends before turning to the task at hand. *Do we just . . . ,* Key starts.

I think so. I take a knee next to the nearest human and pick her up. She must weigh a hundred and fifty pounds, but the full rig takes the weight like it's nothing. I lift her, balancing her midsection along the plane of my shoulder, before bending back down and picking up another one. Wooj and Key follow suit, and Marshal Jesuit stows one of her acquired stunsticks on her belt, keeping the other out just in case as she starts scooping up as many people as she can carry with her free arm.

A broadcast ping rolls through the exosystem. *Breach danger heightened,* it shrieks. *Make for safe spaces immediately.*

My stomach twists. I've thrown my cards in with the Fractionists, and they're venting a ship. I don't understand why. I can't make sense of any of this—it's all happening too fast.

Above us, a klaxon starts to wail, and the tide of the protest falls into shaky confusion. "Hull breach is coming," Marshal Jesuit roars, her enhanced body blasting her voice over the crowd. "Everyone needs to get to a sealed zone *now.*"

The conscious people don't need to be told twice. A cry goes up across the crowd, screams piercing the air around us as people start running. Some know where they're going. Others look lost—my exo identifies them as potential Fractionist organizers, people who might have traveled to the *Aeschylus* specifically for the uprising. They follow the others in a confused jumble.

We reach into our download of the ship's layout, searching for the closest emergency airlock. The nearest one is a hundred yards along the thoroughfare. As we take off toward it, a ping of guilt runs through me for the people we left behind. It pushes my legs faster and faster, and we easily outstrip the humans, who dive to the side when they hear the thunder of our footfalls behind them.

The entrance to the airlock space bottlenecks the crowd into a dangerous, seething jumble. We push our way through, our awareness expanding, our cameras flickering nervously, just in case someone has a stunstick, but it seems that having unconscious Fractionist protestors on our backs is doing wonders for our public image. People even part to let us through.

"Here," Key says, foisting one of her limp humans onto a pair of protestors. "Take them in. Watch their heads." Wooj and I follow her lead until we're unloaded, then immediately turn and start pushing back through the crowds.

As we make it past the bottleneck, we pass Marshal Jesuit, who's coming in with what seems like an impossibly large number of people draped over her back. "There are still a couple unconscious back there," she says. "I think some of the protestors are helping, but—"

"On it," Key snaps. Purpose ignites inside her, and she takes off down the street.

"Where's Praava?" Wooj asks. His worry sears the space between us.

"Best to let her follow that impulse corrupting her. Otherwise she'd be completely nonfunctional." Marshal Jesuit hands off her unconscious cargo to the other people cramming into the breach shelter.

"So she went into the facility?" he says, hitching his head at the building the protestors had gathered around. "All by herself, with her mind a mess, in the middle of an armed protest?"

The marshal shrugs. "She has her breach suit. The ship's management software will clear a path for her, so she won't be ripping down any doors, and no human's going to go after her with the breach alarms going off. You two stick with me. We need to make sure these people get locked down safely." Farther down the avenue, more refugees are racing for the shelter, herded by Scela forces. Some of the Scela have children clinging to their shoulders.

My exo does its best to tune out the klaxons overhead. I glance back, wondering how many more people the airlock can take. They weren't built anticipating this many people in one area—the shelters are supposed to be able to support the ship's population, evenly distributed throughout the living quarters. It's already tightly packed.

The pitch of the klaxons changes, and my heart sinks. The Scela run faster, grabbing whomever they can. Their pounding feet echo my pounding heart. The air draws tight around me. "Get inside!" Marshal Jesuit screams, wrapping her arms around the people nearest to her.

It's too late.

We're too late.

The *Aeschylus* is venting.

CHAPTER 10

KEY

I've never known wind. The air circulation systems on every starship I've ever been on have been gentle creatures, barely noticeable. I'd seen casts, of course, taken from discovered worlds, from inhospitable planet surfaces, from Old Earth, showing the menace of weather that the void has protected us from for three hundred years.

Now the void is reminding us why we need to be protected from it too.

The rational part of my mind knows that I'm in my breach suit. I'm still breathing, even as the air explodes out of the ship.

But something irrational is taking over me as I freeze in the middle of the thoroughfare. It feels like it's rising up out of the holes, clawing out of the emptiness to seize my brainstem. The exo fights back, trying to stuff this worming, strange sensation back where it came from.

My eyes land on a person gasping for breath as the air goes thinner and thinner, and that *thing* bucks and thrashes against my exo's hold. Is it compassion? Concern? That raw emotion the marshal warned us about? But I've felt those things before—admittedly in smaller doses than the others—and the exo never fought me like this. What's so different about now?

My cameras flick erratically from person to person. The Fractionists around me have no protection from the void. The conscious ones flounder and gasp, the unconscious ones going stiller and stiller. My exo urges me to detach from them. It's the only way to save my mind from the horror of the inevitable.

I glance back at the shelter. The airlocks are already sealed. There's nothing I can do for the people around me.

For the second time today, a larger exosystem snaps me up. I plunge into the stream of minds, all of us electrified with the new order pounding into our skulls. I search for the marshal and my squadmates, but none of them are here. We're all the Scela still outside the breach shelters, and we're being ordered to—

No, I rebel. *I can't.*

The twisting, scrabbling *thing* inside me fights against it, but my exo urges me to stoop, and the will of the order bends my legs.

I shouldn't—

My fingers close around the hilt of a protestor's discarded stunstick. They turn the knob to its strongest setting.

All around me, the other Scela move back and forth through the stragglers, dolling out the flash of stunsticks' mercy.

A sick feeling twists in my stomach that the exo does its best to remove. I'm not supposed to have a heart anymore. I'm not supposed to care that we're killing these people left and right. Is it cowardly that I'd rather let them die painfully by the void than easily by my own hands?

It's a peaceful way to go, the exo wills me to understand. A brief, painful jolt is better than the agony of asphyxiation and vacuum exposure.

I lift the stick.

I bring it down. I force my brain to disconnect, force my emotions to quiet, stuff whatever that *thing* was back in the holes that riddle me. But there's some part of it that never goes away. No matter how many times I touch the stick to skin. No matter how gently I do it. No matter how hard I do it when doing it gently doesn't work.

My only consolation is the exosystem. It's somewhere between a current and a song, the voices of dozens of minds in concert flowing through grief and anger and frustration. Some are furious at the Fractionists, their strikes rough and thoughts red-tinged. Others are torn apart at the thought of killing—we're supposed to be *defending* these people, after all. But every last one of them doesn't want to be doing this, and it keeps me steady, knowing I'm not alone. For maybe the first time, I'm truly glad to have other people in my head.

I force myself to watch as I do it. To bear witness to these people's end as they stare right back at me, clutching their throats. I rip back the fetters the exo has slammed down over my cameras and expand my gaze until I can see absolutely everything around me. The quiet, motionless bodies, and the ones that still twitch with life. There's a camera crew creeping through the thoroughfare, breach suits on, but undoubtedly human underneath. Their lenses twist and focus, bending low to catch details on the dead and nearly dying.

Something unsettling rattles through me. Something the exo is trying to keep me away from.

One of the camera crewmembers turns and spots me. She hoists her device, her hands flying over the controls as I find myself pinned by her gaze. An echo of my dreams shudders up my spine. I don't know what I'm supposed to do in the face of it, so I just stare back at her. She seems like she exists in a world completely removed from the one around her. Her breach suit is polished and athletic, clearly not a Fourth District issue.

In fact, everything about her seems First District to the practiced eye. She must have flown out to cover the protests. Of course the First District–based news cycle would want to get prime material for the cast that will inform the rest of the Fleet of what happened here. It'll be a devastating blow for the Fractionist movement—this mindless destruction, this meaningless death. No one even seems to be sure what the objective of the protests was.

The woman turns her camera away, and I let myself breathe easy.

Then the thought hits.

She's wearing a breach suit.

She came from First District.

She's here moments after the *Aeschylus* vented.

Her suit's not from this district.

We're all wearing breach suits. All of us Scela. It was part of our mission. We *knew* it was going to happen.

The machine along my spine reminds me that the General Body is good. I already know this. I know the work they do—the work *we* do for them—is for the benefit of all humankind. The Fractionists are the ones who would vent a ship. They melted the *Kronos,* and they ripped the *Aeschylus*'s hide open the moment the tide of the protest turned in favor of the Scela enforcers. It's them. It had to have been *them.* The General Body wouldn't slaughter a group of

117

people for show. It's part of their mission statement to bring all of the Fleet to the next habitable world when we finally find it.

I try to let that notion soothe me.

It doesn't take. As the order in the exosystem mutates, urging me to move the bodies to a lower deck, the mismatched pieces itch against the back of my mind. I pick up as many corpses as I can carry, and try to ignore the way their fragile deadweight scalds me.

Up above, on the habitat's domed ceiling, a few Scela crawl toward the location of the breach with tool belts and patch kits. The hull will be fixed within the hour, the ship will keep flying, and we'll all pretend this tragedy could have been avoided if it weren't for the Fractionists starting the protests in the first place.

I can see the casts already.

I can hear the rhetoric.

I can feel the cameras on me.

All at once, my drive to defend the Fleet feels like a construction. Like something the exo is forcing into my brain and my muscles and my sense of purpose. The memories I've been striving to recover, the rewards the exo's been doling out for work well done—what if they're just *bait* to keep me from the truth?

My muscles lock tight, and the exo presses down a wave of pain as they strain so taut they feel as if they might rip. Scela strength pulses against what's left of my human flesh, trapping me in the cage of my metal.

I have to get past this. I can't be the Scela I need to be, can't pull myself to the level that'll put me right if I'm doubting.

But the doubt is in my veins, and I can't flush it. Like something's woken in me. Like the edges of my holes are leaking.

I reach out for the exo, and it lends me enough strength to shut down that line of thinking. To push through. I let the exosystem sweep me up and lose myself in the greater whole.

But when I drop off my last load of bodies, the exosystem relinquishes me. In my own lonely brain, my thoughts run wild.

What happened to the *Aeschylus*—I grapple with my exo to fully form my treasonous suspicions. It fights and fights, trying its best to protect me, but I can't stop the puzzle pieces from clicking together. The conspiracy unfolds like this: The General Body is alerted to another uprising. They send in Scela to shut it down, all the while planning to breach the hull and lay waste to the area. If they're lucky, they take out a few important Fractionists among a whole lot of innocents. They send in camera crews to make sure the whole thing gets captured. To make sure it's clear the Fractionists are to blame. The General Body looks like heroes, their masses of hyperpowered soldiers rushing to save as many people as they can. Protecting. Defending. Always acting in the people's best interest.

It's not true. It can't be true. It's treason just to think it.

Besides, with our position in the Fleet so uncertain, now isn't the time to be doubting the General Body that gives us our orders. We're far enough right on the rankings board as it is. I stuff my wild theory down into the recesses of my holes, praying the others won't find it there when we reconnect. I can't put this kind of thought anywhere near Woojin, who couldn't contain the idea if he tried; near Praava, where it might mix explosively with her gut instinct to defend her sister; or near Aisha, who would just use it as fodder for her rampant anxiety.

I'd be better off forgetting it entirely. I seem to be good at forgetting important things—why can't this be one of them? But my theory won't unstick. Not with the crippling uncertainty that grows in me with every breath of reprocessed air I take. Not with the bodies around me. Not with the feeling in my gut that I *owe* something to the people who lost their lives today.

The unfocused eyes of the dead surround me, pleading for the truth. And all around, the void offers nothing but silence.

CHAPTER 11

AISHA

The howl of the breach winds has quieted to nothing as the vacuum takes the place of the ship's air. I'm swallowed by the murmurs and whispers of the humans who surround me inside the breach shelter. We're packed as it is, but as I look around, all I can think is that we could have fit so many others.

I scan the faces around me. Most of the humans have pressed themselves back against the walls, as far from the Scela as they can get. Marshal Jesuit keeps one hand clasped around the hilt of her stunstick, just in case. There's no telling who in the crowd is armed and who among them are stupid enough to try taking us on. The other Scela who made it into the shelter cluster around us, near the doors. Mercifully, the marshal has kept our minds separate from the others, but our exosystems are rattling with an unfulfilled order—once the hull breach is patched and the doors are opened, we're supposed to start making arrests. A transport has already docked on one of the sealed levels of the ship, waiting for us to fill it.

My aunt may not be part of this cell, but these Fractionists are her people. The ones who would rip a ship open the second the tide turned against them. A sinking feeling wraps around my stomach, and the exo shudders under the weight of the secrets it's been keeping bottled up inside me. Aiding the Fractionist rebellion seemed *right* this morning. I thought I understood their point of view. I thought I saw value in doing anything it took to get humanity out from under the General Body's thumb.

I thought it was *worthy*.

But I can't understand any point of view that justifies what's happened to the *Aeschylus*.

Un-Haad, Lih. Marshal Jesuit nudges into our exosystem. *We've got a special assignment.* Her voice is hesitant, still tinged with her anger and frustration at not being able to control us. *Once the doors open, we have orders to regroup with Tanaka and retrieve Ganes. Apparently she's found what the Fractionists were trying to get at. Or rather, who.*

Ratna, we all think at once.

Ratna Ganes and her team, the marshal confirms. *They're at the heart of this, somehow.*

A new connection flares up as our linkage to Praava restores. Her relief washes into the system, and it's easy to forgive her when she's beaming, her smile Scela-wide. *Ratna's safe,* Praava says. *She and her team made it to an airlock within the facility. I'm outside it, waiting for the all clear.*

For a moment we inhabit her body, shivering with anticipation in the little corridor outside the airlock. Ratna hasn't seen her sister as Scela yet, and Praava's scared to pieces of what her reaction will be. Wooj and I push a little encouragement into her exo, and her spine straightens.

When we pull back into the breach shelter, I can feel a hint of an approving smile drifting from Marshal Jesuit. Something tells me we've just moved leftward on the board.

The temporary patch takes exactly twenty-five minutes to install, with another five to restore the ship's atmosphere from the ancillary supplies. The crowd presses closer and closer to the shelter doors, anxiously peering around the Scela as creaks and groans rattle through the ventilation systems outside.

A countdown starts up in our exos. Ten seconds until the doors open.

Every passing moment is a prick against my skin. I know what's coming.

When the airlock hisses open and fresh air comes rolling in, the humans sigh in relief. But it doesn't last. Cries of alarm echo off the walls as the Scela leap into action, pulling away the protestors they've identified.

The three of us slip through the tumult of the arrests to find Key waiting for us outside.

She rejoins the exosystem with her guard up as usual, but even so, it's easy to tell that something's shifted inside her. The emptiness doesn't come from her holes anymore—there's another hollow feeling consuming her now, one she assures us we can't possibly relate to the moment Wooj and I ask what's wrong. The power levels of her enhancements are lower than ours. She spent them carrying the bodies down to the nearest intership deck. Her walls lock her away from the rest of us, and she follows at a slight distance as we make our way to the research center.

As we enter, we pass a team of Scela elites, made distinct by the white striping painted across their exo ridges. They carry unconscious humans in tactical gear by their ankles, making it look as easy as lifting a sack of groceries. *The protests were cover,* the marshal says with a nudge. *While most of the Fractionists made noise, this team of infiltrators was attempting to break into the labs upstairs. The elites got to them before they made it—though apparently the infiltrators benefited from an unmanaged Scela clearing a path through the building.*

Our exos tug us to the third floor, where Praava waits. The doors on the airlock haven't been opened yet, and even though she knows she's on thin ice, she demands to know why.

Because we're here to arrest the occupants, Marshal Jesuit replies.

Praava recoils, and for a moment we're terrified she'll grab us again and pile us onto the marshal to defend her sister. "What's she done?" she asks out loud, pouring her anger into her voice instead.

"It's for her protection," the marshal says levelly. "The protests were focused around this research team. We're still working to unravel the motivations behind the Fractionist gathering, but it's important that we make sure its target is contained."

"*Contained* and *arrested* are two very different words," Wooj notes. He would know.

"I'm giving you four a chance to act of your own free will, but do not hesitate to think that I will force you if it comes to that," Marshal Jesuit snarls through her teeth. *For once, do something the right way the first time,* she presses after a moment, anger turning to exasperation. *You're low enough on the board as it is.* She flicks a command through the exosystem, and the airlock doors hiss open a moment later.

Praava takes point with the four of us behind her as ten humans step out into the corridor's harsh lights. Ratna is immediately recognizable among them—though she's half Praava's height, they have the same rich brown skin, the same sculpted cheekbones. She shies away at the sight of the Scela waiting for them.

"Ratna, it's me," Praava says when her sister draws near. Her voice is soft, projecting just past the breach suit.

Ratna squints. My exo pulls me back from reading into the subtleties of her expression—too human, too nuanced, not for Scela eyes. But I do it anyway, because I need to know. I need to see anything but the terror my own sister felt when she saw me as Scela for the first time. That fear she had in her eyes, the way she flinched—it eats at me. And I still haven't seen my brother.

It takes extra processing, extra wrestling with the thing on my spine, but it's worth it for the moment when the realization breaks over Ratna and her teeth bare in a human smile. "I can't believe they made you even taller," she says, then lunges forward and wraps her arms around her sister.

Something deep and horrible shreds in me, my ugly jealousy flaring out through the exosystem before I can rein it in.

Ratna's hug brings confusion sputtering out of Praava—she doesn't know how to react. Her old human instincts urge her to hug back as tightly as she can, but her exo reminds her what a bad idea that is. So she dips her head, tucks her chin, and lets it rest on top of Ratna's head. A compromise, but it's enough. For a moment, the corridor crystalizes in the moment of love between the two sisters. Inside and outside the exosystem, we feel it. Wooj grins Scela-wide. Key shifts uncomfortably as her walls slip a bit, just enough that we feel the emptiness inside her aching in a way she can't explain.

Ratna's response has mellowed out the other researchers. They don't expect it when Marshal Jesuit straightens and says, "Enough."

Ratna jumps back, Praava's guilt swells, and the rest of the humans snap to attention. "What happened here today is proof that the General Body needs to play a more active role in the work you do."

Her voice is strangled, stilted. The humans can't pick up the subtleties, but we Scela know—her words are being fed to her.

"Your research into the wasting fever and its origins can't be properly conducted where there is public access to both you and the materials you work with. If the Fractionist demonstrators had succeeded in what they aimed to do here today—" She falters, resisting. Whatever she's being fed now, it isn't ringing true for her. The marshal doesn't want to say it, but it isn't the kind of order she can disobey for long.

When her voice comes back, it's even more robotic than before. "They would have destroyed everything you worked for and twisted it to suit their own purposes. They would use your research to spread lies and fragment the Fleet. And they very nearly succeeded in killing a good portion of the people on this ship to cover their tracks. This squad of Scela has been deployed to escort the ten of you to a private transport, which will take you to the starship *Lancelot*. It will serve as a *temporary* holding facility until we can be sure your work is secured."

Everyone can read the truth underneath her words. The starship *Lancelot*, First District, is a prison ship. A holding pen for people the General Body sees as instigators. The conditions there aren't as bad as those tanks on the *Endymion*, the ones Wooj feared enough that he'd risked a Scela integration instead, but no one has ever come back from the *Lancelot*. And from the looks on their faces, none of the humans in this narrow, bright corridor believe that they'll be the lucky first.

Praava's rage erupts suddenly, a thousand times stronger than her fear, and she rounds on the marshal. A buzz hums against our necks, pulling us into Praava's wake as her fists come up. Ratna's supposed to save the Fleet. Ratna's research is the entire reason Praava gave her body away in the first place. *What's left for her if—*

"Ganes," Marshal Jesuit says, her voice dropping to a dangerous, cool murmur. And before Praava can process the marshal's calm, our supervisor is *in* her, locking her limbs in place and then forcing her arms down at her sides. The rest of us snap free from Praava's control and stagger back, watching in horror as the marshal's mind strips Praava down to nothing. *I've never had to do this before—please don't make me do it again. There's nothing we can do but obey right now,* the marshal impresses on her. *Stand down or remove yourself. There is no resisting this order.*

Praava gives a mute nod, and Marshal Jesuit releases her. She doesn't know how to put it into words, to beg for forgiveness in a way that both her pride and the exo will allow. Instead, she turns to her sister and blurts, "What the hell were you doing?"

We all share the sentiment. Plague research doesn't exactly strike us as the sort of thing that would inspire Fractionists to assemble en masse to get their hands on. It isn't the kind of information Yasmin is after either—that's for certain.

A researcher opens his mouth, but one of his colleagues tugs on his shirt and he swallows back whatever he was about to say. They glance mistrustfully between us, and I wish I could read their thoughts as easily as those of the Scela around me. Something isn't right. Something doesn't add up. But no one's saying anything. All we can read from them is fear and resignation. Up against our power, against the will of the General Body—there's no resisting.

Our exos instruct us to restrain the researchers in case any of them try to bolt. Ten of them and five of us means a fragile human wrist in each Scela hand. The humans don't seem too happy about it, and there's a small scuffle about who gets to put their left hand in our grips and who has to offer up their right. Ratna's the only one who doesn't complain, offering her right hand to her sister without hesitation.

A sickening taste sours the back of my throat when we step out the doors of the research center. These people could be helping Amar with their work, and instead we're dragging them away from where they're needed most. And I'm not even sure *why*.

As we march them up to the intership deck and load them into the shuttle where we're instructed to deposit them, I keep trying to wrap my head around what transpired today. Yesterday, the Fractionist conflict seemed distant—a minor scuffle, a simple assignment, one we barely had to touch. Before, it was just the trigger for the opportunity to give up my body and save Amar. Now I see it everywhere, the way it weaves into everything that's happened to me. Somehow the life of the rebel movement is tied to the life of my little brother, to the well-being of my little sister, and to everything I sacrificed myself for.

But my own life is bound to the General Body. They determine how much I'll earn and how much I'll be able to provide for my family. I need to show them I'm loyal to them too. The exo on my back is at its wits' end trying to keep my warring allegiances secret.

Praava bends over Ratna to strap her in, and all of us feel the sudden rush of proximity as her sister leans up to whisper in her ear. All of us hear the words Ratna hisses, barely audible over the stomp of feet and click of harnesses snapping into place.

"The General Body is lying."

A chill rushes over me. If that's true, maybe Yasmin and her movement are on to something. What if the venting of the *Aeschylus* was a necessary measure for the Fractionists? Can the deaths today be justified if it moves us toward bucking the General Body's control over the Fleet?

My thoughts are clouded, and when we strap in after the prisoners, I slap my hand back against the hullmetal and pray. This time, it's not because of the shuttle. This time, I pray for answers.

And I pray I find them fast.

CHAPTER 12

KEY

The starship *Lancelot* scares the shit out of me. Not because of the long, dark corridors, the sterile cells, or the empty-eyed people sitting in them. No, there's something about the ship that makes the gaping holes in me feel even bigger. And I can't look away.

We pass rows of cells that are unlike anything I've seen on a cast. The jail tanks on the prison ships the Fleet launched with are just barely large enough for a human being to tolerate without feeling like they're wearing it. Just enough room for movement, not enough room for living. Rumor has it that a sentence in one of the jail tanks on the starship *Endymion* feels twice as long as it actually is.

But here on the *Lancelot*, the rooms are ... well, room-sized. Probably because the ship wasn't built as a prison transport—the need for something like it wasn't anticipated. The quarters are residential, and the only modifications are the locks on the doors and the transparent walls that make up the corridors.

Some of the prisoners approach the clear plastic, their dull eyes brightening with curiosity. I'm grateful for my breach suit's helmet protecting me from their hungry stares. My exo agrees. It doesn't want anyone here to see my face. To them, I'm just another machine, a weapon in the General Body's hands. They have no connection to me, and they shouldn't be allowed to make one.

But then there's a face I can't ignore. A face that stares at me through ragged golden hair with his gaze no longer trapped behind a camera lens in my mind. With my headpiece on, I know I'm just another Scela. But I see his face, and my whole world is blown sideways.

The boy from my dreams isn't a figment of my imagination.

He's real, and he's sitting in a prison cell aboard the starship *Lancelot.*

My exo clamps down, urging me to keep walking without breaking stride, even though everything in me wants to run to him, smash the plastic of his cell, and shake him by the collar until he explains exactly how he got in my head. I need answers. No more flickers of some life I used to live. No more camera eyes watching in my dreams. For the first time, I have a concrete link to the things I'm missing.

And yet it feels like my mind rebels against the very notion. The holes in my brain are swallowing me. The machine on my back shutters my thoughts from the others, but it can't stop my stomach from churning. The back of my mouth goes sick with bile.

But I keep marching until we've herded the scientists down to their holding cell in the ship's bowels. The light down here is dim, the corridor so similar to the narrow space where we boarded the *Aeschylus,* but my exo gives my brain a little shove before my thoughts latch on to what happened aboard the ship.

I want my breach suit off. I want to breathe again, to convince myself that I won't be trapped in this skintight prison forever. But beneath the layers of sealed fabric is another prison—the structure of the exorig woven into my body. I can feel the creak of my bones in the metal that cages them. *It makes them stronger,* the exo insists, but it's a cage of its own and it knows it.

The boy in my dreams is on this ship. He's not in any of the memories I have left, but he's here. That has to mean *something.* The muscles of my shoulders stretch taut as I try to probe my empty spaces for an explanation.

Tanaka? Marshal Jesuit asks from the head of the squad. She lets her concern nudge into me, reminding me how little I've been paying attention. We're at the holding cell. No problems from the scientists. Our work here is done.

It's nothing, I tell her. I pull my thoughts back, push my holes forward, and try not to let it disturb me how much that puts her at ease.

CHAPTER 13

AISHA

A week after the *Aeschylus* vent, I find myself in the *Dread*'s Master Control Room, facing down either the smartest, most fearless human I've ever met or an utter madman.

"Lopez," he says, by way of introduction. If he has any other names, he doesn't seem to think I'll need them. Most people try to keep Scela in their lines of sight, but Lopez immediately turns his back on me, drops into his chair, and starts jabbing at his keyboard. I might as well be a piece of furniture.

"Aisha Un-Haad."

"I know." He doesn't turn around, and the exo urges on the prickling sense of indignation crawling up my spine. *Humans ought to respect us,* it croons. *Humans who don't respect us are trouble.*

That's the point, I retort. Because apparently Lopez is the be-all-end-all of the *Dread*'s fledgling Fractionist cell. From this tiny room, he monitors the entire ship and controls a good part of it. When a secure door needs opening, one call to Lopez gets you through. When someone needs a camera to go down and needs it to look like an accident, Lopez is your man. And when someone needs to isolate a Scela who's made a bargain with her duplicitous aunt and direct her up to the security center without anyone else the wiser, well, that's how I ended up here.

For something as grandly named as the Master Control Room, it isn't much to look at. Most of the room is dominated by the instrumentation panel and the bank of screens suspended over it. A few printed photos are taped to the machines—landscapes of Old Earth and discovered worlds. I'm guessing Lopez doesn't get much scenery outside of them.

My head's mercifully lonesome—it's another rest day, and the marshal dissolved the exosystem this morning before leaving to deliver her second report to the General Body. In the past week of grueling training, we've been making up for our failures on the *Aeschylus*. I doubt this morning's report is getting us any farther leftward on the board than we were before our last field test, but at least it has the marshal safely shipped off to the *Pantheon,* making it almost too easy for Lopez to direct me up here without incident.

"If the *Dread* is a body, I am its exo," Lopez drawls, flicking through a camera feed so rapidly that even the machine on my back can't keep up. "Anything happens on this ship, I see it. Anything happens on this ship that someone else shouldn't see, I sweep it away."

"That's not really how the exo—"

"Hush. That's not the information I'm supposed to be getting out of you. Though Yasmin was unclear on how exactly the Fractionist movement is supposed to benefit from your little arrangement."

"You talked to Yasmin?" Excitement flushes through me. At last—I've found someone who dances circles around the *Dread*'s communications lockdown. "Could I send a message to my sis—"

Lopez spins in his chair and fixes me with a glare fierce enough to freeze an elite Scela in their tracks. "I will humor you, because you're new at this. This is a communications network people have devoted their entire lives to building. I put my hide at risk every day to encrypt critical information and spread it to the rest of the movement. And you want to use my masterpiece for *personal mail*?"

He pauses.

"I mean, I *could* if I wanted to. But I don't need the validation. You have your job, I have mine. Let's talk about how you're going to be good at yours."

I bristle. The exo urges me a step closer, and I square the shoulders of my rig. I've spent the past week pressing down my pent-up frustration in the wake of the *Aeschylus* disaster and all the unanswered questions it awoke—questions I *couldn't* answer until the Fractionists finally deigned to reach out. I didn't come here to be lectured by some puny human.

The puny human rolls his eyes. "Spirits. I've spent half my life around Scela, kid. Posturing isn't going to get you what you want—just makes you look stupid."

I relent, the exo stifling my blush response.

"So you're insecure. Good to know." Before I can snarl, Lopez claps his hands and spins back around to face his bank of monitors. "As I was saying. This is the extent of my reach." He gestures to the screens as they cycle through camera feeds, reports on the *Dread*'s systems, and telemetry on other ships in the First District tier. "But you can reach further. The cause needs information only you cyborg weirdos have access to. You have that creepy little mind-reading thing going on. You ship out on missions that elude my gaze. I heard tell you were on the *Aeschylus* a week ago."

Conflict simmers through my system as I nod. The casts this

week have been vicious toward the Fractionists, and I've found myself agreeing with a lot of what they're saying. Two hundred and thirteen people died in the breach. The Fractionist movement has fresh blood on its hands. And with the extra maintenance the *Aeschylus* now requires to preserve its damaged hull, there's talk of dropping it down the tiers as far as the Sixth District. I don't understand how venting part of the ship could further the Fractionist cause. If anything, it badly damaged the movement in the eyes of the public.

The confusion must be clear on my face, because Lopez rakes a hand through his hair and mutters, "Yeah, I don't get it either. Breaching a hull has never been a strategy in our playbook, and the *Aeschylus* cell has dropped out of communication, so it doesn't seem like we're getting an explanation any time soon. There's more to that story. Got any missing pieces I should know?"

Even though I can't fully stomach working with Fractionists right now—albeit a different cell of the movement than the one that chose to vent the *Aeschylus*—I know this is what I signed up for. Lopez will report to Yasmin. I need her impressed. And maybe he can fill in the information *I'm* missing. "The Fractionist protestors were a distraction for a team of infiltrators trying to get at scientists in the research quarter."

Lopez's focus sharpens. "Scientists researching what, exactly?"

"The origins of the wasting fever."

He grunts, pulling up a document and logging the information. As I walk him through the details of the deployment, the breach, and our trip to the *Lancelot* after, I keep trying to make it all fit together in a way that makes sense. Why was a small team of scientists the objective of a protest that drew hundreds? Why does the Fractionist movement have any interest in the fever trying to kill my brother? And why—God, *why*—would the Fractionists vent the ship?

When I finish telling Lopez every useful detail, he sits back, a frown deepening the lines on his face. "I don't know what to make of it all," he admits. "But that's not my job. Now it's time to figure out how you're going to make your next report."

"Can't I just—"

"No, you can't just come waltzing up here every time you have new intel. Today was an exception. A rare opportunity. During basic, you get one day a week without"—he sketches a loop in the air next to his temple—"*that* going on, and with time-sensitive information in the mix, we can't wait around for the next time it's convenient for you to disappear."

"Then how—"

"You need a runner." Lopez points to a screen showing an overhead view of Assembly, to the scrawny-looking humans darting back and forth across the deck. Pilots. Maintenance. Doctors. Dockworkers. To most of the ship, they're as invisible as the mechanics of the craft and just as essential. I see what he's saying—I need someone who can slip through the cracks, who can move inconspicuously where I can't. "But since this is *your* runner, you need to find someone who's already in your orbit. Someone who doesn't have to go out of their way to interact with you."

"And how do I find a Fractionist?"

Lopez shakes his head, laughing. "They're all Fractionists, robot girl. They just don't know it yet."

I stop myself from squaring up again. I don't need this kind of flippancy. "Everything about that is too convenient. How'd the Fractionists even recruit *you* anyway?"

Lopez's gaze drops to the pictures taped around his monitors,

137

and his chest swells around a heavy sigh. "Kiddo, I recruited myself. This *room* recruited me. You try being stuck in a box this big for twenty years and get back to me on how you decide to get your kicks. In a Fleet like this, everybody's got something that'll turn them away from the General Body's shining beacon."

I'm halfway to feeling sorry for him.

Then the arrogant smirk is back. "Don't worry about finding a Fractionist—you pick your person, you send them my way, and I'll take care of it. I may not be as pretty as the girls they put in the First District propaganda casts, but I'm *very* persuasive when I need to be."

I suppress the urge to sniff, though my exo is simmering with ridicule. He's got an awfully high opinion of himself if he thinks he can recruit *anyone* to the movement, especially at this fragile moment. But if that's the way he wants to play it, I'll play along.

An idea comes to me, and my exo lights up with glee. If Lopez is leaving the choice up to me, I'm choosing someone he's going to *hate*.

For any Scela with downtime, Assembly is the place to be. As I approach the recreational side of the deck, I spot groups of senior Scela—distinguishable by their long, elegant hair, which seems to be a point of pride—lounging together. Some of them talk out loud, others seem to be absorbed in deep mental conversations, and I even spot what looks like a guerilla tattoo studio set up in the shadow of one of the smaller shuttles.

I move through them uncomfortably, the fuzz on my scalp prickling, trying to avoid their gazes. None of my squadmates seem to be on the deck. I don't want to know what that means Wooj and

Praava might be doing, and I'm glad Key and her silent judgment aren't weighing on me.

A familiar voice carries over the chatter, its tones far too varying and intricate to be mistaken for Scela. I whirl around and spot Zaire the dockworker sitting cross-legged on a blanket with a knot of senior Scela surrounding him. "Folks, folks," he says, raising his hands in the air as an uncanny smile spreads across his face. He looks like a cat backed into a corner by a pack of dogs, but there's something about his posture that's far too relaxed for that.

I take a few steps in his direction, trying not to look like I have an agenda.

"Let's play a simpler game," he drawls, holding up a ball bearing the size of his knuckle. "The cards are too fancy, you know. Let's try this. I'm going to place this ball under a cup." He reaches behind his back and produces three opaque drinking glasses, which he drops mouth-down on his blanket one by one. "You pick the cup with the ball in it, I pay you. You pick an empty cup, you fill it. Who's in?"

Three of the Scela around him raise their hands simultaneously, clearly joined in an exosystem. "Forty-five units," one of them says, and each of them pulls fifteen out of their pockets, dropping them in a neat pile on the blanket in front of the cups.

"Ah, ah, ah," Zaire scolds as one of the Scela starts to flip her headpiece down. "This game is camera-shy."

She retracts it, looking sour.

Zaire glances up and picks me out of the crowd. "Hey, newbie!" he calls. "Want a piece of the action?"

Something sharp twists in my gut at the thought of wasting money on a trivial betting game. I should have pushed Lopez harder about contacting Yasmin and Malikah—I still have no idea whether my salary has made it to the *Reliant* yet. And though some Scela seem to withdraw enough units to carry around and wager, *pocket change* has never been a part of my vocabulary.

Zaire skips right over my hesitation with a cheerful shrug. "Bystanders are welcome to watch, but no hints, got it? Same goes for all of you," he says, waving his hands at the flock of Scela. He beckons the three players with a crook of his finger. "C'mon, you. Pop a squat."

The three of them kneel in unison. I wonder how long they've been together as a unit—how long it must take to get that comfortable with other voices constantly threading through your thoughts.

"No last words, no regrets?" Zaire asks. Seeing none, he cracks a wide, human smile. "And here we . . . *go*." With a flick of his thumb, he sends the ball bearing high in the air, then scoops up two of the cups, spinning them in his palms. When the bearing drops, he swoops one of them across its arc. The ball disappears into the cup, and Zaire's hands disappear into a flurry of twists as he juggles the two cups between his hands.

I've already lost the ball, so I shift my attention to the three Scela staring intently at Zaire's display. If I were them, I'd set one person on each cup to track whether the ball enters or exits it. My exo agrees, and I suspect it's what they're doing. Their focus is unblinking, and all of them lean forward slightly, as if a few inches of proximity will help them win the game.

I edge a little closer too. Not for sight, but for sound—I try to train my exo's hearing processing on the clatter the little metal ball makes every time it hits the wall of a cup. But when Zaire slams the two cups down on his blanket and starts swirling the three of them back and forth, occasionally tilting them up to pass the ball between them, there are too many little noises to distinguish which one comes from the bearing.

Several of the Scela rock back on their heels, letting out groans. Zaire's smile grows wider, and his hands start moving faster. He has no enhanced muscles, nothing beyond what he was born with, but this guy is putting experienced Scela to shame.

Finally he decides he's had enough of toying with them. His hands come to rest with a sudden snap, and all three cups fall still. I notice two of the players cocking their heads, straining to catch any last giveaway rattles, but the blanket he plays on deadens the sound in a way that explains why it's there in the first place.

Zaire lifts his eyebrows at the Scela.

The three of them stay absolutely still. A huge mental volley must be going back and forth between them, because one keeps shaking his head vehemently. It takes them a full minute to reach a consensus, and finally they point at the rightmost cup.

Zaire tips it up, but we all already know from his smile. "Pleasure doing business," he says.

"Cheeky little shit," one of the players replies.

Zaire sweeps the pile of units up, flipping them in the air one at a time and letting them drop into the satchel at his hip. "Any other takers?" he asks, glancing around the crowd. When no one steps up, he shrugs. "Can't blame you. Tomorrow, maybe."

"Cards later?" one of the senior Scela asks.

"Gimme a minute." As the crowd dissipates and Zaire flips the last of his units into his bag, I step up to the blanket. "Change your mind?" Zaire asks without looking up.

I ignore the inevitable pinch of my thoughts flicking to my empty pockets. Dropping to a crouch next to the blanket, I reach out and knock the middle cup over. Empty. I try the leftmost cup, and find nothing but air beneath it. I glance up at Zaire, who holds up his left hand. Caught in the web between his thumb and index finger is the ball bearing.

"You cheated."

"I think you'll agree that cheating against this crowd is a little justified," Zaire says with a smirk. "Also, one of them definitely should have caught the moment I pulled the ball out."

"Maybe they did notice, but they wanted to make you feel better."

"And it worked," he says, patting his bulging satchel.

"Is it good money, doing this?" I ask.

He shrugs. "Doesn't hurt. But it's mostly just how I get my kicks. When you spend all day hanging out with jacked-up cyborgs, it's nice to feel like you have something going for you. Why, you looking to go into business?"

I let a smirk slip past my lips. "Of a sort. Do you know your way to the Master Control Room?"

CHAPTER 14

KEY

The stunstick hums in my hand. If I think too hard about it, I start to pick apart the different resonances—flesh, bone, metal. Nerves vibrating against wires. All of it *me*.

But the point is to stop thinking. My exo flashes the pattern of moves I'm supposed to be working through, and I shift my stance into the start of the set, my focus homing in on the dummy in front of me. The exosystem lines up as my squadmates do the same, our bodies locking in sync.

Go, the impulse whispers down my spine.

I lunge forward, stunstick raised, flowing into the first strike—

And my fingers slip. The humming escapes my grip, the stunstick sailing out of my hand a fraction of a second before it lands on the dummy. *FUCK,* I blast through the system, landing hard on my knees.

I know it's just a dummy I'm hitting. I *know* I'm doing no damage, hurting no one. The exo's been reinforcing those facts over and over. But all I see is the *Aeschylus.* The somber face of Chancellor

Vel, speaking in low tones on a Fleet-wide cast from her seat on the starship *Pantheon* as she offered her condolences for the tragedy. The massive hole blasted in the *Aeschylus*'s hide that they showed on every screen.

The people who fell by my hands.

They were going to die anyway, the exo insists, trying to be kind about it. *You were sparing them from agony. And most of them were just Fractionists. No need to get worked up over their deaths.*

It's been three weeks since the *Aeschylus* disaster. We're two days away from our final assessment. The marshal's past two reports have inched us slowly leftward on the board, but it's nowhere near enough to make the elite ranks I know I should be striving for. Everything rides on our last test. And not once today have I successfully completed a combat set without either dropping my stunstick or crushing it in my grip.

"You just kinda have to lean into the reality of it," Praava observes from my right. She's the only one who paused when I fucked up—Woojin and Aisha are still hacking through their sets. "It's your human side that's causing the problem. Leave it to your exo."

Which is easy for her to say—Praava's never had a problem with her exo. Since our return from the *Lancelot,* she's gotten even better, constantly outstripping the rest of us in training. Her thoughts burn with *purpose,* almost as irritating as Aisha's. If we make a good assignment, if we impress the General Body with our potential, she believes she might be able to secure her sister's release from the prison ship.

To my left, Woojin lands blow after perfect blow on a dummy. His control over his body is beautifully fluid now, but it's only because he's not wearing his full rig. In the metal, he still struggles to keep up with the rest of us. He's been improving steadily. But, as the marshal warns us after every single training session, we're only as strong as our weakest link.

I can't let that be me. I *won't* let it be me.

"If it were as simple as leaving it in the exo's hands, I would have the hang of this already," I snarl. I kick against the mat, my enhanced musculature bouncing me three feet into the air. Aisha sends a burst of amusement into the exosystem when I land with my legs splayed.

I shove her back into her own head. She's been acting weird lately, practicing cloaking herself to the point that sometimes it feels like she's dropped out of the exosystem entirely. Which is a relief, honestly, but I can't help but wonder why she needs to hide herself from us, especially when she used to batter us with every single worry in her head.

Whatever it is, it's not affecting her performance. She's doing better than me.

I stalk across the mats and scoop up my stunstick. Praava nudges a curl of encouragement at me, and I snap back at her.

She shrugs. *Just trying to help.*

I don't need your help. I just need practice. I need to get my mind in order. I need to become the perfect tool the General Body designed me to be, and that starts with clearing my head. Forgetting what I did on the *Aeschylus*.

Forgetting that boy I saw on the *Lancelot*.

There has to be a rational explanation for how he got in my head. He must be an acquaintance from the *Antilles* who fell in with the Fractionists or stirred up some other sort of trouble—the kind that lands you on the *Lancelot* and not in an *Endymion* tank. I suppose he's pretty enough to latch in my subconscious and end up in a dream or two.

Doesn't really explain the consistency.

But maybe I'm just spooked from the theory I had about the *Aes-chylus* vent. Maybe I'm jumping at shadows, finding little conspiracies everywhere to fill up the empty spaces inside me. I still can't shake the thought that there might be more to the breach that damaged the *Aeschylus,* even though I know it's ridiculous. The General Body's kept us safe and kept us flying. We've lasted three hundred years on these ships, thanks to their leadership. Just because we came close to losing another ship to Fractionist terrorists—

Did we?

I hoist the stick over my head and bring it down on the dummy, trying to ignore the shudder that threatens to overtake my spine and cling to the glow of success. The exo nudges me into the rest of the practice set, and I keep my grip tight as I land a flurry of strikes. I can do this. I won't be the weak link.

But then I remember the words Ratna whispered to Praava in the shuttle. I remember how *true* it felt to hear that the General Body can't be trusted. Deep as my bones and the metal laid against them. All these holes inside me, all these uncertain things, and then there's this—and it's completely irrational. There's no foundation in my memories for that mistrust.

Just empty spaces where a foundation might have stood.

I *will* feel complete, the exo promises. I *will* feel whole again. If we come out of our final assessment on top. If I can get my mind together and be the best damn Scela I can be.

But now that I know how a bone-deep truth feels, I'm not so sure about the exo's words.

And the second that thought settles is the second I slip again. Only this time I don't let go of the stunstick. I don't crush it either.

I just follow through on my swing, strong and sure, clear past the dummy I was aiming to hit.

And straight into my other arm.

Oh, fuck me, four minds think in unison, right before the pain whites out the exosystem.

"You're really quite lucky it isn't worse," Isaac says as he limps around the hospital bed.

I stare at the ceiling, not bothering to conceal my scowl. My useless left arm is stretched out, propped up on a series of supports. My exo enforces strict instructions to keep it deadened from the shoulder down. Isaac and his team of juniors have managed to restore the anatomy I bashed and electrocuted. A furious red burn sears across the skin of my forearm, making the metal and resealing underneath it stand out even more.

I almost wish I could feel it. The numbness is disconcerting, made worse by watching the doctors twist and pull at my body with massive clamps until the metal I bent was set straight. A handful of thin endoscopes did all the interior work, burrowing into the flesh of my arm to repair the artificial muscle, tendons, and nerves.

"We were able to make repairs with minimal invasion and no cutting you open," Isaac continues. He tucks his datapad away and sets himself carefully on a stool, stretching out his braced leg. "You'll be sore, of course, but you won't miss your assessment."

"Joy," I grind out. Good to know that on top of competing with Woojin for the position of weakest link, I'll be expected to perform in a test that will decide my entire future as a Scela with an arm that's only been *minimally* invaded.

I purse my lips around a question my exo thinks I should keep bottled up. The last time I was in Medical, Isaac brushed off my missing memories, and after he knocked me out, I didn't bother asking twice. But now it's pretty damn clear that something isn't right about the way I came through the conversion.

I just need *something* to fill the holes.

"Why did I become Scela?" I blurt.

Isaac looks up sharply. His stool scoots back a defensive inch.

"I still don't remember, but it must be— Aisha and Woojin and Praava all filled out forms when they chose to take the metal. There has to be a record for me, right?"

The doctor pushes up his glasses, rubbing his tattooed hands over his face. This close, I can see that the ink sketches the vague outline of Scela machinery over his dark skin, each part labeled with measurements and ratios. "Key, I can't—"

"It does exist, doesn't it? I have a right to know what it says."

"You don't," Isaac retorts, his voice soft with exhaustion. "You voided your autonomous rights when you became Scela. And even if you didn't, I don't have the clearance to—"

"*Fuck clearance,*" I snap. "I don't *remember* voiding my rights. I have to . . . I need to . . ."

"Key, you need to relax."

"Don't tell me to—"

"*Key,* stop . . . *thinking,*" he repeats more forcefully. "Unclench your muscles. Clear your mind, or you're going to rip something."

The pain registers over the frenzy of my thoughts, and I give in grudgingly, letting the exo soothe me until my head empties and the rest of my body is as limp as my deadened left arm. My eyes feel heavy and hot, and something tells me this is the closest Scela can get to crying.

I just want to know. I want a reason for existing.

"Please," Isaac breathes, pushing to his feet. "Be careful. You see what this does to your body. If this gets too out of hand, we might have to cut you open again to put you back together."

He limps purposefully toward the door, then hesitates.

"And if it goes too far, we might not be able to put you back together at all."

I'm released from Medical on the morning of our last rest day with instructions to pay close attention to my arm's alignment and report back to Isaac if anything seems off. The injury is sore, as promised, but everything seems to be in working order, and after the humiliation of my freak-out in front of Isaac, I'm not keen on seeing the head of Medical again any time soon.

I've got one full day to kill before our final assessment. Marshal Jesuit hasn't explained exactly how we'll be tested, no matter how many times Woojin asks, but I don't want to dwell on that particular uncertainty either. Today's the last time I'll be free of my squadmates' minds before we find out our assignment. Before the blame starts piling on if we get some dead-end patrol job.

So I'm going to enjoy this time off as much as I can. Clear my head, just like Isaac wants. I duck into one of the halls that leads to Assembly. Even though it's usually packed with uncomfortable camaraderie, there's bound to be something worth doing on the deck's recreational side.

Only the moment I step out of the hallway and onto the deck, my exo snaps my vision onto a way-too-familiar figure. Aisha's tucked into a corner, out of sight for most of the Scela scattered across the deck. She has her head bent, lowering herself to the level of the human she's speaking to.

Strangely enough, it's Zaire the dockworker hanging on to her every word.

Suddenly I want her in my head. I want to know exactly what she's saying. This doesn't look like nostalgia for where she came from or any sort of sympathy. It looks like she's trying not to be seen. The exo urges the fury rising in me. Who does she think she is, sneaking around and blocking us out? If she's doing *anything* that's going to knock us rightward on the board—

I cross Assembly before I can think better of it, coming up behind them. She's using part of her body to cloak him from sight, which has the added bonus of keeping me out of view until I'm two steps behind them.

When Zaire spots me, his face lights up with a wide grin that barely masks the panic in his eyes. "Hey, your squadmate!" he chirps, his voice cracking high.

Aisha whips her head around, and I see the usual wrath in the flare of her nostrils. "What do you want, Tanaka?" she growls.

"What's going on here?"

"Nothing that concerns you," Aisha says.

"I mean, I'm a little concerned," Zaire interrupts. He tries to worm around Aisha to stand between us, but she holds up a hand, catching him forcefully across the chest.

"Isn't he off-menu for you?" I ask, raising an eyebrow.

"That's not what this is," Aisha snaps, just as Zaire says, "Why, jealous?" She bares her teeth at him, and he shrinks back. "Scram," she mutters, and Zaire immediately turns tail and hustles down the hall.

"I'm flattered!" he calls back over his shoulder.

"So what is it, then?" I ask, folding my arms. My exo reads the twitch of her pulse, even without the neural connection lacing our minds together. She's nervous. Defensive. Hiding something.

Aisha narrows her brows, setting her jaw in an exaggerated Scela scowl. Being confrontational isn't working. Cooperation just isn't a part of her makeup.

"Look, our assignment is coming. If whatever shady shit you're dealing with is going to get the squad in trouble, I deserve to know, at least."

"I don't owe you anything," Aisha says. She steps forward as if she's trying to blow past me, but I catch her by the elbow, my fingers squeezing tight against her flesh. Aisha's face might as well be sculpted from hullmetal—she barely reacts, even as my own exo flashes warnings that the pressure I'm applying might be hurting her.

"You don't know what you're starting," she says, keeping her gaze fixed on the distant launch tubes across the deck. "You don't have any say in anything that matters to me, and if you have any interest in keeping the squad focused, you'll leave me alone."

I want to scream. She has to realize how suspicious she's acting. She has to understand how all this looks. But I keep my face set. Perfectly cool. Perfectly Scela. "Don't blow this for the rest of us," I warn, keeping my tone flat.

I drop her arm, and Aisha gives me one last scowl before she hustles across the deck, her mechanically enhanced strides carrying her as quickly as they can. I glare after her, my thoughts spinning. The exo's right there with me, trying to parse what just happened. In our entire conversation, she didn't give me a single straight answer.

I still have no idea what kind of game Aisha Un-Haad is playing, but if it gets in our way tomorrow, I'm going to rip the fucking exo off her back.

CHAPTER 15

AISHA

Ten minutes in the mess. Then everyone to Assembly. Rigs on. Shuttle's waiting. The marshal's orders burst into our exosystem, snapping me and the rest of the squad awake. Her presence swells to drown out our groggy complaints and I start praying before my feet hit the floor.

Yesterday, for the first time, Zaire was the one passing information to *me* instead of the other way around. He warned me that there was going to be something more to our assessment today, something the Fractionists want me to look into. But then Key interrupted, he bolted, and I never found out what exactly I'm supposed to be looking out for. I don't even know where this shuttle we're being ordered to board is meant to go.

So I keep praying as we dress, rush to the cafeteria, and chug our breakfasts down with somber final glances at the rankings board. We've managed to crawl to the center of the graph, but it's not enough to save us if something goes catastrophically wrong today. And if we have any hope of earning white stripes on our rigs, we'll have to be at our absolute best. I'll need every last drop of God's grace to make it through this test.

We hurry to Assembly and strap on our full rigs. With the energy of the metal humming through me and the cameras fettering my vision, my nerves start to calm. Even my anxiety over the shuttle ride ahead goes quieter than it's ever been in the safety of my rig's cocoon.

I won't let it hold us back. Not today, when it's most important. If we do well, we can put all our struggles in training behind us.

And there's a secret hope brewing in me, one I keep buried far away from where the rest of the squad can feel it. If we get a good assignment, one where our salaries double or even triple, I can get my siblings out of Yasmin's hands. I can stop spying for her dangerous movement and finally put my guilty conscience to rest.

It's been three weeks since the *Aeschylus* vent, and I'm still struggling with the revulsion that rises in me every time I pass information along to Zaire. It all feels like harmless stuff—nothing as drastic as what I gave Lopez on the first day—but I can't stop thinking about how the Fractionists might use the information. What kind of blood could I be painting my hands with, just by giving them facts from missions I hear about on Assembly or the gossip that flickers through my exosystem every time we get popped into a larger body of Scela? That, on top of the constant struggle to keep what I'm doing out of the exosystem, has been keeping my brain spinning restlessly for the past two weeks.

Key nearly caught me. I have no doubt that if she knew what I was up to, she'd hand me over to the General Body on a silver platter. No matter how much I'd plead, that heartless, cold Scela would give up my brother's and sister's lives without hesitation.

The risk is too great, and with her getting suspicious, I need a way out.

Maybe today I'll get that chance.

Marshal Jesuit strides between our bays, her headpiece cocked back and her eyes flashing as she glances between us. A little flicker of pride spreads through the exosystem from her, and it warms me. The exo scoffs its disdain. It doesn't want her pride. It wants her endorsement.

The others' exos chorus in rhyming agreement. Praava's ready to earn a place that will buy Ratna's freedom from the *Lancelot*'s cells and get her back where she's needed. Wooj—well, he'd just be happy to get through this without another glitch, but there's a tiny hope stirring in him that an elite assignment might mean that Medical would look into fixing what went wrong during his conversion.

And Key, predictably enough, just wants the validation. She wants to prove she's worth her metal, to satisfy her greed, to fill those weird holes inside her.

"Today marks your graduation from basic training. There's only one more assessment standing between you and your unit's official assignment. Today, your mission is to deploy to an Alpha world."

My thoughts go fuzzy around the edges as the exo smothers them preemptively. *Alpha world.* The phrase registers.

We're going to a planet surface.

Discovered worlds are ranked on their habitability. Omega-class worlds are impossible for humans to inhabit under any circumstances. Alphas miss the mark by only a couple factors. There are thousands of Omega worlds in the database, and thousands more in the spectrum between Omega and Alpha. There are only thirty-seven Alpha worlds.

There's no class above an Alpha. If we found a world like that, we'd name it something real.

"To the shuttle," Marshal Jesuit orders. If there's any hint of nervousness in her, she doesn't share it. She's probably done this hundreds of times—it's part of her duty as head of basic.

But I'm crushed between fear and excitement, and I feel like my chest is about to collapse. Even if it's not habitable, this world's surface could be the closest I ever get to knowing what it might feel like to stand on the planet God promised. But to get there—

To get there—

The sharp edge of Key's warning, the delicate touch of Wooj and Praava's concern—they can't do anything to pull me out of the terror that grips me. Somehow my legs are working, encouraged by the buzz of the marshal's instruction. With heavy steps, I tramp in rank to the end of the deck, where a massive shuttle is waiting, its bay laid open. We file up the ramp, settle into seats, and wait as a pair of dockworkers checks our restraints.

The moment their backs are turned, my hand slams against the hullmetal behind me. I pray for grace. For strength. For this canister of metal to survive the forces we're about to be subjected to.

A nervous giggle slips out of Wooj before he has a chance to swallow it.

The rear hatch slams shut. Behind us, the engines rumble as they start to warm, and the whole shuttle lurches. We load into the launch tube.

The engines fire. My prayers vanish as gravity does, my focus shifting to keeping my stomach in line.

The hold is utterly empty save for the five of us. We're surrounded by the sway of unbuckled belts as the shuttle pitches and rolls. Out the back window, I spot a ship hull flashing past. We're maneuvering to the outside edge of the District formation, and I don't want to think about what comes next.

"FTL drives ready, engage in thirty seconds," an intercom crackles above us.

In its web of data, the exo generates a countdown.

I wind my fingers in the straps of my restraints.

The ship crawls forward. The gentle push of acceleration becomes an insistent nudge, which leans forward until the drives are roaring mercilessly, tugging us closer and closer to the precipice of light speed.

We trip over the barrier, and my exo fizzles with delight. It tries to get me to share its glee, but I'm too focused on my hold. If I grip too hard, the excess strength of the exorig gloves will rip the restraints right out of the wall. The temptation is all too real as the ship hurtles farther and farther from the Fleet.

My heart feels like it's swelling in my chest as I think of my siblings. Of how much distance is rapidly expanding between us. I never got to tell them I was leaving. If something happens to me—

The exo chokes off the speculation, trapping me solidly in reality as we plunge through the void between stars.

With our only window facing the rear of the shuttle, we don't actually see Alpha 37 on our approach. Our first glimpse of the planet is through the fires of our entry burn, and it's barely more than a glimpse for me—one look and my eyes are squeezed tightly shut, the sounds of my prayer drowned out by the roar of the flames and the rattle of our ship. Even after the deceleration breaks and we cruise the rest of our way to our targeted landing site, I don't dare open my eyes again until we've settled on solid ground and the shuttle's engines cut out, leaving us still and silent.

I unstrap as soon as the exo will allow me and immediately collapse onto the stable floor of the cargo bay, my thoughts smarting with humiliation. My legs feel like jelly, even with the metal supporting them. A hand comes down on the back of my rig, and Marshal Jesuit lifts me to my feet like a kitten. "Real grav, kid. How's it feel?" she chuckles. She walks to the hatch easily, already adjusted to the strange pull beneath her feet.

Real gravity. An actual planet, holding me to its skin. Hundreds of thousands of souls in the Fleet have lived and died and returned to God without ever experiencing this. Three hundred and one years have gone by, and only a small fraction of humanity has stood the way I am now.

"Heavy," I reply at last. *Heavier by a factor of 1.1,* my exo informs me. But with my enhanced body, the extra weight is nothing.

"Trainees," Marshal Jesuit announces as the other three unstrap and get their feet under them. "Masks are located in a bin up front. You'll want them on good and tight before the doors open."

Our exos nudge us into formation and parade us to the equipment. I grab a mask, fit its clear plastic mouthpiece over my nose and mouth, and attach it to a tank, which the exo prompts me to sling over my shoulder. It catches on a set of magnetic hooks, and then it's part of my body, its weight sitting naturally on my bones. I check the seals on the mask once more because the exo wants it and a third time because *I* need to be sure.

Behind me, Wooj starts leaping from foot to foot. He seems outrageously excited about the fact that each time he bounces into the air, an entire planet is pulling him back down again. With his full rig on, his exo's winning over his mind in the struggle to control his body, making him slightly unsteady. Overall, though, he seems stable. His headpiece hides his eyes behind bulbous lenses, but the smile we feel through the exosystem is genuine and Scela-wide, not manic. I hope it stays that way. We have too much at stake today for him to glitch out again.

I let myself share in his enthusiasm. Just a little. I think of the Ledic scripture's descriptions of our promised world, and for a brief second I let myself imagine that I've landed on Paradise with the Fleet at my back, ready to make a new start. It's said that our souls are bound to Earth, that they return there when our bodies let them go. But the great priests of generations past were so in tune with their spirits that they could feel Paradise calling to them, and even though the air outside is toxic, I imagine the gravity beneath my feet is that same pull, calling me home.

Even Key isn't immune. Over and over, she has to remind herself to focus, to not get carried away by the fact that there's a planet under her feet. Over and over, she fails. A rare smile peeks through the distortion of her face mask.

With all of us standing, our masks on, Marshal Jesuit flicks a signal out to the pilot, and the rear door of the shuttle slides open with a whir. Starlight floods in, and our cameras flicker as they rush to adjust their apertures.

And then a world sprawls out before us.

The surface ahead is star-baked and desolate. I heave in a deep breath, my mask fogging when it washes back out again. I wish I could smell it—the rocks, the dust, the thin layer of algae that coats the plain ahead of us. All I get is plastic and bottled air. I squint my apertures, my vision zooming in on the hazy spine of a distant mountain range.

It's so still. So quiet. For the first time in my life, there's no rumble of distant machinery, no whisper of recycled air streaming through vents. The only noise is my breath, my heart, and the internal hum of my Scela power. I try to wrap my mind around the planet's size, the lonely speck we make on it. Our squad, the marshal, and the pilot. No other people within billions of miles. Nothing but the fuel in our engines to save us from the gravity keeping us pinned on this world's surface.

"Welcome to Alpha 37," Marshal Jesuit says. "As far as the scientific analysis from the initial scouting has revealed, the only thing this world lacks is breathable air. Your tank is your lifeline. Pay attention to your levels. A minute without air and you're unconscious. Seven and you're dead."

I check in with my exo to make sure it's reading the tank. It is.

"Your rigs should keep you protected from any dangerous environmental elements, but if any of you get an open wound, report it *immediately*. I'll be at the edge of your system like usual." Marshal Jesuit stands at the head of the exit ramp, her hands on her hips, and information pours into my exo. A beacon, a terrain map, a countdown. "Today's exercises will be a test of how your squad performs in a completely new environment. How cohesively you can function when faced with the unfamiliar. You all now have a deadline and set of coordinates to a location on the planet's surface. Get there before the time expires. Good luck."

Our exos flock us together as we flood down the ramp and out onto the rough, rocky ground, past the glow of heat still radiating from the shuttle's engines. With the same target uniting the four of us, our minds link up in perfect synchrony. Key plunges ahead, taking the point of our formation. Praava and I flank her, while Wooj brings up the rear.

And we *run*.

They try to approximate a sky on the ships. The habitat domes, with their painted, faded blue. I hear in some frontend starships, they even project shifting clouds onto the arched metal ceiling. But now I'm staring at real sky, sky that reaches miles above my head, scattered with graying wisps of haze. Nothing can compare. Even the vaulted ceiling of Gym Deck seems claustrophobic. It has visible boundaries. This world feels limitless.

Our boots plunge into the dirt, leaving deep tracks behind us as we plow across the open plain. The countdown urges at the back of my neck, each number peeling away like a layer of skin.

The target flashes in my vision, distant, but the space between us is closing with every pump of my legs. A boulder field lies ahead. Flat ground to our left. But Key doesn't divert. She runs the squad straight into the uneven terrain, vaulting over the rocks. I feel Wooj stumble, but he catches himself on his hands for two strides and then he's after us again.

The boulders fly past us, our hands skimming over them as we wind and twist. I can feel my exo reading the landscape, taking my vision and transforming it into a map that I flow over like water. My breathing and heartbeat align with Key, Praava, and Wooj, and we push ourselves as fast as we can go. Nothing less will do with this much at stake.

The scattered rocks give way to larger slabs as we approach their source, a towering cliff face that juts out over the landscape. We thin down to a single-file line, and I take the point, dodging back and forth between the massive boulders. At the base of the cliff, I hesitate, letting my HUD map a climbable route.

Every second that ticks by burns into me as I wait for my direction. I can't stand it—even though the path is only half calculated, I lunge forward, my gloved hands digging into the stone as I scrabble for handholds. Praava's fast on my tail, then Key, then Wooj, each of them slotting their fingers into the spaces where mine went before.

The star's heat blazes down on us as we climb, but I savor the sensation of its energy melting into my skin and metal. In the Fleet, starlight is cold and distant, kept at bay behind hullmetal. But here, with dirt beneath me and sky above, the warmth embraces every inch of my body.

The exo loves it too, I think.

There's a crumbling noise beneath me and terror spikes through our exosystem as Wooj latches on to Key's ankle. A mess of conflicting signals floods out of him—none of our exos can make sense of them, but the human parts of us know what's going on. He's getting distracted by the stress of the assessment. It's devouring his thoughts and making it easier for the glitches to slip through. Wooj grimaces, ducks his head, and grabs for a rock hold before any of us can ask a question. He presses us to keep climbing.

So we do.

I summit the cliff, then Praava, then Key, Wooj lagging slightly behind us. Something vicious and animal takes over Key as she lunges to her feet—her urge to reach the target is so strong that she almost takes off. Waiting around for Wooj is weakness, and it's going to keep us from an elite assignment.

Praava stops her, first with a hand locked around the back of her rig, then with a forceful mental grip that keeps her pinned in place. Key struggles to break free, but I lend my strength, and our combined will reduces her to a seething mass, heaving against her casings as we wait for Wooj to make it up the cliff face.

"It doesn't count if we don't make it there together," Praava chides her.

Key bares her teeth. The expression's warped beneath the mask but inescapable in the exosystem. It gets a twinge of sympathy from me or my exo—I can't really tell which. There's something that aligns between us. Even if I don't agree with her reasons, I know in my gut that I want this just as badly as she does.

Wooj is still struggling, his HUD frantically insisting on the path as he tries to grab the handholds. He's so close. But his exo is flailing. It feels like half of him has been torn away, and what's left is scrabbling to keep its hold on his mind. "What—" he chokes, and his exo convulses against his spine.

He can't glitch on us. Not now. I drop to my knees and reach out, my fingers scraping along the ridge of his armpieces. "Grab on to me," I grunt.

But Wooj is locking us out, his exo raging inside him, and his grip slips. I lunge down to stop him, but Praava darts forward and snatches the back of my rig before my momentum takes me over the edge of the cliff. With one last burst of strength, Wooj lashes out and catches an outcropping.

It shatters under his grip.

All our exos flood with his panic, with the sensation of falling. Every rock he strikes on the way down pummels into our nervous systems. When he hits the ground, the exosystem evaporates with a blinding flash of white.

I blink, suddenly and horrifically stuck in my mind and my mind alone.

Praava shakes her head next to me. I reach her mentally, but the system is *gone*. "Did it—" She chokes, muffled through the mask. With her headpiece down, I can't see her eyes, only the flicker of her cameras' lenses as they roll frantically. "Wooj!" she shouts, stumbling for the edge of the cliff.

I grab her shoulder to steady her, worried she's about to go the same way. Key steps up beside us, her lips set in a grim line as she leans out over the edge. "Woojin?" she calls, her voice wavering somewhere between fury and concern.

His body is a small, crumpled speck at the base of the cliffs. I zoom my cameras in, my breath frozen between my ribs as I search for movement, for any sign that he survived the fall. My exo's in a frenzy trying to beat down my distress, but if he's dead, if we *failed*—

He shifts, rolling onto his side, and my enhanced hearing picks up a faint groan. Praava yelps, lunging forward again. "Careful," I shout after her as she starts to spider her way back down the cliffs.

To my surprise, Key plunges after her without a moment of hesitation. "Move your ass, Un-Haad," she shouts, cutting a haphazard path down the crumbling handholds. "We can salvage this."

I'm after her in a flash. I hate that *this* gets me moving so quickly, but Key has a point. If Wooj isn't too hurt, we can get him moving again. We might not be breaking any records, but we still have a chance to finish our assessment and make an impression.

Hand here. Foot there. I let the exo puppet me, the growing distance from our target burning in the back of my mind. By the time my feet hit the ground, Wooj is on his feet, his back to us, turning his arms over and over as he checks his rig for damage.

He turns around. His mask dangles from his chin, nothing but a warped, twisted hunk of metal and plastics.

"*Shit,*" Key hisses.

I check my internal clock. The amount of time that's passed since the exosystem evaporated.

Unconscious in a minute. Dead in seven.

But it's been two minutes since Wooj hit the ground. Praava

fumbles with the straps of her mask, stepping toward him, but he holds up a hand. "Guys," he says. "Nothing's happening."

Praava shakes her head. "Maybe it's slower for Scela, but—"

"No," Wooj retorts more firmly. "My blood-oxygen levels are stable. My exo's saying nothing's wrong with my body. I mean, I'm bruised as shit, and I think my rig's pretty banged up, but nothing's wrong with this air."

At my left, Key inhales sharply, the sound strangled beneath her mask. My exo protests inside me, but its denial just makes the truth more starkly clear.

Alpha 37 is habitable.

CHAPTER 16

KEY

Well, this is bullshit.

With no exosystem between us, I have no way of gauging my squadmates' reactions. Their faces are impassive, their eyes hidden behind their headpieces, their muscles impossibly still. I feel like I should be running, but the target's no longer pulling at my consciousness. I don't know where I'm supposed to go or what I'm supposed to do.

Though the exo resists, I reach up and unlatch the mask from my headpiece. This is it. This is the planet we've been waiting three hundred years for, and I don't care if my neural systems say otherwise—Woojin Lih doesn't get to be the only one breathing its air. I rip the plastic away from my face and inhale.

Something goes quiet in me as the fresh oxygen floods my lungs. For one shining moment, I'm at peace with myself and whatever I've become, because this planet is *mine*. I didn't even know I wanted it so badly. My empty spaces don't feel anywhere near whole, but maybe I don't mind it so much now.

Aisha follows my example, tugging at her mask's straps.

Praava keeps hers on. "They're gonna kill us," she mutters. Even though our exosystem is disabled, my headpiece's hearing picks up the hollow fear in her words.

"Why would they?" I retort. My exo urges me to come up with a logical explanation for what's happening, struggling to keep me away from the inescapable facts. "Maybe it was a miscalculation. Maybe the air is a slow killer. The General Body's been world-searching for centuries—there's gotta be some reason—"

"Fractionism," Woojin says, like it should be obvious. He brushes some dirt out of his rig, swaying slightly. "The General Body wants the human race to assemble neatly under their rule. The seven-district system only works within the Fleet." His jaw tightens, and I know his exo is struggling to accept what he's say-ing. "We land, and all that goes to shit. There's no obligation to be united under the General Body when we're off the ships, free to expand, and we have an entire *world* to settle."

"You sound like a propaganda cast," Aisha spits out. Her tone is defensive, just like yesterday.

Woojin shrugs, a wasteful motion in a full exorig. "I've listened in on my fair share, but I'm just saying—that's what they're scared of. That's why they'd cover up something like this."

"What if they've done it before?" I mutter, and feel the cameras of their rigs snap to me. "Other Alpha worlds. We could have—" Turmoil rises in me, the exo trying to curb my voice. It doesn't feel like part of my body anymore. It's a parasite, I'm the host, and now my holes have never felt bigger.

Aisha nods along with me, and I know she's thinking of her siblings. Of her life in the backend of the Fleet. Of how *unnecessary* the whole system is if we could be building a new way of life on this planet.

"Ratna," Praava breathes, going still like something's just hit her. "Ratna was investigating the origins of the wasting fever. The consensus has been that the fever is a mutation of a different disease that was already aboard the Fleet, but she said they were starting to look into a more niche theory that the disease was terrestrial in origin. They must have looked too closely at the data from the recent discovered worlds and found things that didn't line up."

"And maybe the Fractionists got wind of it," Aisha says with a nod. "And that's why the riots targeted your sister's research center."

And the General Body vented the ship to keep them from reaching it. I don't dare say it aloud. Instead, I heave in another breath, trying to settle back into the exo's embrace.

Aisha's lips twitch like there's something more she wants to say, an extra dot she's connected, but after a moment of waiting, it's clear she isn't ready to share it just yet. It's fine—I'm not sharing everything I'm thinking either.

A nudge from my exo lifts my arms, and I reluctantly press the mask back over my face. The blast of air that hits me tastes sterile, filtered beyond recognition and compressed into nothing, but it makes the exo happy. It sinks back against my spine.

But I can't shake the fact that there was *real* air in my lungs. Molecules in my body that came from a planet's atmosphere. If I had any of Aisha's reverence, I'd call it a holy moment. None of this seems real.

"So," Woojin says, rubbing at a bruise. I'm almost jealous— his full rig protected him from the fall, so much so that he probably won't need any clamps or endoscopes to put him right. "Now what?"

"We have to go back," Aisha mutters.

"They're gonna kill us," Praava repeats.

"We're fucked," I say, just to round it out.

"Hey, there's a whole habitable world out there," Woojin replies with a sly grin. "We could always take our chances."

But I can feel my exo urging me back toward the shuttle, and I'm sure a similar impulse is rattling through my squadmates' systems. The only real option left is to face the consequences of our discovery, whatever they may be. Woojin tests his legs, shifting and flexing until he's sure that his rig is still functional. Then, for the first time, he leads the squad, setting off into the boulder field at a steady jog as the three of us flock in his wake.

The marshal catches us before we're halfway back. She thunders to a halt in front of Woojin, her rig flashing in the starlight as she snaps her headpiece back. "What the hell happened?" she asks, and even without the system, I feel the moment her disappointment shifts to cold betrayal at the sight of Woojin's mangled mask.

Her eyes narrow, and a click at the back of my skull sends me rocketing back into the exosystem. Only this time, we have a fifth participant fully present in all the intimacy of a small system.

Her presence washes over us in a new light. This is Marshal Gwen Jesuit. Thirty-five years old, Scela for fifteen of them. Born in the Fourth District. Mother. But before we can go too much farther, she pulls herself back and takes a step forward, towering over us as she approaches. The exosystem boils—rage from her, fear and anxiety from the rest of us.

"So—" Woojin starts, but Marshal Jesuit's exo throttles his speech before he can get another word out. We're insignificant next to her level of control, and as she yanks us in mentally, all four of us flinch at the simmering fury waiting for us there. A wary hum runs up the backs of our necks, a threat if we try to speak out of turn.

Back to the ship, she orders. *Hurry. Lih, try to hide that thing behind your hands. We have to protect the shuttle pilot.*

If the marshal's afraid too, we're even more fucked than I first thought.

She turns and sets back off the way she came at a punishing pace, and we spill after her. My stunstick wound aches as my arms pump, and across the system, I can feel Woojin's body groaning with near-constant complaint.

And now that we're reconnected, my thoughts flood with Aisha's indignation—not just over the secret we discovered. She had so many hopes for today, so many dreams riding on getting an elite assignment. All of them now lie shattered at her feet. She's looking for someone to blame, someone to punish. Woojin for falling. Me for rushing Woojin.

I don't think Aisha Un-Haad realizes what a profoundly angry person she is.

When we reach the shuttle, the marshal ushers us quickly into the cargo bay and seals the ramp behind us. We're forced to keep up the ruse of the masks as the air filtration systems whine overhead, replenishing the hold. When at last the hum shifts from a low rumble to a steady whine, Marshal Jesuit lets us take them off.

No speaking out loud, she says in our heads. *We keep this as quiet as possible until we know for sure what's going on here.*

We do *know what's going on here,* I retort. *This world is habitable.*

This world is survivable, she counters. *Certainly more survivable than we thought. But "habitable" could be dependent on other factors. We need to stay calm, and we need to lock down this information. If it gets out, it could set off a panic that might not be justified.*

Aisha drops back suddenly. I flick my thoughts her way and find her . . . smaller. Heavier. Weighed by something I don't understand, something she's not sharing. She shoves me away.

My exo informs me that there's a protocol for events like this, the marshal continues. *When we depart from this planet, we'll be handing ourselves over to the starship* Lancelot.

My limbs lock up, a chill running down my spine. After so long fighting to be some of the Fleet's best defenders, we're being ordered to surrender to the ship that carries its traitors. Not to mention that among them is a boy who seems to be blocked from my memories but keeps escaping into my dreams. Isaac's warning echoes in my mind, and a storm of protest rises in me.

Tanaka, the marshal warns, and my spine straightens, my metal snapping to attention. *This order's not the kind you can disobey.*

A thought bursts from Aisha before she can clamp down on it. *I have to tell Yasmin.* She walls herself up the moment our scrutiny swings around. *My sister. My brother. I need to—*

The marshal cuts her off. *You'll do no such thing. We talk to no one until we're on the other side of this. Whatever's going on, we'll clear it up on the* Lancelot. But her thoughts slide to her own family, to the daughter she left behind on the starship *Atreus.* Marshal Jesuit lifts her chin, pressing down her agitation like the expert she is. *I need your focus. Can you promise me that?*

The four of us nod.

Then buckle up. Marshal Jesuit flicks a bit of her consciousness toward the ship's controls, passing her orders along to the pilot. We settle into our seats and pull the restraints over our shoulders.

The moment we're settled, the marshal flips a switch, and our exos go dead.

I try to move, but the weight of my rig is so great that I can barely twitch my fingers. Panic spirals from my brain, expecting an outlet in the exosystem, but it's gone. I'm alone in my skull, no machine keeping my mind in line.

I won't be trapped. I won't be stuck in this metal with no explanation and then have my control taken away with just a switch. That clawing, twisting sensation comes scrabbling out of my holes again, and this time my exo isn't there to combat it.

The others are stone-still around me. I clench my teeth, trying to beat down the tumult on my own. But the only thing that interrupts my spiral is when the shuttle's thrusters fire at last and the soft sound of Aisha praying rises beneath the rumble.

Our exos are still dead when we finally dock with the *Lancelot*. With my vision locked straight ahead and no internal time, it's only the jolt of the airlock sealing that lets me know our journey has reached its end.

A pair of humans darts into the shuttle the moment the door slides open and begins unstrapping us. Outside the Fleet ship's gravity, we float limply as they line us onto a rack where we hang in file by the napes of our necks. A robotic arm extends into the shuttle and drags us into the *Lancelot*'s gravitational field. My rig collapses against me, and I struggle to keep my thoughts in focus as the metal presses down on my lungs.

Without my exo's control, my cameras have gone static and my field of vision has reduced to almost human levels. I can't turn my head. I can't even open my jaw. I'm trapped in the horror of my body, in the monster *they* made me.

They?

The thought is so visceral, and yet I can't place what I mean by that one little word. Who's *they?* A burn aches in the back of my throat. I fight the feeling, but I've forgotten what it's like to have a solitary brain. I can't do it. I can't stop these thoughts.

"Tanaka," Marshal Jesuit murmurs through her wired-shut jaw at my left. "Tanaka, stay with me."

I wonder how she noticed, but then I realize the way my lungs are pumping. My chest expands and collapses so fast that it's a wonder I haven't passed out. More likely, it's a miracle of the way my body's been reworked.

Every time I move, I can feel the metal around me, against me, inside me. Isaac's warning burns stronger and stronger in my memory.

"Tanaka," the marshal grunts.

I breathe in. I hold it, my swollen lungs straining against a biology that doesn't feel right. I breathe out, which helps. Only a little, but it's enough to get my heart's thunder under control. I wish it were the fresh, crisp scent of the planet's air, but I don't think I'll ever smell that again at this point.

Corridor after corridor scrolls past. We've been loaded onto the back of a truck that rushes through the *Lancelot*'s halls. Not along the cellfronts, thankfully. I don't think my mind or body could take it if I saw the boy from my dreams again.

Somewhere to my right, Woojin starts giggling.

"Great," Praava mutters.

"You know how to pick 'em," Aisha says, and the two of them share a quiet chuckle. I try to bury myself in their laughter, try to lose myself in it, but without the exosystem, I'm grasping at nothing. I'm alone with my holes.

Instead I count my breaths, but even that seems harder with no machine in my head. And with no exo to mark time, I'm left to guess how long it takes to deliver us to a cold, sterile room where we wait for another indeterminate stretch. Woojin's giggles keep bubbling up, and roughly ten fits later, the door slides open and a lone person steps in.

Whoever it is doesn't enter our field of vision. We're pointed at the far wall, all our cameras fixed on its sloping plastics. The door whispers shut again, and for a moment all I hear is the hiss of five Scela breathing.

Then a tired-sounding voice says, "This really isn't necessary."

The exosystem snaps between us, and all five of us jolt together in a confused jumble. There's a rush of relief in our minds relinking, but for me, the relief is that the exo is humming against my spine once more, soothing every terrible thought that rises in me. My muscles relax, and I'm unsurprised to feel an ache kneading itself into them.

But something's off—something's strange. An electric crackle—almost like the threat of a hanging order—infuses the metal on our backs. My cameras whirl around, the HUD flaring in my vision as I turn to face the room's sixth occupant. The relief dissolves in my stomach.

Facing us with her arms folded is Chancellor Vel.

CHAPTER 17

AISHA

No one reacts quite right. Wooj lets out a laugh. Key tries to salute. Praava's hands twitch into fists. Marshal Jesuit inhales sharply through her nose and almost snorts. And I convulse in my rig, trying to wrench my head around to get her cloaked figure centered in my vision.

Chancellor Vel.

The woman who's held power over the General Body for most of the time I've been alive, who has dictated our very way of life. I've only ever seen her in casts or at a distance—I always assumed they used the cameras to make her look taller. In the training room she was a far-off shadow looming above us. But here in person, she towers without the assistance of heels or an exorig—nowhere near as tall as Scela, but impressive for a human. The elegant robe that marks the Chancellor's rank shines as bright as starlight, a stark contrast to her richly dark skin.

A sacrilegious thought flickers through me. *Scela may be built with Godlike strength, but this woman looks the part.* The eerie buzz hovering on the back of my spine gets keener. None of us are sure what to make of it. It's like our exos are primed to receive an instruction, despite the fact that so far, none has been given.

"This isn't necessary either," Chancellor Vel says, and a moment later the clamps on our necks snap open, dropping us unceremoniously to the floor. Marshal Jesuit is the only one to land squarely on her feet.

Straightening and turning, she pulls the rest of us with her as we get our legs under us. When all our cameras fix on the Chancellor, Vel smiles.

It isn't a kind one. My cameras pick up on the little human subtleties that sour her expression, then flick to the techy-looking manacle locked around her wrist. The exo seems to know what it is and what it does even before she raises it. It clamps down on a shudder of anticipation, and the uncomfortable hum on my back sharpens to a bladed edge.

Chancellor Vel flicks her hand, and all five of us drop to our knees in unison.

"Remove your headgear," she orders.

The back of my neck ignites. A ripple rolls through my exo, and before I know what's happening, my headpiece is retracting from my face, ripping my cameras' sight away. My systems press down my panic, reassuring me that there's nothing wrong with the way she's controlling me, that the Chancellor, by nature, wields full control over Scela.

That I *belong* under her command.

No, I rebel internally. My autonomy's been ripped away like it's nothing, and I can't ignore that. I try to push back against her control, try to bring my headpiece back down, but my exo locks me in place. A tinge of alarm washes out from me, joined in the exosystem by Wooj's heady wave of fear. He chose the metal to avoid confinement. And the Chancellor's pinned him with a mere flip of her wrist.

This is nothing like the marshal's orders. Not even like Praava's override of our system. That was gentle, a tug on the hand compared to the intensity of the Chancellor's will yanking us into place like beasts on leashes. Praava understood us—she was Scela. But now we're at the mercy of a mind that can't possibly understand our bodies, our brains, the way we mingle with the machines on our backs. The Chancellor sees us the way humans do, the way I used to see Scela. We're tools. Weapons. Things to be wielded with force.

"I want a report of what happened on that planet," Chancellor Vel says, nodding to Marshal Jesuit. "Spare no detail."

She turns her back to us. Strapped to the base of her neck is a device with wires that plunge into the underside of her skull. My exo identifies it as a neural transmitter in communication with her cuff. A master node in the Fleet-wide exosystem. No communication flows into it, but through it, the Chancellor can bend all of us to her will.

We don't get her thoughts through the conduit—only her orders. And I nearly thank God out loud, because she doesn't get our thoughts either.

Marshal Jesuit falters, but we all feel the moment the Chancellor's command rips her speech away from her control. Words pour out of her mouth, her intonation flat and lifeless. In the system the marshal fights to stay calm as the facts rush out of her.

She tells the whole story with no breaks, save for a moment of hesitation when she tries to describe what went wrong with Wooj's exo that caused his fall in the first place. She settles for the word *malfunction,* a compromise from the exo's preferred *glitch.*

When the marshal finishes, Chancellor Vel closes her eyes. I can't read any sort of intent in her expression, and the exo has to corral the terror that grips me. She could kill us so easily. She could probably do it through the freakish device on her wrist.

But when Vel speaks next, her voice is soft and almost friendly. "The pilot never found out?"

"We made sure the pilot saw nothing. He no doubt wonders why we returned so abruptly, but he hasn't been given any reason to suspect that . . ."

"That Alpha 37 is habitable," the Chancellor finishes. "Which, unfortunately, it is."

The confirmation hits our exosystem like a lightning bolt. It's true. There's a livable world out there. Humankind's great purpose has been fulfilled. The urge to fall to my knees and praise God is tempered only by the cynical wave that overtakes me from Key's end of the system. The Chancellor confirmed it too easily.

Which means either she trusts us to keep the secret, or she's not letting us leave this room.

None of us think it's the former.

Chancellor Vel meets each of our eyes in turn with an even stare. "The Scela are the pride of the Fleet," she says, beginning to pace back and forth along our line. "Now it seems the Fractionists have made their most insidious disruption yet. They're using our own protectors against us."

My walls are up in an instant, even though I know Vel can't read my thoughts. I pray the others are too focused on the Chancellor to pay attention to the way I've snatched myself abruptly away from the rest of them.

"You were never meant to carry out your assessment on Alpha 37 in the first place," she continues. "That planet's been

177

removed from the approved sites. It appears a Fractionist hack swapped the target into your flight plan. We'll find its source soon enough."

Zaire's warning yesterday. I can almost see Lopez's smug little grin as he brags about his control of the *Dread*. No doubt he was the one responsible for making the switch. I was supposed to investigate Alpha 37's secret and pass the information along to the Fractionists.

So much for that.

"Fortunately," Vel continues, "the coordinates themselves aren't accessible outside the shuttle databases—otherwise we might have a much larger crisis on our hands. I'm deeply sorry that you got caught up in this. I want to thank you," Vel says, breaking off from her pacing. "For your honesty. And for your continued discretion."

I never dreamed the word *continued* could make my legs feel like they're about to melt from sheer relief. She's letting us live. The tension in the air lessens as understanding sweeps over us. The burn at the back of my neck goes cool.

Then Wooj snaps. "How the *fuck* do you justify this?" he yelps, lunging to his feet. The rest of us gape, stunned that *this* is what he chooses to do the second her hold loosens. Chancellor Vel waves her hand, and he collapses on his knees again, utterly in her thrall.

She doesn't flinch. She doesn't even blink. Maybe that's why she's been able to keep her position for so long. She hasn't once looked at the messy knots of skin around our protruding enhancements or shrunk back from the sheer power that rolls off the rigs. The woman who stands before us is fearless.

"Woojin Lih, is it?" she says, lifting her chin.

"Yes, Chancellor," he replies, but his voice is hollow and forced.

Her voice drops to a dangerous whisper, her words crystal clear in our audio sensors. "I have the names of every single person in the starship *Orpheus*'s underbelly who has ever shown you kindness. All those people who took you in, who gave you jobs, who helped you claw your way out of a life of nothingness. Raise a hand to me again or breathe a word about Alpha 37's true nature, and I will cull them from our population."

Terror blasts out of Wooj as he stares unblinkingly up at the Chancellor. When he speaks again, his words are genuine, filled with as much emotion as his exo will allow. "It won't happen. I swear."

"Good." Chancellor Vel pivots, her eyes settling on Praava, who ducks her chin slightly under the weight of the Chancellor's attention. "Your sister is already imprisoned on this starship. Don't give me reason to move her to a tank on the *Endymion*."

Praava shakes her head. "I won't," she says immediately.

Then the Chancellor's gaze lands on me. Outwardly, I stay Scela-blank, but inside I'm struggling to keep my composure. *I'm* the reason we ended up on the planet. I'm the reason we found out that God's promise of the next good world has already been fulfilled. I'm the reason my squad is being threatened and forced into silence. All because I'm trying to—

I almost start laughing. The Chancellor's impending threat is so predictable. So inevitable. They know exactly where my salary is going. They know exactly what my pressure point is. And since Amar and Malikah's lives already depend on me, it's not like her threat is anything new. I'll endure it. I've *been* enduring it.

But when the Chancellor opens her mouth, it's not the words I'm anticipating. "I don't expect we'll have much trouble from you, Aisha. I'm sure you, of all people, know exactly why we cannot have the rest of the Fleet aware of Alpha 37's status."

My throat goes dry. "I don't—"

"You should understand better than any of them." The Chancellor pauses, and my exo recognizes the moment of quiet, thrilling anticipation before a blow comes down. "You know firsthand what panicked people do in close quarters."

She has her hand raised like she's going to snatch my next words away, but there's no need. I don't have any words left, because she's right.

The memory hits like a sucker punch. Two years ago, a rumor started circulating on my birthship. People said the General Body had decided the *Reliant*'s population overgrowth had gone too far, and they were going to cut off its food support. It wasn't true, but it lit a fast-burning fire in people. They packed the streets, crushing anything in their path on their way to empty the granaries. I still remember the noise of it—the constant clamor outside our windows, the snap of stunsticks in the streets below, the screams and shrieks, the heavy thunder of Scela footfalls. It took two days for the noise to quiet down. Two days for the streets to clear. Two days for them to identify my parents' bodies.

"Riots," Chancellor Vel continues, "benefit *no one*. And that's what this Fleet faces if word of this world leaks."

I can see it. Exactly how it unfolds every time.

Crowds sprinting and pushing, seething masses of people pounding on hullmetal, screeching for a freedom they've felt entitled to their entire lives. I see the thousands of children who will have to know exactly what I went through two years ago. Another little girl on another backend district street, waiting at the window for the inevitable as the noise in the distance grows louder and louder.

I nod. My heart feels torn and raw, but the exo soothes it into an even beat.

"When our ancestors lived on Earth, it was as a fractured people. The Fleet gives us unity and we have found our strength, our common ground. If the Fractionists get their way, we fall back into the chaos that we left Earth in. That is humanity divided. Humanity turning against itself. Humanity's final extermination."

I bow my head. Earth was Paradise unearned. Humankind wasn't ready for God's grace, and we had to leave, to travel, to become worthy. My exo cringes at the Ledic teachings pouring from my memory, but Chancellor Vel doesn't notice.

"If the Fractionist threat recedes, there may be hope that we'll be landing on that planet within my lifetime. But if they continue to insist on splitting the Fleet, continue to take measures like the *Aeschylus* vent, the General Body cannot allow information about the planet to leak." Vel's eyes soften, and she takes a step back. The humming of the gauntlet's presence eases. "This is for the protection of everyone under my care," she says. "Under *your* care—not just the people you love, but the people you serve as Scela. I don't like making threats like this, and I'm deeply sorry that's what it's come to, but as the leader of the Fleet, it's my duty to keep it safe at any cost."

"I understand," I concede, head limp against my chest. In the exosystem, I feel the others—Wooj especially—pressing me to reject everything she's saying, to rebel against her control. But I *do* understand. And I'm halfway to agreeing with everything the Chancellor has said. Yasmin threw me into this blind. I didn't have a chance to think things through before I started doing her Fractionist dirty work, and I let my fear govern me before my reason could.

Now I'm starting to see reason.

"Unlike the Fractionists who put you in this mess, we value

Scela," the Chancellor says. "Too few survive the integration process to put any to waste—we *need* you to help combat this growing threat, and we can't have you out of commission. So we'll be equipping your exos with blockers that will keep you from joining any exosystems outside your own. With the blockers in place, your thoughts won't leak the information anywhere you can't control, allowing you to continue your duties. And you, of course, will not *choose* to leak this information under any circumstances."

At my left, Key lets out a derisive snort, and the rest of us tense in unison.

The edge of the Chancellor's smile disappears, and she pulls her gauntlet up, forcing Key's spine to straighten. "Key Tanaka," she says, low and level. "You aren't like your fellows. But that's no surprise to you, is it?"

The Chancellor steps right up to Key's side, leaning close to her face. In the exosystem, we feel Key's urge to flinch, to take a step back, but Vel's gauntlet has her pinned in her metal. Pain burns through the system, radiating from the back of her neck.

Through her ears, we hear every word the Chancellor says. "It would be a more intensive process to block the planet from all your memories, but unfortunately, that won't work with *you* in the mix. We can't risk it on a brain that's already had memory blockers installed, you see?"

Key's lip curls. A faint whimper leaks from her throat.

"It was a mercy that we chose to suppress those missing pieces. Being Scela with them still there would be a tormented existence—you likely wouldn't be able to stand it. But mark my words, if you tell anyone outside your squad about the planet in our grasp, we'll put those memories right back in and let you live with it."

Key's always been hollow. An empty thing, a girl with holes.

But nothing has shaken her before this. Nothing made her so uncertain—or if it did, she never let us feel it until today. Now we feel the Chancellor's words blasting her thin. We feel everything she knows about herself wavering. She's always desperately wanted to know who she was before she took the metal.

Suddenly that information's no longer a reward—it's a threat.

Her exo's the only thing that keeps her upright, and she can't meet the Chancellor's steely gaze.

"I'm here to serve the General Body," she mumbles, but predictably enough, there's no certainty behind anything she's saying. "I'm here to be the perfect soldier, to hold this Fleet together with my bare hands if necessary. Take my word or take my body—whichever serves you best."

"Smart girl," Chancellor Vel says, baring her teeth almost Scela-wide. "The technicians should be ready any minute. And once they're done, we can put this whole fiasco behind us."

This time, none of us make the mistake of laughing. This fiasco is far from over. And whatever comes next, I know one thing deep in my bones—it's only going to get worse.

CHAPTER 18

KEY

The holes are on purpose.

I'm not damaged goods like Woojin. I'm being protected from that *thing* that came crawling out of me when the exo shut down. I should be relieved. Grateful, even.

Instead I'm burning. I'm out of alignment with the others as we make our way to a nearby medical ward, my exo putting up walls again to protect them from the scorching confusion cycling through my brain. What could be locked down in my head? What's so horrible that unlocking it could destroy me? My exo screams in my ear not to pursue it.

I don't know whether to believe it.

Wrapped up in the war inside me and shuttered by my head-piece, I don't realize we've stopped until I run right into the marshal's back with a clack of colliding metal. A burst of her consternation hits me, followed by a brief squeeze of her will on the back of my neck that forces me to straighten up and step back. After the unrelenting violence of the Chancellor's gauntlet, her mind's touch is shockingly tender.

My cameras whirl, taking in the sterile white room we've entered. I'm surprised to see Isaac limping back and forth among the team of humans setting up the blocker installation. An unsteady fury rises in me—he *knew*. Or at least, he must have known *something*. There must have been more he could have told me before the Chancellor turned the past I've been seeking into a nightmare I have to escape.

I watch him shout orders, clutching his datapad to his chest as the technicians unpack a massive set of ugly, thick wires and plugs. They look familiar.

I reach for the memory and instead feel the edges of my holes twisting and aching. So they're another thing I've lost. *Another thing I'm being protected from,* the exo wills me to understand. It's pushing out calm, but I'm not buying it.

What if the Chancellor wasn't telling the whole truth?

My breath goes shallow, and for a moment I feel as if the air in the room has vanished, as if I'm back in the silent hell of the *Aeschylus* vent.

Isaac turns and faces us. "We'll be rewriting the permissions on your interexo protocols, making sure you can't jack into the greater Scela system. Jesuit, yours is a little more complicated, since we need you in communication with the rest. You'll be the nexus point for access to these four. You'll be taken care of last."

"Then I'm going first," I say, stepping toward the technicians. Anything to get away from the vile, twisting thoughts, from the doubts and insecurities, from everything that might make me unworthy of the metal I wear. One of them hoists up a plug, and my body already knows what to do. I bend forward, crouching to expose my neck as I flick a panel open at my nape.

The tech hesitates, and that prickling familiarity intensifies. I've done this before. Somehow I've done this before, and somehow I *know* that's part of my missing pieces. The exo's stress triples—over and over, it warns me to be careful with what I'm chasing.

Isaac stares at me from across the ward, a wary spark in his eyes. He glances at the tech and nods.

The plugs jack into my port with a harsh snap, and Marshal Jesuit dissolves the exosystem. As I adjust to my solitary headspace, my exo recoils from the thought of what's about to happen. It hates even the *notion* of being forced to change. A moment passes as the technicians swipe furiously at their datapads, and then my cameras cut out, leaving me in total darkness.

The pain ignites inside me like a star gone supernova. My body rocks and shudders, my hands clench into fists, and then I lose myself entirely in the cold, white light. I feel the exo's muted attempts to shield me, but there's nothing it can do to stop the horrid sensation of someone brute-forcing my brain to comply. The new protocols slice through me like a sharp knife through flesh. They're twisting, pulling, rearranging.

I feel the familiarity here too.

Finally it fades. Finally my cameras click back on, my muscles relax, and my exo grabs hold of my body again. I rip the plugs out of my neck before the technician can get to them, my exo flashing warnings about improperly ejected hardware. The port flips closed. I toss the limp cords to the ground.

"Wasn't so bad," I say.

Even without the system between us, I know the others can tell I'm lying. And even worse, the install's done nothing to combat the sinking, empty feeling of my holes and what they might be for. I stagger back toward the door as Aisha steps up for her turn.

Everything's rising inside me. Who I am. What I was. What I

saw on the *Aeschylus.* The exo swats it down, but I swat it back. I want it to consume me. I want to understand what's going on in the Fleet. Why the General Body would vent a ship and blame it on the Fractionists. It's even easier now to believe that they were the ones who vented the *Aeschylus,* knowing that they've covered up an entire livable world to maintain their power. I want to carve through all the lies that surround me, but there's one lie at the heart of it all. One thing I need to know.

One thing that feels like it might tear me apart if I find out.

The door is right there. The exo doesn't stop me from walking through it. I square my shoulders, brace myself for the order that will yank me right back into the room, and wait for the marshal's reaction.

"Tanaka," Marshal Jesuit warns, but when I don't stop, she mutters, "All right, you need to cool off—I get it."

I round the corner unhindered, my heart racing faster than a shuttle at light speed.

I'm free of the exosystem. Free from the chatter of my squadmates and how incomplete I feel in their presence. Free from the marshal's will and Isaac's warnings and the Chancellor's vague threat. Without all of them breathing down my neck, I take stock of myself. Of the mystery inside me, this thing that was done *to* me.

I won't let myself be controlled by it.

And there might be answers on this very ship.

My exo digs in its heels, but without the exosystem, there's no willpower for it to enforce apart from my own. I snap back my headpiece. It takes me a moment to adjust to seeing with eyes instead of cameras, to only have 180 degrees of visibility from side to side and even fewer up and down. I run one hand over the place where my exo ridge meets my skull, my fingers brushing over the stubble of my hair growing back. In the nearest plastic wall, I catch a warped, faint image of my reflection.

I remember what I looked like before my conversion. I was built lean and willowy before they carved me apart and stacked me with the buildings of a mechanical god. I used to have hair that swept down to my shoulders, cut severely at a dramatic angle. Now there's metal squaring my jaw. The ridge of my exo carves my skull in half. I'm an animal. A monster.

But I still remember that look on Aisha's aunt's face on the *Reliant*. She'd mumbled something—some word I didn't quite catch, but somehow it was meant for me. She's a backender, and yet she seemed to recognize me.

Keep away, the exo warns, but that warning only spurs me forward. I stalk through the halls of the prison ship, the doors parting as easily for me as they did for Praava on the *Aeschylus*. The ship's management software knows better than to get in the way of a Scela on a mission. I move down the rows of cells as their residents peer curiously through the glass. The location I need to get to is seared into my memory, into a space the holes can't touch.

It might destroy me. Or it could fill the holes at last. All depends on whether I trust the Chancellor.

So I run toward it.

Keep away. Keep away. Keep away, the exo chants in my head. The uncomfortable hum on my neck is back, enforcing orders I don't remember being given. I fight it. Throw my own will against its insistent buzz. My legs go unsteady beneath me, and I sway like a drunk as I round a corner to another row of cells. This is the hall. Three blocks down. My footsteps thud at uneven intervals.

Just a little farther. Just to the plastic of the cellfront.

I lift my eyes and find a familiar face staring back at me.

No, it's not, the exo screeches in my ear.

But it is. It's the boy from my dreams, this boy standing in the cell—

It's rising in me again. The metal around me, the metal inside me—it's not my body, it's not a body I chose, it's *not supposed to be like this.* The boy jumps back from the cell wall as I sag against it, warping the plastic with my weight. My fingers dig into my skull, pressing along the line between my exo's ridge and the flesh and bone of something that should be *mine* and *mine alone.*

"Hey," a voice says, muffled slightly by the cellfront between us. I squeeze my eyes shut, my audio inputs ringing with confused signals. I know that voice.

You don't, the *thing* on my back shrieks.

I'm stronger than this—that's the worst of it. They built me with all this strength, and what use is it if I can't keep myself together? What's the point of jamming my head with blockers and patching me up and throwing me into a fight I can't quite justify? Why did I do this to myself?

And maybe it's finally remembered that we share this body, because the exo actually gives me a clear and truthful answer to that last question.

You didn't, it whispers.

My eyes snap open again. They find the golden-haired boy approaching the plastic, his expression halfway between horror and holy reverence. I lock up my muscles, holding myself perfectly still as he comes closer and closer. *Keep away,* the exo whispers one last time, just in case I haven't gotten the message already.

"It's you," he breathes, his lips barely moving. "Spirits alive, Key—"

Only I don't hear how he finishes that sentence, because

suddenly I'm lost in an onslaught of memories. This isn't a controlled leak, one of the exo's rewards for a job well done. This is white water in a flooded Earth cast. My head goes under, and there's no coming back up for air. His voice is all around me—*Key, Key, Key*—soft, harsh, fond, frustrated. I've heard him say my name so many times, and every single one of them is trying to claw its way out of the dark spaces in my brain.

Some of them sharpen, images flickering in my head. An outstretched hand, a wild party pulsing around us, an easy smile. *Nice to meet you, Key.* Breath on my cheek, my name said like a warning, just before I kiss him. A camera lens, studio lighting, hands on my shoulders. *Key, you can do this.*

"Key!" he's shouting now, pounding a fist against the plastic barrier. I've sunk to the ground, propped up crookedly against the cellfront, and I can feel my exo at work in my head, trying to keep my muscles from seizing up. They spasm against my will, clenching and unclenching ferociously. My mismatched teeth grind together.

I don't know which way to run. I've come so far for my memories—if this is my only chance to recover what I'm missing, to make my head make sense again, I have to see this through. But it's ripping me apart to be this close to what used to fill those holes, and I don't know how much longer I can last.

The Chancellor may be a liar on some fronts, but I never should have believed she'd make an empty threat.

My eyes roll, meeting the piercing blue of my dream boy's. His mouth drops open, making a shape I've seen before—as a Scela, in an orphanage cafeteria, on a ship I never want to go back to. Only this time I hear the sound that was missing when Yasmin spoke.

"Archangel," the boy says.

Oh fuck.

I'm gone, I'm gone, I—

"—really don't see the need for the new costume," I tell Kellan as he circles around behind me.

"It's about effect," he says, straightening the banner that serves as a background for our makeshift set. I flinch as one of the other crewmembers adjusts a light, accidentally pointing it directly into my eyes. "Besides." He crouches low next to me, close enough that his breath teases along my neck. "Looks good on you."

I crack a savage smile, nudging his chin away with my knuckles as the tips of my ears go hot. "Save it for later," I hiss, then go back to fidgeting with my skirts. A small red light glows to life in the darkness.

It's over the top, but the costume works. Today I've been decked out in shimmering white, the bodice cut with sharp angles and a neckline that takes no prisoners. With my lips painted crimson and the camera settings adjusted to make the contrast pop, I'm unrecognizable and ethereal. I look ready to hold my own on the floor of the General Body Seat.

The General Body Seat would never host the likes of this, though, and that thought puts a slight smile on the edge of my mouth as one of the crewmembers holds up the first cue card. Kellan ducks behind the camera, his golden hair briefly backlit by the studio lights. "Scramblers are live. Standing by to jack the cast channel," one of the tech guys announces. "Ready when you are."

Kellan settles the crew, fidgets with a few settings on the camera, then holds up three fingers.

On two, I breathe out.

On one, I breathe deep.

The green light glows. "Citizens of the Fleet," I announce, my voice calm and clear. "This is the Archangel, once more coming to you live from the heart of the stranglehold."

It's a hell of a speech. I got giddy just rehearsing it, and it's an effort *not to let the words get to my head as I plow through the cue cards. My chin tilts at an angle Kellan would call "downright cocky," and I know he's going to tease me for it the second we lose our hold on the channel. I can't let myself think that far ahead in the future—I sink into the immediacy of my performance.*

I'll use everything I've been given. Every little piece of the privilege I was born into. My charisma, the schooling that shaped my voice, my disarming looks. Even my parents' money—they think I'm blowing it on fancy First District parties, not propaganda cast production. Kellan does the same.

But I'm the one in front of the camera. The one who's poured her heart into dozens of speeches performed on hastily arranged sets as the techies in the background jockey to maintain their hold on the Fleet-wide cast system. The one they paint into the guise of an avenging angel, some kind of ancient and holy retribution for three hundred years of wrongs.

I'm the face of the Fractionist movement. The voice that announces its message throughout the Fleet. I'm the Archangel. I'm—

"—Tanaka. Tanaka, *look at me.*" Scela hands jostle my head unkindly. The voice keeps repeating my name, and I feel myself being rolled over and pushed upright, my back propped against the cellfront. Every muscle in my body feels raw and sore, like my integration's brand-new again.

My head spins, my exo doing its best to guide me back into the realm of rational thought. I'm on the starship *Lancelot*. I'm sitting outside the prison cell of a boy I was in love with two months ago. I'm still made of holes, still empty inside, still missing so many of my pieces. But now I know why that is.

Finally. Finally, finally, finally.

I was a rebel. I was a Fractionist collaborator, and the General

Body stripped me down and rebuilt me into their weapon. They gave me this exo to quash my loyalties and my memories, to bend me into obeying them without question. They took away everything that mattered from the girl in that memory. All because what? Because I dared to be the movement's face? Because that stupid First District girl got in over her head? Because she was dumb enough to get caught?

It's so difficult to see myself in her, even if the exo weren't running frantic damage control, twisting my thoughts away from the missing year inside me. The Key Tanaka who was willing to help the Fractionists sounded so hopeful, so *idealistic.* Maybe my cynicism is a side effect of being stuffed in Scela metal. Another symptom of being made from blank spaces.

And suddenly my memory floods again, not with my lost pieces this time, but with the people who lost more. The bodies going limp around me on the *Aeschylus,* Fractionists who were there to give voice to what they believed in, not to do any serious harm. They just wanted answers, justice, to find the information that was promised to their ancestors when they boarded these ships three hundred years ago.

There's a world out there. A world they should have stood on.

"I'm going to fix this," I mumble. I've never been more sure of anything since the moment I woke up in this body. My eyes slide open, and I roll my head to find Kellan crouching next to me, his fingers splayed across the plastic dividing us.

"Key," he breathes, and I clamp down on the flurry of memories, terrified of what might happen if I chase them again. In concert with the exo, I force myself to stay empty. No more of the past. I've seen enough. Felt enough. Any more than that one memory might tear me apart the way Isaac promised. But I know what it means and what I'm supposed to do with it. There's a future for me ahead, and I think I finally know the shape of it.

"I'm so sorry," I tell him, my voice growing stronger.

"You—*I'm* sorry. I dragged you into all this. I had no idea they would . . ." I see love in his eyes. I see horror. I don't know if I deserve either.

Kellan deserves an explanation, but right now all I can give him is a promise. "I'm going to find a way to make it right." I may not be his Key anymore, may not be their Archangel, but I'm Scela now, woven with the strength to rip through hullmetal. What good is it if I don't use it?

I grin, Scela-wide.

Then I look up and find Aisha Un-Haad glaring down at me.

CHAPTER 19

AISHA

"I can't believe what you've done," I snarl the moment I've dragged Key into the service elevator, away from any ears that might hear us and any cameras that could pick up the words I'm thinking of screaming at her. I thank God that Lopez has taught me the ins and outs of dodging most ships' security measures—the main elevators are always monitored, but the freight ones have made for convenient rendezvous points with Zaire.

My skull's still rattling from the blocker installation, but Key seems twice as disoriented. I wish I were linked to her, just so I could slam the weight of my fury into her brain. I have to settle for locking my hands around her wrists and squeezing them as tightly as the exo will allow, forcing her to face me as she sways on unsteady legs. The elevator doors slide shut behind us, but with no buttons pressed, we go nowhere.

"Yeah, well, you believe a lot of wacky things, Un-Haad," Key drawls, but there's venom behind the casual lilt of her voice.

"Shut up. You'd better thank your spirits that *I* found you instead of the marshal or worse." I wrench my grip a little tighter. If she feels the pain—*She must,* my exo insists—she doesn't show it. "What were you thinking? What happened?"

"Fuck off," Key snarls.

"Tanaka."

"Un-Haad." She knows she doesn't have to answer to me, even if I were able to hit her with my will. She can match me blow for blow—she's been in my head long enough.

"You have no idea what you're doing. What's at stake for me if they suspect—my aunt . . ." I break off, my exo warning me. It can help with the barriers in my mind, but it can't stop me from spilling the truth through my lips. I'm the one who ordered it to keep this secret. But if Key's going to understand, maybe she needs to know exactly what's going on.

She needs to know exactly why we ended up breathing Alpha 37's air together.

"My aunt is a Fractionist leader. In exchange for my siblings' care, I've been feeding them information—including what we found out when we arrested Ratna. They must have found the Alpha world to target from the data in Ratna's lab, and they arranged for our field test to go there, hoping that I'd be able to confirm its nature. And thanks to them, with this whole *habitable planet* thing happening, we're under even more scrutiny. There's probably no way we'll ever get assigned above patrol, so I'm probably never going to get my siblings away from Yasmin, and if we step out of line, the General Body has zero qualms about using them against me. And knowing we're being watched, *knowing* how it would look, you literally just went straight to a Fractionist prisoner the moment you had the chance!"

"I didn't tell him anything," she mumbles. Her hands twitch in my grip, and her eyes avoid mine.

"Looked like you two were plenty friendly."

"Because he *knew me*," Key retorts. She twists her arms, snapping free from my hold. I anticipate the shove that sends me flying into the elevator wall, but not the dent my massive body leaves in it. "You can snoop in my brain all you want, but you'll never know what it's like, missing the core of who you used to be. You don't know what it's like, having to guess at what's supposed to fill those holes, at why I'm suddenly seven feet tall and wearing Scela metal for no fucking reason. Seeing him, hearing him . . . it unlocked one of those memories. It nearly killed me—I don't know what would have happened if you hadn't pulled me out. But now I know what's buried in my head. I know . . ." She trails off, giving me a wary look.

"Know what?"

Her lips twitch, and her eyes dart to the elevator doors.

"Either you tell me now or I force it out of you the second we're back in the system, I swear."

"Fine," she mutters. "What's one more Fractionist in the squad anyway?"

Something must be wrong with my audio processing—she can't have said what I think she just said. But then Key starts explaining, and my mind goes numb. This is just perfect. On top of *everything else,* suddenly we have a brainwashed Fractionist *leader* in our squad? It's so outrageous that half of me wants to reject it outright. But then there are the parts that make too much sense to ignore. No wonder the Chancellor herself came to observe us at the start of basic. No wonder Key was sent with me to Yasmin's— she was sent to be *seen*. To send a message.

And this Key Tanaka in front of me—this flustered, ranting lunatic so unlike the cool, hateful girl I know—she'd have to be a Fractionist nutcase to believe half of what she's spouting.

I inhale sharply when she finishes. "First things first, *I'm* not a Fractionist. I'm being *used* by the Fractionists—it's not the same thing. And you ... Well, clearly you're not the Archangel anymore—"

Key's mouth opens to protest. She gets out a strangled sound, then closes it, and it tells me everything I'd know if we had the exosystem between us. Her eyes drop, betraying her uncertainty.

I can't afford any doubt. "This Archangel was a Fractionist conspirator. You were trying to rip the Fleet apart. First the *Kronos*, now the *Aeschylus*—"

"Don't talk to me about the *Aeschylus*."

I snap my headpiece back, forcing her to absorb the wrath that's simmering in me. "What?" I seethe.

"Don't. Talk. To. Me. About. That. Ship." The exo brings out the animal in her, enough that she finishes that sentence with teeth bared.

Unbelievable. "So you want me to ignore the tragedy that just—"

"At least you weren't a part of it!" she roars. "You didn't watch them die—you didn't mercy-kill them, and you have no idea what ... how powerless ..." She breaks off, hissing. "If there had been any way I could have saved them, I would have. I should have. But now all I can do is make it up to them. So maybe that's what I'm gonna do. I'm gonna be the Archangel they deserved. And I'm not gonna let *you* get in my way."

My blood runs cold. I have to shut this down—whatever's gotten into her head, it can't be allowed to leave this elevator. "Can you even *hear* yourself right now?" I snap. "The Fractionists caused the breach. They're dangerous, and they have to be stopped before more tragedies like this happen. What's next? The *Reliant*? That First District palace ship you've sloughed off? I can't stand by when people like ... like *her* have their way with the Fleet. With our *lives*."

I want to go on, but something in her expression makes me pause. Something's wrong with what I've just said—there's something she wants to correct me on. If I were linked with her, I could reach into her head and try to force it out, but with nothing but air between us, I have to wait. My distant consciousness prickles—I know I'm ignoring the marshal's orders to bring Key back to the shuttle. But I don't move a muscle.

"I don't think the Fractionists caused the breach on the *Aeschylus*," Key confesses at last. Her eyes flick up to mine, sharp and wary. Her body's gone still and steady.

Those memories must have really warped her. I shake my head and brace myself for whatever bullshit she's about to spew. We don't have much time, but she clearly needs to get it out of her system before we return to our squadmates and the uncertain fate awaiting us.

"We were warned about the threat of breach before we left the *Dread* and had time to suit up. There were First District camera crews in breach suits on the *Aeschylus* before the vent happened, when it was only supposed to be a riot. I think the *General Body* might have caused the vent. Think about it. Why would the Fractionists vent at the location that would cost them the most? Why would they vent at all?"

I groan. "Because they were *losing*. Because their aim is chaos in the Fleet. They want humanity to turn against itself, to doubt itself, to rip itself apart."

"Their aim is to break the General Body's hold on the fate of the human race," she snarls back.

"Where'd you hear that one?" I scoff. From the confusion that flickers over her face, she isn't quite sure. Maybe the Archangel is surfacing in her again. The notion is terrifying. If she could come all the way back from what the General Body made her, what would happen to her? A true, righteous Fractionist in Scela metal—what would she be capable of?

"Look, you saw that planet. You know what they're hiding from us. You don't think that—"

"I also saw my sister's hands dyed the color of her blood. I gave up my body to protect her, and turns out I also dropped her right in the hands of a woman who's using her as bait to force me into a revolution. The General Body knows she's my weak spot, and if you think for *one second* I'm going to risk her safety for some idealist's cause—"

"What kind of world do you want her to grow up in, Aisha? One where people die the way your parents did?"

Key's fully expecting the shove—she almost welcomes it. I throw her back into the elevator wall, my exo urging me to go further, to rip her throat out, to spill her no-good, traitorous blood. "Say another word about my parents and I'll tear the exo right off your back, you worthless Fractionist piece of shit." I keep her pinned to the wall, my face inches from hers. Our breathing is out of sync, mine hitching with fury.

"Answer the question," she replies.

"What?"

"You'd resign your sister to a life in this Fleet?"

My hands clench tighter around her shoulder pieces. I pour my will into the exo, forcing my eyelids back, making my stare unblinking and unyielding. In place of language, it feels natural to resort to this kind of posturing. Maybe we're more animal with the metal. I grasp for the right words, the ones that give me an upper hand.

But the Fleet's been downright cruel to girls like me and Malikah. Maybe on a planet's surface, with stars above and dirt below our feet, with a new order no longer dictated by ships and tiers and three hundred years of precedent, we could have a better future. A future where Malikah's brilliant little mind could grow with her hands unstained.

There's a good way to answer Key's question, the exo insists. A loyal way.

But not a truthful one, and I think Key sees it in my eyes. She jams a finger down on the buttons, and I rock backward as the elevator starts moving. "That's what I thought," she says.

I punch her. I'd never thrown a punch before becoming Scela, but the exo has the movement locked and loaded, and it unleashes with force that would be lethal if she were anything near human. Key's head snaps to the side, my knuckles meeting the edge of her exo with a dull thud. She gives me a second—I know she's giving it because of the way the wicked smile creeps over her face—to realize what I've done.

Then she strikes back.

We're raw and rattled and ragged. It doesn't matter. She slaps a blow across my face that makes me see spots. I dodge the next one, and my exo does the smart thing, flipping my headpiece up. It slams down over my vision as I swing blindly, waiting for the HUD to engage. It's no surprise that my strikes miss, and when my cameras flicker on, it's just in time to catch Key's returning blow. I sweep an arm up into an instinctive block that catches her fist on my forearm plating. She transfers the momentum into a whirl that doesn't seem possible in the narrow confines of the elevator, and my exo berates me for not looking down in time to catch the leg that knocks my feet out from underneath me.

I hit the ground with a force that has me checking the elevator's carrying capacity in the back of my exo's information, but apparently it's built to handle several times what we can produce.

Before I can recover, Key grabs one of my arms and twists. I try to yank it from her grasp, feeling the full rig's power cells depleting little by little. At this rate, we'll drain them. More accurately, I'll drain them first. The move doesn't seem to be costing her anything, as my exo helpfully points out. I writhe and twist, my face planted firmly on the elevator floor.

She plants it deeper with a foot jammed into my back.

"Yield," Key Tanaka breathes.

I don't budge.

I *won't.*

All my life, people like her have done this to people like me. Knocked us down, pressed us into the floor, and demanded that we give up. That we roll over. All my life I've had to go along with it. I had no power to stop it, no power to take back what belongs to me. But now I have this body. Now I'm a living weapon.

I'm just as Scela as Key is. And she's just put herself off balance.

I jam my knee up into the leg she's not using to pin me down. The motion would have shattered my old human body, but my strength and flexibility are limited only by the enhancements woven into my muscles and the metal attachments that make up my outer skeleton. Key tries to anticipate, tries to shift some of her weight back onto it, but it's not enough to stop me from buckling her.

Her grip loosens, my arm pops free, and I immediately twist over, lunge up, and catch her by the throat. Key manages a strangled grunt around my fingers, her arms swinging as her legs snap rigid, but when my grip tightens on the tender, unenhanced flesh I've managed to catch, she holds up her hands in defeat.

Serves her right for not equipping her headpiece.

Serves her right for thinking she could say *anything* about my family. The callous mention of my parents plays through my head again, and the exo draws all the rage and grief into the tension of my muscles as I draw my fist back.

"Don't," Key chokes, but it's as good as telling me to do it.

Several things happen all at once. The pieces of my arm enhancements flash a final warning as the power cells sputter. I ignore it and ram my fist into Key's face once. On the second time, it's accompanied by the pneumatic hiss of the elevator doors opening.

On the third time, I punch Key in plain sight of Marshal Jesuit, with Wooj and Praava at her back.

The shuttle ride back to the *Dread* feels like it's never going to end. With our exosystem unlinked, we're left stewing in our own heads. I sit in the fore of the ship, my deadened, powerless arm limp at my side. Key's hunched over in the back, her fingers alternating between worrying at her throat and picking at the stunstick burn on her forearm. Wooj and Praava slump together in the middle, occasionally throwing us worried glances. Marshal Jesuit sits across from them, her arms folded, her headpiece still covering her face.

There's an unspoken agreement in the air. We don't have to be in each other's heads to understand it. No one speaks until the marshal does.

She finally exhales. "What did I do to deserve you lot? Is there some huge past sin I'm supposed to atone for and you all are the way I'm meant to do it?" When no one gives her an answer, she snaps her headpiece back. Her eyes are livid. She's not exhausted—she's enraged. "I thought having a glitchy integration in the batch was going to be the worst thing I had to deal with. Then there was the emotional override, and I then thought that would be the worst of it. But today proves that apparently *none* of you are capable of behaving like functional Scela."

None of us have anything to say, so none of us say anything.

"Lih and Ganes, your training will continue. Tanaka and Un-Haad, you're on suspension pending psych evals."

Key bristles, and I brace for her to rat me out as the one who started it. "You didn't suspend Praava when she got people *killed* with her outburst aboard the *Aeschylus*."

"Because we left her problem behind on the *Lancelot*," Marshal Jesuit snaps. "Whereas with you two, the problem seems to follow you wherever you go. And with . . . *new information* now in the mix, I *really* don't need more problems. So until either one of the psychs sorts you out or we reprogram your exos entirely, you're grounded."

"What about our salary?" I blurt before the exo can advise against it.

"Suspended," Marshal Jesuit says. "No work, no pay."

My hands quiver. Even with the metal woven through them, keeping them steady, I can feel the tremors starting. I can feel the dyeworks ink sinking into them, staining them irrevocably red. I inhale, and my breath feels tainted too, my throat scarred by the thick, smoky, impossible-to-filter air of the *Reliant*'s sublevels. And suddenly the weight on my back isn't my exo's metal—it's a lifetime of work in the darkened hell of the textile plants. It's everything I've just inflicted on my sister. I bow my head and whisper thanks that no one else can feel the crushing wave of panic settling over me.

There's no time to wait.

I have to act.

CHAPTER 20

KEY

The marshal didn't really specify what "grounded" means. I notice that at some point on the shuttle ride back to the *Dread,* she relinks Praava and Woojin, so I suppose being isolated from the exosystem is part of it.

I'm not complaining.

When we unload, some sort of instruction takes over them, and they immediately depart without so much as a look, leaving me, Aisha, and Marshal Jesuit on Assembly.

"Dock your rigs," the marshal says. "You'll still be bunking with the rest of your unit, but outside of the dorm, I don't want to see you within twenty feet of each other until after the psychs clear you. I'll schedule your evals."

"What are we supposed to do in the meantime?" Aisha asks.

The marshal shrugs. "Keep out of trouble. If you can manage it." She turns and thunders off across the deck, leaving me and Aisha in the shadow of the shuttle.

We ignore each other through the rote task of disassembling and docking our rigs. Each rattle from her bay makes my exo bristle territorially, but I focus on stripping my enhancements off my body, feeling more and more drained as each one loosens out of my plugs. Between the strain on my muscles from my stint with the Archangel's memories and the sore spots from Aisha's fists, my body has been through a hell of a lot more than it was built to handle today.

And my body hasn't had the worst of it. My mind's been turned inside out several times over, each revelation more shattering than the last. In my exhaustion, the notion of a psych eval is running circles around my head. No doubt they'd discover that I've unlocked—if not the actual substance of my memories, the actual *self* they've buried—the general gist of what's locked down in my head. What would they do to me for that?

Considering that they were willing to take an unwilling girl, flay her, and rebuild her into a Scela body, I'm not sure I want to entertain the possibilities.

But if I'm going to avoid that outcome, I have to—

I should—

The exo's digging its heels in, trying its best to protect me from that line of thought, but I argue against it. My exo's supposed to keep me safe. The General Body's threatening me. *Please, spirits alive, just let me try to save myself,* I groan internally.

It relents.

I check to make sure Aisha's left her bay and find her skulking toward the halls that lead to the main body of the *Dread*. She won't be any help, as the bruises on my face testify. But there's no way she's getting information off this ship without help, and I think I know exactly who one of her conspirators is.

* * *

"Holy shit, Tanaka," Zaire says when he sees me. I've managed to keep myself hidden in the crowd gathered around his ball-and-cup game, but as the rest of his watchers start to disperse across Assembly, he picks my swollen face out of the crowd. "I take it the assessment was rough?"

Assessment? I almost blurt. After all that's happened in the past day, I nearly forgot that this morning was supposed to be our final test. "Nothing we couldn't handle," I reply as I approach his blanket. As he continues tucking his winnings away, I kick over the middle cup—I'm so sure it's in the middle one.

"Nope!" Zaire grins as I reveal nothing but worn, slightly stained fabric beneath. "Guess again. Or don't. Actually don't— nothing to see here." He bundles in the blanket, sweeping away the final cup before I can kick it over. "To what do I owe the pleasure? My charm? My good looks?"

"A mutual friend," I tell him evenly, tapping the side of my exo ridge.

His eyes narrow, his posture hunching slightly as he beckons me closer. I take a knee next to him. "Is she . . . *in* you right now?" he whispers.

I bite down on a consternated sigh. The bruises on my face smart, and my exo is sputtering with quiet humor over this charade. "Aisha got it worse than me in the assessment. She's stuck in Medical, but this can't wait. She's telling me that if you don't help me—if you're standing between her and the duty that keeps her siblings safe—she'll shuck your ribs from your spine."

"Well, that does sound like the Aisha we know and love," Zaire says. His eyes have lit up. Seems like he's the kind of human who can't resist a challenge, which is exactly what I'm banking on. "I'm gonna need one thing from you before you tell me anything else," he says, his tone darkening.

"What's that?"

"Your first name." He flashes his human grin again.

Surprisingly, I find it halfway charming. Maybe I'll never understand what the old Key had with Kellan. The feelings I had for him have been wiped from my brain, and I don't even know if there'll be any recovering my capacity to feel like that. But—and I'm so glad no one else is in my head for this thought—Zaire kind of makes me want to try.

Zaire navigates Assembly with so much grace and ease that I start to suspect he could do it blindfolded. And he can't be much older than me. I'm about to ask how long he's been working this deck when he throws up his hand, catching me across the chest. I follow his push back behind the wing of a shuttle—the exo's amused at me letting a human steer me around—and we duck out of sight as a dockworker walks past.

"Why are we hiding?" I hiss. It takes a certain amount of control to get my voice down to something quiet, no thanks to the exo. "You're a dockworker—no one's going to suspect you're up to something."

Zaire rolls his eyes. "Yes, but if you really want to make this clean, you make sure people don't even suspect you were anywhere near the thing you're trying to get to."

The exo prickles, urging me to reprimand him for daring to talk back to a Scela, and I almost hush it out loud.

"C'mon," Zaire says once the dockworker's out of range. He

grabs me by one of the ports on my wrist and yanks me off across the deck. I try to keep my footsteps light, which is a tall order given the extra metal—and spirits know what else—weighing me down. Trying to sculpt my motions into anything close to "sneaking" just makes me feel like a horse.

We pull up against the hull of a shuttle. The shape and size seem right to me, but I never got a good look at the ship's ID number. Fortunately, Zaire knows his deck. "This is the one," he says, pressing a palm against the hull. "Shipped out this morning, mission was aborted, returned unexpectedly early. Interrupted a very nice nap I had going on."

"Fascinating," I deadpan. "Get me inside."

"Easy, robot girl. I like to go slow on a first date." Before I get a chance to react, he swings around the docking struts and up to the pilot's door. "Now usually you need a fob coded to the door to get inside these things, but—" He ducks under the hull, rolls onto his back, and flips open a panel. "In an emergency, say, a fire on deck, there has to be a way to get into the ship from the outside and rescue the pilots. Hence—"

He twists something, and the door pops open with a dull *thud*.

I bare my teeth in the closest thing I can approximate to a human grin.

"Just smile your normal way—it's okay," Zaire says, his gaze turning soft. My exo snatches an embarrassed blush back from my cheeks. I guess he's used to working with Scela, enough so that he can read our faces as easily as any other human. I offer him a hand as he crawls out from beneath the ship.

He takes it, realizing his mistake too late. I pull him to his feet with a force that lifts him nearly a meter off the ground. Zaire's limbs flail every which way, his eyes bugging out. At the sight, a sharp, excruciatingly loud peal of laughter bursts out of me. I clap my hand over my mouth as he lands.

So much for stealth.

Zaire stares at me for a breathless moment, his legs bent like a newborn foal. "Get in the shuttle," he whispers, and I don't need to be told twice.

He slams the door behind us once we're both inside, then ducks to the front-facing windows, peering out to see if any of the noise we made attracted any attention. After a moment, he nods. "Okay, we're in. Now what?"

I step up to the controls. "We need coordinates of the planet this ship went to this morning. Or something like that." I glance up at him.

A beat of silence passes.

Zaire holds up his hands in defeat. "Key, I'm a dockworker. I appreciate your faith in me, but I don't know anything about computers. I got the tricks of the ship's mechanics down, but as far as this . . ."

A second wave of embarrassment washes over me and I order my exo to shut down my facial muscles, just in case I have any uncontrollable notions of expressing my mortification. "Sorry," I mutter.

"I'm flattered, though," he offers, the edges of his mouth quirking up. "Hey, there may still be hope. You're the one with the computer thing wired into your brain—I'll bet *you* can do it."

I consider it. "If the exo knows how, I'm not sure it would tell me," I say, peering over the instrumentation as I rush through the data my systems have on this type of shuttle. There's really only the bare minimum—an emergency protocol for an event where I might have to fly the ship on my own, and not much else. I run my hands over the controls as if touching them will jar the information I need out of the recesses of my exo. Nothing comes to mind.

Then my hearing pricks up—footsteps.

Scela-heavy footsteps.

Walking straight for our shuttle. I meet Zaire's bulging, panicking eyes. He hears them too.

"Hide."

CHAPTER 21

AISHA

It took me way too long to track down Nani. With the raw wound of losing my salary rending holes in my rational thought process, it was nearly impossible to figure out which of the hundreds of bays was hers, even with her name and pilot status marked clearly on the tag chained to the mesh. But God's luck was on my side—Nani left her fob collection hanging undisguised on a hook in her bay.

So much for security.

Now that the pilot's ring is safely tucked into the pocket of my uniform, it's just a matter of identifying the ship we flew out on. I approach the long-range shuttles, scanning their identification numbers with holy reverence humming through my veins. I wonder which one of them was the first to travel to Alpha 37, the first to fulfill our grand destiny before the General Body swept that destiny under the rug.

I swipe the jangling mess over the scanner and the pilot's door pops open with a low *thud*. I check over my shoulder again, then clamber inside the cockpit and pull the door shut behind me. My nerves feel overloaded with equal parts anticipation and dread.

The ship's interior is dark but for the subtle glow of emergency lights. I move to the pilot's chair and perch myself on the edge of it, scanning the instrumentation for the fobhole. This part does require a bit of guessing. I know the right fob's on the ring, but it takes twenty-three wrong guesses to find it. When I slide it into the socket, the instrumentation glows to life, and my exo shivers along with me. It's thrilling to think that I have several tons of metal and explosive force under my control. A ship's a hyperpowered body with a few exponents attached, and the machine on my back *loves* that notion.

Something shifts in the rear of the shuttle, and I nearly jump out of my exorig. *It's nothing. Just some equipment not strapped in right,* I chide myself. But there's suspicion curdling in the exo, urging me to check just in case. I never expected it to be the more paranoid one.

"Hush," I breathe.

I don't know anything about shuttles, and the exo hardly knows more. This is the first time I've been in the cockpit of one—before, I'd only really seen this area on casts. I can't let that unfamiliarity freeze me. Can't stop imagining what will happen the moment Yasmin knows my money isn't coming. Can't stop thinking about my sister's hands getting redder and redder. Can't stop seeing my brother waste away on the lower levels of the *Panacea*.

I'll give Yasmin something better than money. Something she'll value enough to keep my siblings safe. Something that will clear my debt to her forever—that will put her in *my* debt. If she wants a planet, I'll give her a planet. I'll gift-wrap the new world for her. *Anything* if it will keep Amar and Malikah safe.

But that requires extracting the coordinates from this machine—if they haven't been wiped already. I refuse to consider the possibility. Right now, the only obstacle I'll allow is the fact that I have no idea how this thing works. I reach into the exo, straining to find something relevant about this ship. It suggests a button on the instrumentation panel, and I press it, reading the label above a split second too late.

"Ignition sequence started," the ship announces.

"No, no, no—" I groan through my teeth, jamming the button again, but that doesn't seem to do any good. A low rumble starts up from deeper in the ship. It's quiet, barely noticeable outside the shuttle, but in my head it sounds like the rattle of reentry. If the engines fire, I'll be caught for sure. I flail into the exo again, and again I'm offered a button to press. I don't care about labels—I jam my hand down on top of it, and mercifully the pitch of the rumble breaks. The ship falls silent, and I lean back in the pilot's chair, pressing one hand over my rapidly beating heart.

A prayer flashes through my head, but I don't dare voice it.

Frozen in place, I scan the deck outside the windows. No one seems to have noticed the ship that just nearly flew out of here unbidden. I let myself relax, the gentle cushion of the seat cradling me as I slide my eyes shut.

Then someone sneezes. Someone who's very much *inside* the ship. It's quickly followed by a familiar voice whispering, with the deadened resignation of someone who already knows they're busted, "Fucking *human*."

I whirl around in the pilot's chair as the divide between the cockpit and the shuttle body slides open. Key Tanaka and Zaire spill out, the most unlikely pair in God's domain. It looks like it was an honest miracle the two of them fit in the tiny space, and I can't help but notice the dents on Zaire's warm brown skin where Key's metal pressed into him.

I meet Key's eyes. "You."

"Me," she replies. The swelling is starting to settle and darken on her face. I don't regret that it's there.

"You two . . . ," Zaire says slowly, " . . . are *not* working together."

But Key ignores him, a spark lighting up her eyes. "After that whole rant about not going anywhere near the Fractionists for the sake of your family, *this* is the first thing you do?" she says, gesturing to the glowing ship controls humming guiltily behind me.

The urge to punch her is rising again. My exo feeds me memories from the elevator, whispering the joy it would give me to slam her head into the shuttle wall. She's going to mess this whole thing up for me—ruin my chance to secure my siblings' safety— and that's the thought that catapults me from the pilot's chair. My headpiece snaps halfway down, and she recognizes the threat enough to step back, tucking the human behind her as her own headpiece creeps down her forehead.

"You wouldn't," Key says, low and even.

It would draw attention to the shuttle. It would get us caught. But it's so, so tempting. So tempting that it hurts when I pull my headpiece back up and force my fists to unclench.

Key raises an eyebrow.

I purse my lips, mind spinning for an explanation that doesn't make me look like a hypocrite. *You're on your own,* the exo snickers.

"They're pulling my salary because I'm on suspension for something *you* started. Now I need something to head off Yasmin. To keep Malikah out of the dyeworks forever. To keep Amar away from the experimental treatments. For my family, I'd . . ." I pull up short, dropping my gaze to the human interloper peering from behind her. "She brought *you* in on this?"

Zaire shrinks a little closer to Key. "She said *you* were the one who told her to do it. Though she wasn't clear on why we're after the coordinates."

I shake my head. "But *you* were the one who was supposed to pass along the order to—"

Key rolls her eyes. "Un-Haad. He had vague orders. The Fractionists never give someone the full picture. It's all puzzle pieces. Only the people at the top get to put it all together. Zaire doesn't know what you were supposed to discover on the planet."

She turns to Zaire, slapping a hand on his shoulder.

"This morning, this ship made a voyage to Alpha 37. It returned early, because a particular squad of newbie Scela found out the world is habitable. Certain interested parties within the Fleet need this information. So we're here to snatch the planet's coordinates and declassify them before they're deleted from the system. Or, at least, that's what I was going to do." She lifts an eyebrow at me.

I sigh. "Yeah, that's what I was going to do too," I confess, hating every second of it.

"Oh" is all Zaire says. At first. His face falls, his brow furrowing as he tries to process what we've just admitted. He pulls out of Key's grip and takes a step back toward the door, then seems to think better of it. His hands start shaking—he clenches them into fists, but it doesn't help. Something shines in the edge of his eyes as he glances frantically between me and Key. "A *habitable planet*? An honest-to-spirits, actual habitable planet in our reach?" His voice is even shakier than his hands. "You're sure?"

"We breathed its air," Key says. She keeps her voice low, coaxing him like a spooked animal. "And from the General Body's reaction . . . yeah, I'd say we're pretty damn sure."

Zaire takes a deep breath, leaning back against the shuttle door.

His hands steady, and he closes his eyes. "Well shit, I guess I really am a Fractionist now."

"Good. We're wasting starlight," I snap, sinking into the pilot's chair again and spinning it back to the instrumentation panel. "If you're going to work with me on this, help me figure out how to access the ship's logs. We've only got so long before the marshal comes looking for us."

Key steps up behind me, leaning over the panel as she rests her hip on the edge of the copilot's chair. From the knit of her brows and the depth of her scowl, she's just as thrilled about this as I am. "Right, well. Good job on getting the ship booted up. I guess we can start . . . here." Her fingers skim down a list of functions on one of the touchscreens, and she jabs something before I have time to read it.

On my other side, Zaire's fidgeting with the fob ring, still looking a little dazed. "Nani's going to kill you for this," he mutters.

"She can get in line," I retort, the exo's frustration fueling the words that pour out of me. Zaire tucks his hands behind his back, taking a nervous step away.

"I think this is it," Key says, sliding herself fully into the copilot's chair as her fingers fly over the screen. "It's not coordinates, but it's the flightpath. The destination's probably wrapped up in . . ."

"There," I say, smacking her hovering hand out of the way and pointing at the screen. It glows under my finger, and I flick it up, pulling a swath of numbers and letters onto the display. Universal coordinates.

"Praise God," I breathe, just as Key whispers, "Thank fuck."

Now that we have them, I'm not sure what to do. The only way our exos have ever absorbed information has been through a jack or a download broadcast right into our brains. The coordinates are massive, too big for my organic mind to memorize them reliably. A quick calculation by my exo puts them at 256 characters, without punctuation. I sink back in the chair, searching the data structures for a blank space, a way to commit this information to memory.

"Got a pen?" Key asks Zaire.

"Actually . . . ," he says. He looks like he's trying to memorize the sequence too, but he breaks his eye contact with the screen long enough to dig into his pockets. "Yeah, right here." He tosses it over me, and Key snatches it out of the air, baring a grateful smile.

I frown. Since when has Key Tanaka ever been grateful for anything?

She pulls up the sleeve of her uniform and starts scrawling along the lines of her enhancements on her wrists with precise, elegant strokes aided by her muscle control. The dark of the metal disguises the letters—from a distance, even with eagle-eyed Scela cameras, they'll look like a tattoo.

Zaire snickers. "This is the most low-tech thing I've ever seen a Scela do."

But it's devious, I'll give her that. As Key continues to write the sequence as fast as her hand can manage, my exo presses down the urge to fidget. I almost open my mouth to ask if Zaire has another pen, but my exo prickles at the thought. *Have some pride,* it whispers.

So instead I peer out the shuttle windows, scanning the deck outside, and pray for Key to write faster. Once we get the information transferred onto a more stable source, Zaire can run it up to Lopez, and he can transmit the coordinates to Yasmin and the rest of the Fractionists. We're so close. Everything is finally in my grasp.

And then the cockpit door yanks open.

Marshal Jesuit sticks her head in.

CHAPTER 22

KEY

"Zaire. Run."

He doesn't need telling twice. Zaire bolts for the door on the opposite side of the cockpit, throwing it open and nearly tripping down the stairs and onto the flight deck. His poor, spindly little human legs carry him as fast as he can go.

It isn't fast enough. The marshal hangs back a second, and I catch the edge of a sly smile—she's giving him the distance. Like a cat toying with a mouse.

And when she springs, she moves so quickly I'd need my headpiece's cameras to properly track her. Marshal Jesuit catches up to Zaire in two strides. She ducks low, snatching his knees together, and hoists him up over her shoulder in a fluid movement that leaves Zaire dangling against her back, blinking like he's not quite sure what just happened.

She turns to look at us through the shuttle's cockpit, and my exo ticks off three full seconds before I wrap my head around how thoroughly fucked we are. My thoughts stutter and snap as we're both swept into an exosystem with the marshal at the nexus. I wince, scalded by the simmering fury behind the command she slams against us, pinning us motionless in our seats.

With a stunned Zaire dangling loosely in her grip, she saunters back toward the shuttle, every ounce of her oozing predatory grace.

Aisha's the one who swiped the pilot's keys, I blurt.

Across the exosystem, a familiar rage rises from Aisha's head-space. *Key was the one who got here first. She's the one who used to be a Fractionist figurehead before—*

As if you're not in the pocket of your Fractionist ringleader aunt—

At least I'm trying to get away from the Fractionist movement instead of running headlong toward—

Both of you shut up, or so help me I will order your exos to stop you from thinking, the marshal hisses as she mounts the stairs, ducking slightly to keep Zaire clear of the door frame. *Back of the shuttle, now.*

Unfrozen by the order, we're able to follow her obediently through the narrow passage Zaire and I hid in and down into the cargo bay we loaded into this morning. I glance over at the equipment rack, finding the mangled remains of Woojin's mask. The sight of it just hammers home the exhaustion dragging at my metal-built bones. It's been a long-ass day.

The marshal closes the cargo bay door, slips Zaire off her shoulder, and lifts him up by his collar until he gets his feet underneath him. "Sit," she says, and he sinks obediently into one of the chairs he usually straps us into.

Aisha and I hold our breath, our racing heartbeats slipping in sync. In the exosystem, I feel her anger coalesce into a burning knot.

And then she tucks it away. When she speaks again, it's just tired resignation that floods into us. "I have a daughter, you know? She's a couple years younger than you three. She's back on the starship *Atreus,* Fourth District. I haven't seen her since she was an infant, and she's never seen me in this body. I chose the metal partly because it was the easiest way to care for her, partly because I was scared shitless that I couldn't do the motherhood thing. All through the pregnancy, I thought the instinct would come when she did. But I never quite knew how, and it got to be so bad that I decided I had to remove myself from her life entirely—give her a chance at something better. She has foster parents now, two guys who give her everything that I couldn't. But I still love her more than life itself. Still send all my salary to them to fund her upbringing. And if the General Body has reason to harm *one hair* on her head, I'll skin you two alive and rip your exos off your backs," she finishes, her eyes gleaming with malice.

"I'm sorry," Aisha says immediately, bowing her head. "I don't want you implicated in any of this." She pushes her own feelings for her family out into the exosystem, letting the marshal see how similarly she burns.

"But your daughter—wouldn't you rather she have a better life, one free from the General Body's control?" I ask. The thought feels awkward, half formed, and I know it came from the part of me that desperately wants to claim my history as the Archangel. The echo of my memory looms—studio lights, camera eyes, and Kellan's smile glowing in the dark.

But then it's gone in a flash, snapped in half by Aisha's voice. "I want a better life for my siblings," Aisha growls. "But that starts in the Fleet, not on some distant, undeveloped planet. Do you even *get* family, Key? You don't know what it's like to put your life on the line for people you care about, because you don't care about *people.*"

Wrath burns through me, encouraged by the exo. It urges me

to pummel Aisha senseless, to give her bruises that match mine. I don't know how I'm supposed to feel about my family, about the parents whose perfect daughter turned out to be a Fractionist collaborator. They were General Body loyalists. I have a pretty good guess as to how they feel about me now. And the way I feel about them? It's lost deep in my holes, deep in the abysses of what I used to be. The same goes for everyone else in my life before I took the metal—Kellan, the Fractionists, all of them. There's no one left. Nothing left for me except my exo and this new purpose I found in the fragments of myself.

Zaire's pen is still in my hand. My grip winds tighter, threatening to crush it. But before I can translate my fear and anger and confusion into a good, solid punch, Marshal Jesuit steps between us. "Spirits alive, could you two possibly get any more wrapped up in yourselves? Two minutes ago I found you working together to get the Alpha 37 coordinates. Now you're at each other's throats again." She pushes me back, just a nudge on the shoulders that sends me reeling into the wall. "Both of you need to calm down and listen very closely."

She waits until we've done just that—I can feel her attention on my heartbeat.

"I won't say I'm a Fractionist—"

"I know a guy who could help with that," Zaire interrupts from his seat, then flinches away from the marshal's glare.

"But I do believe there's some good that can be done if the knowledge of a livable world leaks," she continues. "And the Fractionists are the ones with the greatest chance of bringing that change about."

Aisha's doubt seeps into the system. She doesn't know if her aunt is capable of "good"—not after the way she's been manipu-lated. I shove her noise back. I'm holding my breath, waiting for the marshal's next words.

Marshal Jesuit's hand slips into a pocket on her uniform. "I have something that will make the data transfer much easier than transcribing the gibberish you were writing on your arm."

Aisha moves to take it from her, but the marshal's fingers snap shut around the little device.

"No such thing as something for nothing," she says. "So you three had better tell me exactly what stake each of you has in this and why I should trust you with it."

Aisha and I share a look, our headspace reeling as we wage war over who talks first, who explains what, who blames whom for which element of the disaster that's unfolded over the course of our basic training.

The marshal is patient, and bit by bit we recount the story, sometimes talking over each other, other times falling into silence when none of us have the right words. When I confess the truths I learned about myself, I feel something click in the marshal from across the exosystem. She understands. She and Isaac were both warned about how to handle me but never about what I was. And she sympathizes. I like the way her pity feels, so I go ahead and tell her about the way my memory unlocked on the *Lancelot*, even though it triggers a rant from Aisha about why I shouldn't have gone anywhere near the Fractionists to begin with.

I steal a glance at Zaire, who's had little to contribute, anticipat-ing the sight of him looking sorry for me—bracing for it, really. But the only things I read on his face are horror and anger, and some-how that's so much better than what I was expecting.

When we finally run out of things to say and accusations to

hurl, Marshal Jesuit holds out the data jack. Aisha lunges for it again, but the marshal swats her away, instead offering the device to me. "You get this loaded up. And you two—" She nods at Aisha and Zaire. "See if you can get us an audience with your man in the Master Control Room. Starlight's wasting."

She doesn't need to formalize the order. We move like it's burning down our spines.

Three Scela, two humans, and all of Zaire's personality were never meant to fit into a room this small. I wedge myself into a corner as Zaire lunges forward to clap the middle-aged man sitting at the controls on the shoulder. "Lopez, buddy! It's been too long," he crows.

Lopez fixes Aisha with a cool stare, a long-suffering sigh wheezing out of his nose. "This had better be good."

Aisha nods to me, and I pull out the data jack. "Alpha 37 is habitable," I tell him. "These are the coordinates."

He lets out something between a scoff and a laugh, his eyes widening. For a moment, I'm worried he's stopped breathing entirely. Ironically, it seems to be the kind of thing everyone does when they find out a planet has breathable air.

But then he does something worse. As he presses a shaking hand over his stubbly jaw, Lopez slowly starts to cry. In the exosystem, all three of us feel our mechanical counterparts recoil at the sight of tears, utterly human and utterly foreign to the exos. Zaire lets out a nervous little laugh, crouching by Lopez's chair and patting him awkwardly on the back. "Hey, man. Didn't you send them out to see if the world was habitable in the first place? You knew this might be coming, right?"

Lopez rubs his reddening cheeks. Somehow it's even worse that he's smiling through all this. "I know, kid. Seems stupid to be so worked up," he says thickly. "But when I was small, I wanted to be an explorer. One of the folks who shipped out on the shuttles to study the planets we found. Instead, I got stuck in this little box the second they discovered my aptitudes skewed toward a job like this. Been here twenty years. And now . . ." His eyes move up from the jack to find my face. The smile fades, recognition plowing through his joy. "Spirits," he mumbles. "You're . . ."

"The Archangel," I tell him. "Sort of."

And then the tears start falling heavier. "I'm so glad," he hiccups. "So glad you're okay."

"Okay" might be pushing it, I almost tell him, but there's no way in hell I'm giving this man more to blubber over. I try to summon the part of me that Fractionists used to listen to and say, "We need you to broadcast these coordinates to Aisha's aunt on the *Reliant* immediately."

"No," Lopez replies. I'm almost certain I misheard him, but then Aisha's muscles tense. The marshal tugs her back before she can leap forward and carry out her impulse to shake the man by the collar. Lopez pinches back his tears, oblivious. "That shit's not going to fly. We can't just *blast* information across the Fleet at all hours. It's late at night—there isn't much communication going out from the *Dread* to begin with, and certainly none going to the *Reliant,* of all places."

"Doesn't this qualify as a special case?" Aisha grinds out, prickling internally from the perceived slight on her birthship.

"Broadcasting those coordinates would expose the network entirely. I'd be questioned. They'd tear through my machines and find out who else I've been talking to. Poor Zaire here would probably end up on the *Lancelot* or the *Endymion*."

"But it's a *planet*," Aisha seethes. "Humanity's next home."

"And I'd very much like to set foot on it someday," Lopez says, drying his eyes on the collar of his shirt. "Fact remains—we're going to have to wait. Maybe tomorrow afternoon, we'll be able to encrypt it in some data going out to another ship with instructions to deliver it to the *Reliant*. We can't put it in Yasmin's hands tonight."

But that's not good enough for Aisha Un-Haad. The exosystem ignites with her frustration as she draws herself up tall. "I'm not going to sit around and *wait*. That's just asking for the General Body to pick up on the fact that we swiped the coordinates. There has to be another way."

Lopez swivels in his chair, finding the marshal leaning casually against the back wall of the control room. "There *is* another way," he says, catching her eye.

"A shuttle?" I ask.

"Can't," Marshal Jesuit says. "Too closely monitored. Even with Lopez suppressing the *Dread*'s alarms, a shuttle's bound to be noticed once it leaves this ship."

"Then how?"

The marshal's eyes drop to Zaire. "Tell me, kid. You ever supervised a void jump before?"

I don't know what those words mean, but Zaire seems to like them. The nervous pinch of his brows wipes away, replaced by a wicked, wild grin. "Once," he says, like he's begging to do it again. His expression is almost Scela in its exaggeration and uncertainty. There's something oddly handsome about it.

In the system, Aisha's sidled up to the marshal's mind and

found the definition waiting. At first she thinks it must be a joke. *I'm not doing that,* she says.

Marshal Jesuit scoffs. Lopez spins back to his instruments, pulling up the camera feeds he'll need to loop to get us out of here. Zaire lifts his eyebrows at me.

I'm not doing that, Aisha repeats.

CHAPTER 23

AISHA

"I'm not doing that," Wooj says.

"*Thank you,*" I sigh, pointing at him. The six of us are packed into our narrow sleeping quarters, and part of me is fidgeting at our four unmade beds in plain sight of the marshal. "There *has* to be another way."

Zaire shakes his head. He's perched on the edge of Key's bed, his gaze bouncing nervously among the five Scela in the room. "The only way this information ships across the Fleet tonight is if we do the void jump."

Marshal Jesuit nods, leaning against the door frame. "And the only way you make that jump is if you've got all four of you. It's too much of a risk—Un-Haad and Tanaka can't do it alone."

Praava stares at her feet. Our exosystem reels with her confusion, her fear. This morning, her biggest worry was that Ratna was still imprisoned on the *Lancelot,* still trapped in a cell Praava put her in, unable to continue the work that's supposed to save the Fleet. And now there's a planet out there, waiting for humanity. Now there are the four of us barging in on her and Wooj and asking for not only treason but also for her to put her life on the line in a maneuver that could leave her drifting endlessly through the black.

Honestly, the treason scares her more. Dying in space she could handle. But Ratna's already in prison in part because of her. If anything worse happened to her sister, Praava would gladly drift into the void.

So she's a hard sell.

Then there's Wooj. He has his own crop of people to worry about after the Chancellor's threats, but he's far more terrified of the jump itself. His control over his body is loose, and if he runs into another neurological glitch like the one on Alpha 37, he could compromise everything we're trying to accomplish. Even though the marshal says we'll need him, Wooj thinks that his presence is a guarantee the mission will fail.

We've never had an argument like this clouding the space between our thoughts, and I can barely keep my sense of self in the torrent. On one side, there's Marshal Jesuit's hullmetal will, bolstered by Key's weak-legged fanaticism, and on the other, there are some very solid arguments.

And then there's me in the middle. I know what we have to do. I know that we *have* to do it, and fast—before the General Body gets wind that we have the coordinates. But I'll take any excuse I can get if it keeps me safely within the walls of a starship.

So I throw my own tumult into the mix, hoping it stalls us. Every time one side of the wordless argument seems to pull ahead, I drag my mental heels until we've circled back to the same place.

The third time I do it, Marshal Jesuit snaps. *"Un-Haad,"* she thunders out loud, and Zaire nearly topples backward in surprise. Key throws out a hand to steady him.

"Sorry," I huff, but even Zaire can tell that's a lie. "We're not getting anywhere internally."

"We're not getting anywhere period," Wooj groans, slamming his face into his hands with a little more force than he intended. Praava flashes him a sympathetic grimace. "Look, nothing you say is going to get me out that airlock."

"For the future of humankind!" Key says. "For humanity's—"

"This is the thousandth time you've shoved that notion through our heads," Praava retorts. "And I will say again—for the *thousandth time*—"

"That you're not risking Ratna, *we know*," I say.

"So what's it gonna be?" Marshal Jesuit asks, and in the exo-system she locks us still, forcing us to face her question head on as the backs of our necks buzz gently. "Inaction? The four of you just go back to your duties, following General Body orders?"

For once, our system slips into alignment. For once, all of us agree. We *don't* want that. We don't want to serve the very people who have lied to the entire Fleet for the sake of maintaining power. We don't want to be responsible for another three hundred years of wandering among the stars, waiting to discover a habitable planet we've already found.

We *do* want the same thing. We want to strike at the heart of tyranny. We want to point this Fleet toward something that could be *home*.

The marshal smiles, slow and wide, feeling the hum of our agreement. "If you four make this jump, we have a chance of doing just that. Our window is closing. Un-Haad's man in the Master Control Room can pop doors and cover cameras, but it's only a matter of time before someone clues in on what's happening. I need to start heading off suspicion before it starts, and you four have to get off this ship and pointed at the backend."

She opens our door and steps through. *Report to Assembly. Suit up. Unless you want to start the cycle all over again?*

There's no need to respond. No need for her to press an order into our minds.

Wordlessly, we all follow her out the door.

I can't believe I'm doing this.

The four of us are once again armored up in our full rigs and suited up in our breach suits. I'd thought I was rid of the stale taste of processed air for the day, but once again I'm trapped in the keen scent of my own breath. I think I can detect the edge of my fear in it.

Mine tastes better, Wooj thinks, and Praava checks him with her shoulder. The other three don't seem nearly as nervous about what we're about to do, and it's only making it worse. They should be wetting themselves right now, if that kind of reaction were still within our bodies' capacities. The only ones in this corridor who shouldn't be wetting themselves are Marshal Jesuit and Zaire, because they aren't about to jump out of a starship.

A void jump, as the marshal has explained, is a stealth tactic used by Scela to board ships when they don't want to be seen arriving by shuttle. Or when shuttle decks are locked down. Or in other extreme cases. It's rarely put to use, and with good reason—a void jump is the most dangerous maneuver I can think of. A last resort.

One wrong move and you're sailing into the black with no way of saving yourself. Drifting endlessly, until your breach suit's battery dies or you find some other way of creating a quick exit. There's no room for error.

At the end of this corridor is an airlock, and on the other side of the airlock is nothing but airless terror. Marshal Jesuit hangs back as Zaire presses forward, activating the datapad by the airlock door and tipping a salute up at the camera in the corner. A moment later, the door gusts open with a slight hiss. The base of the chamber is filled with greasy, dusty footprints from its primary use—letting maintenance workers out to do external work that keeps the ship flying.

"Right, you four in here," Zaire says. He hasn't stopped grinning since the moment we decided that we're doing this. We tramp inside, our exos organizing us in pairs along each wall. Across from me, Key's already having second thoughts, but the feel of the data jack in her uniform pocket grounds her in a purpose that's hard to shake.

That purpose hums through the system—annoying, persistent, just shy of unpleasant—and I wonder if this is how the others feel every time I pray. Praava assures me it isn't, just as Key shoots over that yeah, it kind of is. I tighten my jaw.

"In the hip of your breach suit is a harpoon," Zaire continues, oblivious to the back-and-forth happening between us. "Long string with a big hullmetal-tuned magnet at the end, basically. If you start to float off course, toss it at the nearest hull—as long as you're close enough for it to reach. Once it's secure, you can reel yourself in and then use the magnets in the fingers and feet of your suits. Your exos should know exactly how to work them."

I probe inside the exo to make sure it knows what he's talking about, but there's no way to test the protocols until there's hullmetal within reach. All four of us are slightly perturbed that we never even knew the magnets existed before today. How many other secrets have been built into our bodies?

"You know the mission specs," Marshal Jesuit says. The District formation. The target. The access hatch on the *Reliant*. The marshal drilled all this information into us while we were suiting up. "It's just point and leap. Keep a tight formation and focus—you're going to need all four of you to get to the backend."

"Yes, ma'am," we say in unison, our voices crystal clear through the comms in our ears but muffled through the shielding of our breach suits.

Zaire moves around each of us, checking the weak points in our suits and inventorying the equipment. He pulls a piece of hullmetal out of his pocket and waves it in front of each of our hands and feet, and our exos respond instinctively, switching on the magnetic current and yanking it out of his grasp. When he motions for it back, there's another instinctive switch flipped, the magnetism drops, and Zaire snatches the hullmetal before it hits the ground.

All these checks and drills and reassurances are only making my anxiety worse. I feel like a coiled spring, like an engine on the edge of ignition, like every enhanced muscle in my body is winding tighter by the second. Praava urges me to relax, partly for my own good, and mostly because I'm dragging everyone else in the system along with me. Her own thoughts are in a similar sort of turmoil, but there's a different focus. After her certainty that Ratna was meant to save the Fleet—certainty that drove her to take the metal—she's not quite sure how to process humanity's salvation riding on *her* shoulders. I want to reassure her, but words escape me. So instead I push the intention her way, and Praava grins, thinking of that day on the *Porthos* when she comforted me and realized that maybe she could live up to Ratna after all.

Zaire tucks the hullmetal into his pocket and finishes the last of his checks. Then he steps up to the doors and turns back to face us.

"All right, fuzzheads, looks like you're all set. Have a nice flight." A subtle smirk plays over his lips, and all but one of us are repelled by it. "Key, I had a good time tonight. Let's do it again sometime," he says, then darts out of the airlock and seals the door before she has a chance to retort.

Not a word, she snarls through the exosystem, but we can all tell she's pleased.

Now is not the time for distractions, Tanaka. All of you, grab the straps on the wall behind you, Marshal Jesuit instructs. *Hold on until the vent's done and the airlock is equalized.*

I turn and wind my fingers in the plastic straps, clenching them as tightly as the breach suit will allow. Next to me, Wooj rolls his head back. He's struggling with the full rig, with giving over his loose control of his body to the machine inside him. If it were up to me, I would have left him behind on this, but the marshal insisted, and Lopez backed her up. Wooj is wrapped up in this too, and we need as many Scela out there as possible, as much backup as we can manage.

In his headspace, he hums in concert with Key. Wooj has spent his whole life turned inward, focused on nothing but his own survival, and he's been lost as a Scela, unsure what to reach for now that a stable life is a given. He's a little thrilled to have found something worth risking everything for. Terrified, too, but that's part of the thrill.

"Hold on, robots," Zaire says over the comm. "Lopez, you have a go."

I close my eyes, even though the exo screams not to.

The outer doors open with a gentle *whump* that gets sucked away as all the air explodes outward and nothingness rushes in to replace it. Across the bay, a sickly feeling pours out of Key as she relives the sensation of the *Aeschylus* vent, but she puts a stopper on it before any of us can comment.

"Airlock is clear, proceed to hull," Zaire confirms.

I slide my eyes open and turn toward the stars. They shine harmlessly, their fiery light billions of miles away, and strangely enough, the thought of it makes me feel huge. Makes me feel bolder.

Key and I are the first to exit the airlock, pulling ourselves along by handholds until we edge out of the ship's gravity field and into the open, weightless void. I immediately slap my hand down on the hullmetal, my magnets switching on as the force of it pushes me back. Though there are magnets in my shoes, the exo suggests using our hands for the hullcrawling. Much finer control, and much less chance of launching us into the nothingness.

As we wait for Wooj and Praava to make the transition, I dare to lift my eyes from the belly of the ship. The airlock we chose puts us on the front end of the *Dread,* and from here, I can see some of the other First District ships. The elegant lines of the *Pantheon* lead us, and for a moment I try to wrap my head around the speed with which that ship guides us through the black. It feels like we're completely still, but it's an illusion produced by the vacuum that surrounds us and the distance between stars.

On the other side of the airlock door, Key stares at the First District and notes how arbitrary it seems. That this set of ships leads, while the backend follows. That this mere formation, necessitated by the engineering needs of the ships, produced rigid social strata over time. That she happened to be born at the top of it, and I happened to be born at the back.

It's difficult, but I keep my thoughts to myself.

"Holy shit," Wooj wheezes. He's managed to get himself out

onto the hull, and Praava drifts near him, her exosystem filled with a silent vow that she'll get him to the backend in one piece.

I lean into the exosystem, searching for Marshal Jesuit's next instructions, but then I remember the hullmetal that stands between us, impeding the exosystem link. We don't hear from her again until we're inside the same ship. The four of us are on our own.

"Starlight's wasting," Key reminds us, and starts her crawl.

It takes a few minutes to figure out the optimal mechanics for this kind of spacewalking. Praava, the natural, lands on it first. With one foot, she pushes off the hull and extends an arm, her magnets spun up just enough to keep her close to the hull without sticking to it. She skims along the hull by her fingertips, her exo shedding waves of joy at the feeling of flying. Wooj doesn't trust it—he scrambles along by his hands in a lizardlike motion, his magnets at full power.

I'm more like Wooj, less like Praava. The thought of what I'd lose if I accidentally launched into the void is too much—it keeps my magnets firmly anchored as I crawl along the surface of the *Dread*. I'm surprised that Key isn't trying to outdo Praava. Instead, she keeps her pace conservative, letting Praava arc out farther. It makes sense, I concede grudgingly. Key carries the linchpin of the entire mission. She doesn't want to jeopardize it.

We round the hull in a matter of minutes, arriving at the rear end of the *Dread,* where the ship's long-inert engines rest. It's been years since the last time the *Pantheon* dictated a change in Fleet direction, and the massive thrusters on all our ships have gone cold, leaving us to coast on the momentum of that last burn. As we pull ourselves over the crest of the *Dread*'s shape, we pause.

All four of us take in the Fleet as we've never seen it before.

The bay windows on starships and shuttles have offered us narrow glimpses, but we've never had an uninhibited view of the ships that have bounded humanity for the past three hundred years. With our headpieces on, our exo cameras weaving their images between us, we can see *everything*. These ships have borne the human race through the universe, arranged in seven tiers, seven layers, seven districts. Tiny shuttles glimmer between them, dwarfed by the scale of the starships. We bask in the faint glimmers of light and life within, stark against the blackness of the space in between stars. This is our home. *This is our pride,* the exos sing. This is what we fight to protect.

Except we're on a God-given mission to land this Fleet. To destroy this balanced structure as we bring these ships to berth. To uproot the General Body's control and plant new seeds on a planet we can finally call home.

And slowly, viciously, we start to smile.

Who wants the first jump? Key jokes, her cameras flickering to each of us. But that's not how this is going to work. If any of us veers off target, the only way to correct that is if we're all in the void together. So we line up along a flat stretch of hull, our toes pointed at the tier of Second District ships directly ahead. A countdown blooms between us as our HUDs zero in on the starship *Icarus,* our first target.

I whisper a quick prayer, then give myself fully to the exo, pushing my will against it and letting it do the rest. All thoughts and feelings get swept to the side as the machine in me winds my muscles, pushing me into a squatting stance. Across the system, we align, our bodies adjusting to match each other. The countdown ticks back.

Three . . .

Two . . .

One . . .

The magnetism in my feet vanishes. My muscles snap outward. We launch off the hull and into nothing. My HUD lights up as it locks on to our target and confirms I'll hit it.

Wooj's flares red. Panic floods the exosystem, but none of us can do a thing about it—any attempt to grab him risks adjusting our momentum, throwing off our course. There's nothing for him to latch on to, nothing for him to push against to bring him back to us. As we drift, he starts drifting farther away. The *Icarus* is a massive target, so massive that it seems ludicrous he might miss it. But all the math swirling around in our skulls agrees.

Wooj grapples with his harpoon, swinging the magnet around on its string until he's worked it into a fast-spinning circle. For a moment, I think he's going to try to hit the *Icarus,* to reel himself in, but then his intention comes through the system. He's got his sights on the starship *Margrave,* adjacent to the *Icarus* in the Second District tier. A much smaller target, but one that will be within reach for him in a matter of seconds.

Focus, he says, both to himself and to the rest of us. The mission matters more than any of this. So for the time being, I block out Wooj and bring the whole of my consciousness onto the approaching hull of the *Icarus.* My fingers tingle as the magnetism returns, reaching, yearning, readying me for the moment of impact.

I hit the ship with nothing but a muffled *whump,* the only noise coming from the brush of my body against my suit and the subtle creak of my enhanced skeleton as it arrests my momentum all at once. My lungs compress, flattened against hullmetal, and my gasp is accompanied by two others as Praava and Key slam into the *Icarus.* Our magnets hold. Our lungs refill with another breath of processed air.

And somewhere, distantly, Wooj snaps to a halt on the end of his harpoon line. He yanks hard against it, and a second later, his feet slam down on the hull of the *Margrave*.

One jump down. Five to go.

The second goes easier. Once again, we target the largest, most obvious Third District starship, and this time Wooj manages to land on it with us. There's still that weird note of resistance cropping up in his exo from his glitchy integration, making every motion more difficult, but he's powering through it. The cliff face, he swears, will be the last time his full rig gets the better of him.

When we round the hull of the ship, Key freezes, staring at the Fourth District, at one ship in particular. From this distance, even with our cameras, we can't see the blown-out section of hull, the patch job covering it, or anything else that would indicate that three weeks ago, the *Aeschylus* spilled itself into the void. Key's purpose hums louder.

A swell of relief-tempered pride rises from Praava at the sight of her birthship, still sailing. It's quickly dampened when she remembers that her sister isn't there, and her thoughts cast backward to the *Lancelot*.

Hey, focus, Wooj reminds them. *Still four more jumps left.*

We recenter ourselves, and the leap to Fourth District goes off without a hitch. It's starting to feel natural, giving my body completely to the exo, letting it take over my legs and catapult me into the blackness. Bit by bit, the fear slips away, replaced by a cool confidence that isn't entirely mine. I'm happy to wear it anyway.

But by the time we're leaping from Fifth to Sixth, we've gotten too comfortable.

Wooj spots the starship *Orpheus,* his birthship, floating on the distant edge of the district formation. He twists to get a better look at it, right at the moment we leap, and his momentum skews, sending him sailing into Praava. They bounce off each other, their courses adjusted, and suddenly our targeting system goes wild as it tries to latch on to something, anything. Praava fumbles for her harpoon, but she's so far off course that it won't do her any good. A sinking, horrible feeling rushes through all of us as we watch her drift steadily farther away.

My hand drops to my waist, fueled by my exo's instinct. I grab my harpoon and wheel it, spinning it into a frenzy until the moment my exo screams for me to let go. The magnet end sails through the void and drills into Praava's back with a thud that knocks the air out of her. She twists around and grabs the line, and my internal targeting pings worriedly as I start to drift off course with her.

But Key catches my drift. Two seconds later, her harpoon slams viciously into my side, and I wrap the line twice around my free arm. "Woojin," she snaps, and waits for three breathless moments before his harpoon rockets past her. She reaches out and grabs the line.

We're a confused tangle of momentum, the lines between us tightening and slackening as our system tries to establish equilibrium. I try to lock my targeting on the Sixth District ship we're trying to hit, but it's out of our reach, and no amount of flailing is going to get us there. "We're going to miss the ship," I hiss into the comm.

"We're not aiming for *that* ship," Wooj replies, and his glee nearly flattens the exosystem as we sail right through the Sixth District tier.

I watch the hulls of the ships go by, accepting my fate a little more with every window we sail past. I wonder if anyone's looking outside—if anyone would spot the flash of four tethered Scela flying through the void. It's late at night, and many of the cabin lights are dimming to their lowest levels as the ships bed down. It isn't likely that anyone's up to see what's happening outside. I scan for faces, but the windows are so few and far between, the chances so astronomical, that my exo nudges me, reminding me to focus. I fix my attention on the next tier of ships coming up.

Seventh District looms, and my cameras immediately fix on the *Reliant*. We aren't going to hit it—it's not the largest ship, and it's not the one Wooj has us sailing toward. A collective sigh of relief passes through our system as the target grows closer and closer—a smaller ship on the upper edge of the formation. Wooj turns in the void, orienting himself so that he sails feet first. His magnetism spins up until the metal in his legs aches.

Three seconds to impact, the exo warns.

I close my eyes and grip the lines tighter.

Wooj slams into the hull, his magnets latching on with everything they have. The line between him and Key snaps tight, and pain lances through the system as Praava and I come to rest, our arms stretched as taut as the lines between us. A tug from Wooj is all it takes to bring us floating down to the ship's surface, and if it weren't for the exo, I'd cry with relief the moment my magnetized feet hit hullmetal.

"See," Wooj says the moment his heart is beating slow enough to let him. "Wasn't all that bad."

"Key," Praava groans from farther down the hull. "You're closest. Please punch him for me."

Key obliges—once for Praava, and once for herself.

I crouch against the hull, press my hand down, and start muttering every prayer of thanks I know. God is on our side tonight. The worst of our travels is over. All four of us made it safely through.

Malikah won't ever go back to the dyeworks. And the Fleet will come to berth.

Key knocks my prayer askance with an aggressive burst of her willpower, strong enough that it scorches the back of my neck. Annoyance snaps through me, but I curb the impulse to hit her again. She has a point—starlight's wasting, and we should get to the *Reliant* before we start saying our thank-yous.

I stand up and give the others a short nod, taking a deep breath that echoes in my breach suit's helmet. We're so close. Just a little farther, just a few more jumps. And as we shake the reckless energy out of our system and launch once more from the skin of this starship, I let myself start believing that for once, things will go right.

When my feet land on the *Reliant* at last, I don't pray.

I don't have to.

CHAPTER 24

KEY

My exo unclenches when we reseal the airlock behind us and take our first steps on the *Reliant.* I feel like I'm taking my first steps as a Scela again, my legs shaky and unsure of how they should move with gravity tying them down. The others aren't doing too much better—not even Praava.

"Did we really just . . . ," she gasps, snapping her headpiece back as her breach suit's seal crawls down her neck. She sucks in a deep breath of the *Reliant*'s air. It's still uncommonly warm compared to the *Dread,* even at night, but Praava's lungs are greedy for something that hasn't been reprocessed in the curdle of her own sweat.

Woojin throws an arm over her shoulder, leaning against her as he struggles to put his mind in a place where he doesn't have to fear every moment. "We fuckin' *did that,*" he mutters, glancing back at the airlock hatch.

Ahead of us, Aisha stares down the night-dark corridor, apprehension building in her. *We're in the upper levels of the ship,* she thinks. *The main body of the habitat is below us. I've never been up here before.* Her exo spins for a connection to the ship's network but fails to grab anything. We don't have a download of the ship's layouts waiting for us here, because no one expects us to be here in the first place.

Probably better that way, I tell her. *Don't want our fingerprints all over the network with no magic man in the Master Control Room to wipe them away. Speaking of, time to haul ass before someone wonders why an airlock just opened.*

Aisha nods, then starts off down the corridor. The taste of her birthship's air is grounding her in the mission, and her thoughts turn repetitive—not a prayer but a vow. A steady chant drives her forward as she swears that she *will* pay off her aunt, she *will* keep her sister out of the dyeworks, she *will* keep her brother alive.

I glance back at Praava and Woojin, who are still clinging to each other for support. "C'mon, you two. We've got some treason to commit."

We make our way through the *Reliant* with far more stealth than our massive bodies should be able to produce. The ship slumbers around us, corridors emptied, doors locked. Every move we make feels too loud when the only other sound is the gentle hum of the ship's machinery, the noise we've been living with our entire lives. This morning was the first time I've ever experienced silence free of any sort of mechanical rumble—save for the airless hell of the *Aeschylus* vent. The thought of a future free of starship noise is somehow both suffocating and thrilling.

Aisha leads the way through the upper levels, but we can feel her guessing. Several times we take turns that end in dead ends, and it takes her nearly an hour to get us down to the level of the main habitat. The vacant streets feel eerie without the crush of people that inhabited them last time I was here, and the absence of leftover decorations from Launch Day make them feel even emptier. We wind through the marketplace, pressed close to the shadow of the buildings in the dimness of the night.

Praava and Woojin take it in with fresh eyes. Neither of them has been in the Seventh District before, and it's a lot to process. Before I came here, it was easy to believe that all starships are equal in the eyes of the General Body. But this one bears the brunt of the frontend's negligence and suffers under the weight of the backend's overpopulation. The *Reliant* seems to be made of frayed edges, stitched together.

I press my hand against the pocket in the breach suit where the data jack rests. Maybe tonight we can take some steps toward changing that. The sentiment feels reckless and new, but not untrue.

Aisha's steps quicken as we get closer, her stealth forgotten in her rush to get to her aunt's door. She hits the buzzer without hesitation, and the rest of us cluster around her, pressing close against the stoop. Just in case, I flick my headpiece down and scan my cameras for any hints of motion. There's no telling who might be out at this hour. Who might misinterpret the sight of four Scela at a Fractionist leader's door.

Our enhanced hearing strains, but we can't detect any noise within the apartment. Aisha frowns and presses the buzzer again. *Malikah has to be in there, even if Yasmin's out,* she reasons.

Something edges at the corner of my camera's vision. I whirl, trying to target the little flicker of motion, but it whips out of sight before I can home in on it. *Someone's out here,* I warn, and the rest of the squad goes on alert.

Aisha's thoughts turn to a steady stream of *Malikah Malikah*

Malikah as she leans against the buzzer, and all of us wince at the grating, distant sound inside the apartment.

Maybe she's a heavy sleeper? Woojin suggests.

There's another whisper of movement down the street, and this time Praava spots it too. Her cameras and mine zoom in on the figure that's just emerged from an alleyway. He trudges toward us like it's the last thing he wants to be doing, and everything about his posture screams fear. I square my shoulders, just in case he needs any extra inspiration.

As he draws nearer, our images sharpen into a gaunt-looking man in his late forties. He keeps his eyes lowered until the last possible second and his palms raised above his head. There's a stunstick attached to his belt, but from the way his body moves, I doubt he has the muscle to use it properly.

Local enforcement? Praava asks Aisha. *Night watchman?* All four of us have frozen, our exos holding us still as our system mulls over exactly what to do about this man.

No uniform, Aisha notes. *And why would he have his hands up?*

Fractionist, then? Woojin suggests. *Only, why would a Fractionist approach a Scela squadron knocking on the door of one of their leaders?*

Because we're knocking, not breaking the door down, I reason. *I'll handle this.*

As the man stops a wary twenty feet away, I step forward to meet him, cocking back my headpiece. In the dimness, he has to squint to see my face. It takes a moment, no thanks to my bruises, and I'm banking on the hope that he's one of the Fractionists who's seen me without the Archangel makeup. But then the recognition flickers in his eyes, and triumph lifts inside me. His whole stance changes from one of fear and caution to one of reverence. Of worship.

Please don't start crying, I beg.

Aisha's disdain burrows into the edge of my mind, but I can't let myself be too bothered. I feel *right*. Like claiming the Archangel has put me into alignment. Like this is what I'm supposed to be doing. The holes still gape in my memories, but I feel whole in spite of them.

"We're looking for Yasmin Un-Dul," I announce. "We have some critical information she needs."

"I'll take you to her," the man says without an ounce of hesitation.

So being a brainwashed rebel figurehead has its perks.

Even with the infamous Archangel reassuring the man, his nervous air clings to him as he leads us through a makeshift hatch in the wall of the *Reliant*'s habitat. Can't really blame him when he's got four Scela breathing down his neck.

Within is a glowing, narrow space run with cables that have to be brushed aside to move anywhere. The man slips through them easily, but our bulk doesn't follow well. We end up pushing and shoving and hoping we don't do any permanent damage to the ship's workings.

After what seems like an eternity of squirming through the walls of the ship—though my exo curtly informs me it was only six minutes—we spill out into an open area filled with the chug of machinery, where a small crowd has gathered. Several of them spook when they see us, scrambling away, and my ears fill with the crackle of stunsticks. Aisha, Woojin, and Praava shrink back, but I step forward into the light, trying to give my face the most human set possible.

The stunsticks fizzle out, replaced by whispers of "Archangel" that get swallowed by the steady churn of the machines around us. I snap my headpiece back down once they've all gotten the picture.

"Yasmin?" I ask.

"Here." She steps forward, her face made gaunt by the light they've strung up overhead. Aisha's aunt looks tired, ragged. These past weeks must have been difficult for the movement, even those who were nowhere near the tragedy. I wonder how many of the people who died around me on the *Aeschylus* were people she knew. Fellow Fractionists. Friends. From what Aisha thinks of her, I doubt Yasmin has many of the latter. Her life is full of carefully calculated distance, the kind you learn when you grow old in the backend.

I meet her gaze with my cameras. Aisha's mistrust of her aunt curdles through the exosystem, but all I see is a woman who's taken the worst of the Fleet's injustices and turned them into fuel for her fire. A woman willing to do whatever it takes to defy the General Body.

A woman who's never going to get her hands dirty, Aisha scoffs. I shove her thoughts away and pry open my breach suit's pocket. The little data jack tumbles into my palm.

"This morning, we shipped out for our final assessment, but a Fractionist hack changed our target to a world the General Body has kept tucked away from the public eye." I start. "But you already knew that, didn't you?"

Yasmin's lips thin. She nods.

"What you didn't know—what you wanted us to confirm—was whether the world was habitable." I pause, forcing back a ludicrous grin. I'm here. I found my way back to what I once was, and

I'm doing something that must have been the Archangel's wildest dream. "The planet *is* habitable. And these are the coordinates," I finish, holding out the data jack.

A rush of pride glows through me as Yasmin's eyes light up. A soft smile breaks over her features, and I return it with my closest approximation. Whispers chorus around us as the Fractionists absorb the impact of my announcement.

Wait, Aisha says behind me. She's been glancing around the room, searching the faces. Her will explodes, rattling the back of my neck as she reaches into my exo and forces my fingers to snap shut around the jack. "Where is Malikah? We rang the buzzer several times—it should have woken her up."

Yasmin acts like she didn't hear, her gaze fixed hungrily on my closed fist. "This couldn't come at a better moment, Archangel. This is truly incredible." She turns around to the rest of the Fractionist gathering. "With this, we can strike back at last. Start the preparations!"

Hushed cheers reverberate through the crowd and some of the humans dart off immediately, twisting back through the pipes and wires. Others lean over their datapads, their fingers flying over something that my cameras can't quite make out. I swear I can smell a nervous, fearful scent pouring off them.

Yasmin turns back to me and holds out her hand, expectant. "The coordinates, Archangel."

Suddenly Aisha isn't the only one keeping my fingers locked around the little device. I scan her face, looking for the usual indicators of deception. Maybe Aisha's right not to trust her aunt. "What are you putting in motion?" I ask, trying to sound commanding, and pull my hand back.

Yasmin's eyes narrow. "Retribution."

"For the *Aeschylus*?"

"You must know that wasn't us—the General Body's been spinning the casts to make us look like monsters, when *they* orchestrated the hull breach. They pinned it on us, but we had nothing to do with it."

Yasmin is telling the truth—or at least the truth she knows—that the Fractionists weren't involved in the breach of the *Aeschylus*. My suspicions were right. But there's something sinister about the way she says it. Something that sets my instincts bristling, the same instincts that made me question the *Aeschylus* vent. "Yasmin, what are you putting in motion?" I ask again.

"We're going to flip the narrative. Use the General Body's tactics against them. Get the Fleet on our side. We're going to avenge the *Aeschylus*. And we need your help to do it."

It's all I want. All I know I want for sure. My fingers slip open, and before I can second-guess myself, Yasmin plucks the data jack out of my hands and sweeps to the nearest table. She plugs it into a datapad, and with a few elegant twists of her fingers, the data distributes to the other Fractionist devices at the table, which ping with the incoming information. "With this," she says, "we can convince the people of the General Body's deception. And after tonight, it will be nigh impossible to side with our so-called benevolent leaders."

"What happens tonight?" Praava asks. Our wariness twines together in the exosystem.

"Tonight, as far as the Fleet knows, a squadron of Scela deployed to the *Reliant* on an unauthorized, off-the-books mission. The General Body had been alerted to a gathering of Fractionist leaders on the ship, which every single one of us can vouch for."

"But we're not—" Woojin begins. The rest of us hush him.

"With the blow dealt to the Fractionists by the *Aeschylus* vent, the cause was clearly weakened. One more drastic measure might eradicate them entirely. So the General Body decided to use those horrid Fractionists' tactics against them, to punish them for their destruction of the *Aeschylus*. They decided to vent the entire *Reliant* and wipe out the cause once and for all."

Alarm and fury burn through our exos before any of us can fully grasp what she's just said. "That's— You can't—" I stammer. "People will *die*."

"Not if you alert them all first."

A sudden, horrible stillness settles inside the exosystem as we wrap our heads around what she expects us to do. The Fractionists' ruse is ruined if they go running through the streets, urging the ship's population to get to their breach shelters. But if four Scela do it . . .

"You're a monster," I snarl, fully aware of the irony in that statement.

Yasmin draws back, her face written with genuine shock. "I thought you were with us, Archangel."

"I don't . . . It's not . . ."

"It's not your place, is what it is," Yasmin snaps. "You did well getting the information to us tonight, but you've only ever been a mouthpiece."

Her words knock me silent. Something else surfaces from my empty spaces—a deep, unavoidable familiarity. This is the same sinking feeling that enveloped me when I was sitting in a chair in front of a camera, reading words that were written for me. My own head swirled with ideas, with opinions, and none of them mattered. All I was supposed to do was look pretty and read the cue cards.

I remember Kellan's apology suddenly, and resentment flares hot and heavy in my thoughts. He said he dragged me into this. Did I let him? Follow him? Want to impress him? Ever since I woke up in the metal, I've been turning myself inside out to prove myself to the people around me. The exo's been telling me all along—that's who I am. That's what I do. And all at once, I understand what *made* the Archangel. The exo wipes away the impact, urging me to stay grounded in the present, but the sour aftertaste of the realization remains.

I wasn't an icon. I wasn't a figurehead.

I was a tool.

And nothing's changed.

Before I can get my wits about me, I find myself swept to the side as raw fear rises from Aisha. She lunges forward, towering over her aunt. Yasmin meets her cameras coolly. "This Fleet goes nowhere without sacrifice. If we lose the *Reliant,* we gain a world. The charges are in place, and there are too many of them for you to stop us. Everything's already in motion. In thirty minutes, we breach the hull, so you'd better get to—"

Aisha's hand snaps out, grabbing her aunt by the throat. Yasmin yelps and squirms in her grip. The Fractionists at the table move for their stunsticks. As the crackle of electricity fills the air, we flock against Aisha's back, pushing our wills through the exosystem to restrain her as she urges her fingers to tighten, to crush Yasmin's neck into nothing. *It's not worth it,* we tell her. *We're outnumbered, and we'll get dropped by the stunsticks. We'll be just as bad as her. It won't stop what's started.*

"Aisha, please," Yasmin begs, her tiny human hands scrabbling against Aisha's massive enhanced ones. "You have to understand—"

"I don't *have* to understand anything. I only need one thing from you," Aisha snarls. Yasmin's feet lift off the ground. A deadly intention curls through the system. None of us are sure if we can stop it. Aisha pulls her aunt close until her headpiece is pressed into her forehead. Yasmin's terror reflects in the lenses of Aisha's cameras as she rumbles, *"Where is my sister?"*

CHAPTER 25

AISHA

I should have snapped Yasmin in half.

The regret pounds through me as I race through the sublevels of the *Reliant*. It wouldn't have solved anything. My sister would still be in the dyeworks, the Fractionists would still have charges placed around the ship's hull, and we still would have been utterly helpless to stop the chaos that's about to descend on the *Reliant*. But it would have felt so good to take the fury boiling inside me out on her. I don't care that she's my mother's sister. Our blood ties have never mattered to her. Now they don't matter to me either.

At least I'm not like Praava. Our exosystem is full of fear and panic right now, most of it mine, but I'm not dragging the other three along with me on my mad rush to Malikah's side. Instead, they're running through the streets and upper levels, warning the *Reliant*'s residents to get to their designated breach shelters. My exo reminds me that I ought to be with them, maximizing our reach.

But I don't care if my destination is inefficient. My sister is in the dyeworks, and I won't rest until she's safely tucked inside a breach shelter.

Twenty-eight minutes and counting, the exo reminds me.

The underbelly of the *Reliant* is where the ship shows its age. Up above, it's hard to believe we've been flying for over three hundred years—everything gets rotated, polished, patched. The signs of wear get swept away. But down below, where only the forgotten go, the signs of wear are inescapable. It's damp and cramped and rusted, and the whole corridor is filled with noisy rumbles.

Down here is the dyeworks.

It sounds fairly innocent, and I think that's half the trick. But the truth is a Fleet doesn't fly for hundreds of years without intense resource management. Meticulous recycling. And nowhere is that process more brutal than in the textile plants in the bowels of the *Reliant.*

I round a corner, throw open a door, and balk as the heat of the place washes over me. If it weren't for my breach suit—already sealed, just in case—the smell of molten plastics and old rags might knock me over. I stare out over the dyeworks, and the dyeworks stare back. Hundreds of red-handed children fix their eyes on the monster who's just thundered into their midst. But none of their little red hands stop moving. They have quotas to fill, far more important than the threat a Scela might bring.

I throw the exo's power into the strength of my voice and shout, "The *Reliant* is in danger of hull breach. Get to your designated shelters immediately."

"What's going on?" a pale, sickly looking woman shouts back, staggering from her perch on the overseer roost. "There aren't any breach sirens."

I grit my teeth. "All of you out, immediately." I don't have time for humans playing games—not when my sister's life is at stake. *Twenty-five minutes.* My cameras flash through the faces in the crowd, the exo trying to pin down the one it knows.

"They aren't going anywhere unless I give the say-so," the overseer replies.

She's awfully high and mighty for a backend dyeworks hag, the exo sneers in my head, but I push its voice to the side. Its nastiness doesn't have any place in a situation this dire, especially with none of the children moving from their stations.

"I said *now*!" I thunder back, trying to channel the marshal's hullmetal will with nothing but my voice. "Evacuate these kids—there isn't time to argue."

My cameras flash. They've found her. I whirl, my focus zooming in on a bench by a mechanical loom, on one girl in particular. Malikah's keeping her head down and her fingers moving, just like the kids around her. I storm over, my exo tuning out the protests of the overseer. "Malikah," I say, kneeling by her. "We have to go."

Her hands are ruby red, covered in the dyeworks' marks and more than their share of blisters. As my little sister whirls to face me, I'm almost knocked backward by the defiance in her eyes. "But the mistress said—"

"I don't give a damn about what the mistress said," I growl, grabbing her by the shoulders. "If the rest of them won't come, I'll get you out of here."

"No!" she shrieks, reaching out for the loom as if it's a tether. I feel a tug on my shoulder pieces that must be the overseer, but I ignore it, staring down at Malikah as I try to process her resistance. "It's not fair if only I get to go. We all should go," my little sister insists.

Unbelievable, the exo shrieks, but I can't help my exasperated grin. I've always loved my sister for her kindness, *encouraged* her to be just and fair. She has all the makings of a General Body representative who could do some good in the Fleet. Of course that instinct within her would work against me now.

I turn on the mistress, drawing up to my full height, and satisfaction curls through me as she shrinks back. "You'll get every last one of these children out of here, or I'll beat you until you won't be seeing anything *but* red."

"Production—" she starts.

I snap my headpiece back, unveiling my snarling, metal-threaded face, and the mistress has the sense not to say anything else. My lungs burn as my nostrils flare. The dyeworks' smoke sears my eyes, but they'll never tear up with my new Scela biology. "Give the order. Halt production. This ship is about to vent."

The last drops of her resistance evaporate under my monstrous glare. She shuffles back to the overseer tower and throws switches in a frenzy. All throughout the dyeworks, machines clatter to a halt—possibly for the first time in days, though with the accident rate down here, that's not likely. An eerie calm descends as the silence melts into the noise of hundreds of shifting, confused children. "That will be all for today. Evacuate to the breach shelters," the mistress announces into a loudspeaker.

Twenty-three minutes.

The children move like a Scela unit, filing in even ranks toward the narrow exits. I try to grab Malikah again, but she jerks and thrashes when my fingers close around her wrist. I let her go without a fight—I'm too scared of breaking her. "If I carry you to the shelter, it will be faster," I urge.

She glances around at all the other kids that surround her. None of them have Scela siblings offering to rush them to safety.

"Get all of us out, Aisha," she says, defiance sparkling in her dark eyes.

Damn her courage. Damn her justice. I straighten, then sprint to the doors, weaving through the lines of trudging kids. "Let's *move!*" I yell, and at least this time they listen to me. The kids start running, streaming out into the corridors, little red fists pumping up and down as they hurry.

Dread sinks down my spine as I watch them go. The *Reliant* was supposed to be primarily transport, with a textile district in the rear of the ship's body. Population imbalance set in after a few generations, and the ship's industry was forced lower and lower to make room for all the new people. But the ship's structure never adapted to match. The lower levels simply weren't built for this kind of capacity.

And their emergency systems never changed. The dyeworks have only a handful of breach shelters, meant for scenarios where a couple maintenance workers might be trapped down here. The nearest large-scale breach shelters—the ones that can accommodate all these kids—are a few levels above us. And the corridors are so, so narrow.

In the distant reaches of the exosystem, I feel Key's terror. She didn't expect to be reliving the horrors she experienced on the *Aeschylus*. She didn't expect to be the direct cause of them. *We'll make it to the shelters,* I snap, as if my thoughts can make it so. *There's time—twenty minutes.*

This would be easier if you were pulling your weight, she accuses me.

The thought lances through me like a needle. *Someone had to warn the dyeworks,* I fire back.

Great, she growls. *And we'll just handle . . . the rest of the entire fucking ship.*

"Faster!" I shout, exasperation nearly cracking my voice. I've lost track of Malikah in the crowd, but we're so close to the breach shelter that already I feel as if a great burden is lifting off my shoulders. These kids are all going to make it.

But then a sudden torrent of klaxons hits Praava, then Wooj, then Key, and a second later, the alarms are in this corridor too. Shrieking, wailing sirens, flashing lights, and underneath them, the petrified screams of the children around me.

The breaches have already started. The *Reliant* is venting.

No. It's too soon. We have to—

My exo slams my headpiece back down, the breach suit's seals snapping in place as reprocessed air floods my lungs. I'm surrounded by the crush of smaller bodies, and I do everything in my power to avoid hitting them. I scan the faces rushing past for Malikah, but my cameras can't find her in the crowd. Is she ahead? She must have made it into the shelter already.

Steady, Key warns in the back of my mind. She's surrounded by the chaotic whip of escaping air, and it's too much for her—she's sunk down on her haunches in the middle of the main street, trying to block out the screaming world around her by slipping into mine. Praava and Wooj are sprinting somewhere in the upper levels, running alongside people who still have time to make it to a shelter.

Unable to do anything for herself, Key directs her will into me, forcing me to focus with a gentle hum. If I don't do *something,* more of these kids will die.

A little boy stumbles over his own feet, and I bend down and scoop him onto my back before he has a chance to get his wits about him. The shelter's within sight ahead. Other kids are getting the picture—I feel the little red hands finding purchase on my back and shoulders as I wade through the crowd, weaving back and forth.

I plunge through the shelter's doors, and immediately the weight drops from my back. There might be a small chorus of thanks, but the exo tunes it out until it's nothing but buzzing in my ears. It needs me sharp. It wants to save more. I rush back out into the corridor.

But then there's a change in the pressure of the air around me. A subtle *whump,* and suddenly the wail of the sirens is bending in pitch as the air rapidly thins. The doors of the breach shelter slam shut, an automatic reaction to the inevitable truth. The Fractionists have breached down here too.

My cameras switch off, my audio cuts out, and the exo goes dead against my spine. It knows I can't take this. It has to protect me. I thrash against my enhancements, but my skeleton is locked in place by the metal. I have to move. I have to find Malikah. I have to make sure she made it inside. But I'm powerless against the preservation instinct controlling my body. I'm trapped in a blackened, claustrophobic world with nothing but my fear and my guilt and my hatred.

It's for your own good, the exo insists, but just because it's right doesn't mean it has to do this to me, has to leave me not knowing. I'm frozen and useless, and all I can feel is the rush of air against my breach suit as the vacuum pours in around me.

Aisha, Praava thinks. *It's going to be okay.* My mind floods with images from the breach shelter she's in, surrounded by humans. But I can't help but notice how much extra space there is around her, how few people have made it, considering the *Reliant*'s overstuffed population.

I got a lot of people in here, Wooj offers. He's in a different shelter, this one a little fuller than Praava's. He notices a cast camera filming, and for a moment the exosystem braids with four parallel desires to crush it. Everything is playing perfectly into the Fractionists' hands.

Key's still crouched in the middle of the street, her cameras fixed on the ground and her hands curled over her head. Her exo is urging her to get up, to be proud and tall and Scela, but her will is unshakable. She can't find any pride in being one of the direct causes of the chaos that surrounds her. She reaches out to me—me, the other reason for all the air being sucked out of the ship—and after a moment of hesitation, I let myself join her. My mind detaches from my body, from my circumstances, from everything but the system that twines through my consciousness.

It isn't fair, that we get to retreat into our minds like this, that we get to ignore what's happening around us. But the alternative is to purposefully wound ourselves, and after what Key went through on the *Aeschylus,* I can't see any point in doing that.

So I let my exo blind and bind me. I stop fighting. I wait it out.

When my cameras snap on at last, after ten full minutes of utter darkness, I'm immediately stunned by the brightness of the lights. I keep my gaze fixed on the ceiling of the corridor as I take my first steps. My soundless footfalls confirm the vacuum that surrounds me. My exo tells me to turn my head, and a moment later, I understand the reason why. Through the window of the breach shelter, I can see dozens of children milling about. Children I saved. The exo wants them to be the first faces I see. For a moment my heart lifts.

Then it lets me see the rest. The hallway is littered with what I want to pretend are tiny bundles, curled in on themselves. My Scela body has stolen my ability to vomit, but the feeling is still there, a churn in my stomach, a taste in the back of my mouth. Suddenly it's horrifically clear to me why Key snapped at me over the *Aeschylus* earlier. This is how she felt—trapped in airless silence, surrounded by the dead, and utterly powerless.

I will kill Yasmin. I don't care that it doesn't change anything. I don't care if the early breach was an accident. She thought this was the way to get the Fleet on her side. She deserves to die in the most painful way possible. The thought burns through my mind as I wander down the corridor, unsure of what to do next. It burns as I notice the overseer woman, her eyes open and red with burst blood vessels, and feel a jolt of sick satisfaction that she didn't make it to the shelter in time.

It burns until it consumes me. Until I'm nothing but fire and rage and pain.

Until I find my sister's body, crumpled against a wall just twenty feet from the breach shelter doors.

CHAPTER 26

KEY

By the time I feel like I can move again, the rescue shuttles have arrived. Breach-suited Scela and humans move soundlessly through the streets, headed for the shelters to start evacuations. A message linked into my exosystem a few minutes ago, broadcast to every Scela on the ship. The *Reliant*'s damages are beyond repair, it announced impassively. Everyone's being evacuated from the shelters and relocated to other ships. Seventh District ships, of course.

My exo keeps urging me to join the teams working to move people to safety. Breach-suited Scela are unfurling tunnels that attach to the shelter airlocks and pressurize, creating an artificial vascular system, a safe path to get the survivors down to the *Reliant*'s intership deck, where the rescue shuttles wait. I fight the impulse, sharpening my will against the order until its hum fades from the back of my neck. It would be smarter to help. Less likely to incur suspicion.

But none of it really matters anymore.

Instead I wander through the streets, following a slight tug from one end of the exosystem. Praava and Woojin are both trapped in shelters elsewhere for the time being. Aisha's the only other one on the outside.

I'm the only one who can go to her.

So I go.

I drag my feet. I don't want to look her in the eye. It feels so silly to think that when her grief and pain is in my head already. But something about seeing her makes it real, and I can't cope with it being real.

I can't cope with what we've done.

Because this is our fault. Completely ours. If Aisha hadn't been so desperate to pay off Yasmin. If *I* hadn't believed that the Archangel was a person worthy of being when all along she was just a pretty puppet in Fractionist hands. If both of us hadn't gone looking for the coordinates in the first place.

We dragged Woojin and Praava into a bloodbath far worse than the one aboard the *Aeschylus*. The marshal put her faith in us to carry out this mission, and instead we've ensured the deaths of thousands. The General Body could punish Marshal Jesuit as this tragedy's originator, and what would happen to her daughter then?

As I mount the stairs to the sublevels, my head starts to ache from the weight of my fury. I want the Fractionist leaders to answer for what they've done here. Once again, I find myself doubting the conditions of a breach. Yasmin said we had thirty minutes. We took her word for it and found ourselves with only ten. It could be an accident—a charge detonating prematurely that forced them to trigger the rest of the breach.

Or it could have been intentional. Nothing gets people going like a martyr. I've seen that enough in the way the Fractionists look at me now. Maybe it's given them ideas.

And who knows what their next move will be?

I swallow back the bitterness in my mouth. Will there be another *Kronos*? Another *Aeschylus*? Another *Reliant*? What other ships have to suffer before our feet hit solid ground?

I trudge down a set of narrow stairs and round the corner into a scene I've seen over and over through Aisha's cameras. There are so many of them, each of them so small, so still. I raise my eyes from the bodies of the children and find the one living thing in this hallway. Aisha's slumped against the wall, her legs sprawled out at careless angles. Her head is bent, and as I get closer, I see that she has her fingers carefully wound in the hair of the girl next to her. The child is facedown, her red hands matching those of every other kid in this corridor, but I know it's Malikah from the numbness that radiates out of Aisha's exo.

There's nothing I can say, and nothing I should. Instead, I cross to her other side and sit, my back sliding down against the wall, my shoulder inches from hers. With a nudge into her headspace, I listen to the feedback from her audio processing. We're still in a vacuum, with no air molecules between us to carry the sound, but inside her suit there's air enough to carry the gentle brush of her massive, enhanced fingers over the limp strands of Malikah's hair.

For a moment our thoughts go quiet, both of us listening, as if that little noise is the only thing in the universe.

She didn't want to wear the scarf, Aisha whispers in my head. *She didn't see the point of it. But she felt so guilty seeing me wear mine—I think it made her feel like she wasn't mourning our parents enough. So she started wearing her own too. The morning I left, she was wearing it, but I guess sometime between then and when we visited Yasmin, she decided to stop. I should have asked her about it. She has such beautiful hair.*

Aisha pauses, her fingers going still.

I had just started thinking that maybe it wouldn't be so bad, not

wearing the headscarf. That it was a chance for me to move on. Leave be-
hind that chapter of my life. And now . . . Though she can't physically
cry, a bubble of emotion that feels like a sob wells up, stealing away
her thoughts.

I wait, still listening.

Now I think I need to start wearing it again.

I bow my head, rushing through the whole of my experience for
something that might not be useless to say. I can't recall a loss like
hers, and I shiver at the thought that this isn't the first loss of this
kind she's had to endure. Her parents, her sister—and her little
brother is on the plague ship. The universe has a track record of
taking everything that's ever mattered to her, no matter how hard
she fights against it.

My own experience is nothing in comparison. What have I lost?
Myself, I suppose, but that doesn't really count. I still have some
semblance of myself, even if the General Body ripped out the core
of the Archangel. My parents are alive, healthy, and probably better
off with me in Scela metal.

I don't have siblings. Growing up, I didn't even have friends
who had siblings. It's a First District thing—if you want to repro-
duce, you're supposed to have one perfect child. You don't get do-
overs. There's pride in having one child, raising them the right way,
and having them alone carry on your legacy. It keeps the population low, so more people can fill the frontend starships and diver-
sify the genetics. In the backend, it's different. There's more risk, I
guess. Factories like the dyeworks can take people at any age, so the
families here are bigger to compensate.

Aisha was right. I don't *get* family. Not the way she does, not the
way she feels. I can dip into her thoughts, pull out every emotion
that passes through her, and it still wouldn't be enough. I can feel

her hurt, but even with her guidance, I can never fully understand it. That much is clear by the way I tried to use her parents' deaths to *motivate* her just a few hours ago.

I'm going to have to do a whole lot better.

So instead I lean. Let my body slump to the right, just enough so that my shoulder is pressing into hers, and through the system I will her to understand what it means. *I'm here. I know what you're feeling, though I won't pretend to comprehend it. I'm not going anywhere.*

And Aisha leans back. Her head rocks to the side, limited by the support struts of her rig and the inflexibility of her suit, but she manages to set it sort of on my shoulder, and I set my head on top of hers in turn. In her exo, I feel Malikah's hair slide between her fingers as she lets go. There's a dark emptiness growing in her. A massive absence. That I understand. That I know how to handle.

You just build yourself back around the holes, I tell her. It's nowhere as simple as that, and I don't think I have it entirely figured out myself, but it's a start.

Her cameras roll, taking in the rest of the hallway, the rest of the children. *I could have saved so many more,* she starts, a count rising in her system as she identifies the individuals. *If I'd been in the habitat instead, I could have—*

Stop, I think forcefully. *No one else was giving these kids a chance. You did. That's what matters.*

Aisha's jaw pulses. *You know what's messed up? If this had gone the other way, if I had saved her . . . I probably wouldn't care about how many we let die. I would have been so relieved that the rest of it wouldn't have mattered. I feel like I care more about the rest of them because my sister's among them. I hate knowing that about myself.*

I shutter my cameras. *Family makes you stupid. But I don't think that stupidity's a bad thing. I mean, yeah, it put us in some bad situations this week. It got . . . It got people killed, is what happened, but that's not useful for either of us to hear. It's so easy to be apathetic. To tell yourself that you don't care about anything and you won't do anything—I mean, look at me. There was so little I cared about before today that when the slightest inkling got in my head that I could matter to something and something could matter to me, it drove me into all this.*

Actually that doesn't sound too great either. There's no way to win when caring about shit gets people killed. A burst of my frustration jolts into the exosystem, strong enough that it shoves some of Aisha's grief aside. I'm tempted to unleash more, to distract her from the hurt that overtakes her. But denying her this moment, when her pain is freshest, would be cruel.

Our exosystem seethes with Aisha's urge to take her vengeance on Yasmin and the rest of the Fractionists. They'll be revealing their next move soon. It probably starts with the footage of the *Reliant*'s destruction, footage we'll be at the center of. But it'll give us a sense of where we stand and what *our* next move is going to be.

Because we can't stand by and follow orders like we were made to. Not when our Fleet is steered by leadership that would vent part of a ship to stop a protest. Not when it's being influenced by a group that would vent an entire ship to swing the public's opinion. The four of us have seen this mess evolve. Have helped it along unknowingly. And as long as we can avoid the willpower that might compel us to do otherwise, we have to try to stop it before it rips the whole Fleet apart.

I don't really know where we start. Despite who I was, I'm kind of new at this, and it shows. I let the question drift into the system between us. Aisha takes it in and digests it. *They can't get away with it. Neither of them. Not the Fractionists and not the General Body,* she thinks. *Not while I still live. Not while my brother . . .*

269

Another swell of emotion.

He's still alive, I know it. He's so strong. I mean, I know for little kids it's supposed to be much harder to beat the plague. But I just can't be the only one left. After everything I gave . . . Her hand drifts back down to Malikah's hair, but she stops herself just short. If she lets herself get dragged back into the past, she'll be useless. *I can't forget him. I can't stop fighting for him just because I lost her.*

On the distant edge of the exosystem, I feel Woojin finally being freed from his breach shelter as rescue squads reach him. He picks up the orders being broadcast and chooses to follow them, seamlessly joining the flow of Scela escorting humans out to the intership deck. With his body occupied, he reaches out in the back of his mind and finds us. There's a moment's pause as he takes in the situation that surrounds us, the way we've settled, and then he thinks, *And you two gave me and Praava so much shit.*

Oh, fuck off, Woojin. Our system fills with the soft warmth of Aisha's quiet, hesitant amusement, and that more than anything convinces me. We're going to make it through this. We'll start somewhere.

Aisha nudges my head with hers. *We'll start by getting up,* she says.

And that's exactly what we do.

CHAPTER 27

AISHA

I see the last of my sister when the rescue crews wrap her in a sheet. They only have so much material, so she's laid side by side with seven other dyeworks kids, their raw, stained hands pressed into each other. A worker bundles them up with slow reverence.

Prayers for her soul's journey pour from my lips. A proper Ledic burial service isn't possible, and a dull ache builds in my chest as I wrap my head around the fact that these little words are all I can give Malikah in the end. My eyes feel too heavy. The exo wants me to forget that I have them, wants me to just use my cameras for everything I need, but they haven't yet built a camera that can cry, and that's all I want to do right now.

I'm sick of being trapped in this suit. Sick of the recycled air being pumped into my helmet, sick of the way my footsteps don't make a sound, save for the creak of my feet inside the boots. I'm tired of these empty halls, the cold, hollow husk of my birthship. It doesn't feel like it's gone, but the vacuum is a constant reminder.

We've lost ships, historically. Most recently the *Kronos* to the

Fractionists, but before that, there were others. More, in the early days of the Fleet, before we figured out how to preserve our vessels over hundreds of years of flight. But when the *Kronos* was destroyed, it was so fast. The FTL drives burned and warped the ship, and then it just wasn't there anymore.

The *Reliant* is still here, and that's the worst part. It feels like it should be fixable. Like maybe there's a way to go back to how things were. But it's beyond repair, according to every assessment that flickers through the exosystem. The Fractionists knew what they were doing when they blew out the hull in all the critical areas. They hit the auxiliary supplies. They ensured there would be no backup to restore the ship's atmosphere once it was gone, and no point in doing it with the hull so badly damaged. They must have studied the ship for so long with that one purpose in mind, and the thought of it adds to the churn of my stomach.

The *Reliant* will continue to drift with the Fleet for as long as we keep our current course. On our next adjustment, we'll leave it behind.

We reunite physically with Praava and Wooj in a rescue transport on the intership deck. They sit side by side, their heads hung, in the part of the passenger bay designated for Scela. The tragedy has overtaken everyone's priorities, and thankfully no one has questioned our presence on the *Reliant*—they're just relieved to have help. The rest of the ship is stuffed with humans. So many living. No dead. Relief pulses through me.

It seems like there isn't any room left, but more appears when the dyeworks children arrive. There are a few shrieks of delight, and I have to force myself to turn away from the sight of families coming back together. Even with my exo suppressing my physical responses, the phantom sensation of bile creeps up my throat.

Steady, Key pushes into my exo. Not in a cruel way, but as a reassurance. Part of me wants to warn her not to go soft. We need her sharpness, her brutality, that *purpose* that carried us through the void jump. But I can't deny that *I* need softness, even if it's from the most surprising person in the squad. I let her know that I appreciate it.

That's everyone, Praava says once the last red-handed child leaps through the airlock. A countdown starts in our exos as the shuttle makes ready to depart. Three other ships on the intership deck are making similar preparations. Out the window, I watch the other Scela deployed to rescue the *Reliant* board their ships. We're the only ones on this transport.

The shuttle maneuvers into its launch tube. As the engines behind us spin up to a teeth-rattling rumble, we strap into our harnesses. My stomach turns, but after leaping clear across the Fleet, a shuttle ride is nothing.

Then the screens in the shuttle start to glow. Confused murmurs run through the passengers, but our exos already know exactly what's happening. A Fleet-wide cast blasts into our system. Only this time instead of the Chancellor addressing the Fleet for Launch Day, it's my aunt's face flashing in front of us, popping up on every screen. For a moment my rage swells so much that I have to fight back the urge to smash every cast device in this shuttle, my own exo included.

Yasmin looks shaken. To all the humans, it seems like she's devastated, but the four of us pick up on something more in her expression. She wasn't expecting this. The early breach must have been a mistake. She didn't mean to kill so many.

And yet she did. I watch carefully as my aunt decides exactly what she's going to do about it.

Yasmin lifts her sorrowful eyes to the camera and starts to speak. "Citizens of the Fleet. Just three weeks ago, a horrible tragedy rocked our formation. Portions of our proud Fourth District starship *Aeschylus* vented, and hundreds of lives were lost. The General Body would have you believe that the Fractionist movement, which was organizing on the ship at the time, was responsible for this event. The General Body is lying to you. They breached the ship with the express purpose of disabling our movement. They didn't care that it would cost innocent lives. Those lives, to them, are just the cost of maintaining control."

My fists winch painfully tight, skin pulling so taut against my metal that my exo warns me I might tear it. She's not apologizing. She won't admit what she did. She's plowing full speed into the plan she laid out, despite the way it's already gone wrong.

"The General Body knew our movement was weak, and that we would be struggling to piece ourselves together in the wake of the tragedy. They discovered that a concentration of our leadership was meeting aboard the starship *Reliant*, Seventh District."

Across the bay, the humans are still as statues, still as the void. As the shuttle slips out of the *Reliant*'s gravity field and into weightlessness, their unblinking eyes remain fixed on the screens. Images of the *Reliant*, of the vent, of the four of us running through the streets flicker, cut with the rough strokes of an editor on a tight deadline. Over them, my aunt's low, furious voice continues to narrate.

"Blaming the Fractionist movement for the breach of the *Aeschylus* worked once. I suppose the Fleet's leadership felt that a more devastating action would work again, even more powerfully than the first time. They sent a team of Scela in a fly-by-night mission to place charges along the *Reliant*'s hull and vent the entire ship.

As part of their treachery, they went as far as to have the Scela alert some of the citizens in an effort to appear like they weren't behind it."

The humans start to murmur. Eyes flick in our direction. The four of us stay frozen, drifting aimlessly in our harnesses. The instinct for self-preservation is overwhelming—all our exos want us to leap out the airlock. But we have to hear the rest of Yasmin's broadcast. We have to find out what she's doing next.

"Fortunately, our informants alerted the leadership to the venting. It broke our hearts to flee, but . . ." Yasmin delivers a dramatic sigh that almost convinces my exo that she's telling the truth. "We knew if we seemed to have knowledge of the hull breach, it would be easier for the General Body to pin it on us again. Those who escaped before the ship venting share in my grief over the lives—the *families* we have lost."

You murdered them, I rage, bones creaking against my metal as my artificial muscles strain with fury. *You killed them all—you killed Malikah, and now you're building a lie to incite people against the General Body on the backs of dead children.*

And it's working. The narrative is set. The trap is laid. All Yasmin has to do now is announce her next course, and the people on this shuttle will be behind her.

She nods slightly, pulling her composure together before her pause gets overlong—likely aware that her engineers are fighting to maintain their hold on the cast before the General Body wrests it back—then stares into the camera. Her brows lower in determination. "The reason the General Body was so desperate to shut us down is this—they have been lying to you a hundred times over. They maintain the illusion that humanity must still wander the stars, not because we haven't found a livable world, but because it allows them to keep their absolute power over our entire people. The truth they've been hiding, the truth we only just confirmed tonight, is that a livable world is out there, disguised as an Alpha world in their records. The Fractionist movement has obtained the coordinates to this planet. But we can't take the Fleet there alone. We need everyone, every district to support us, to rise up against the authority that seeks to bend humanity to its will. We'll take this information to the starship *Pantheon,* to the governance of the Fleet itself, and we'll put humanity on a course to its destined home. All we ask is that you stand with us, so that a tragedy like the *Reliant* never has to happen again."

The screens cut to black as the cast ends. Our heads fill with a swarm of confused thoughts. Yasmin and the Fractionists are headed for the *Pantheon.* The small ships within the Fleet can move independently, but the starships' Fleet direction is set by a control room in the General Body seat. If Yasmin gets hold of those controls, she can use the data jack we gave her to point every ship at Alpha 37. We can put humanity on track for the planet we were always promised.

But we'd be doing it with Yasmin at the helm. Yasmin, who's positioned herself as the Fleet's savior in the wake of a tragedy of her own making. She's no more fit to govern than the General Body that did the same to the *Aeschylus.*

Today I lost half of what I'm living for. I gave up my body to save Amar and Malikah, and it didn't matter for my sister. The universe isn't just. God's grace can strengthen me, but it isn't enough to pray to Her, to put it in Her hands and hope for the best. Balances don't work out because we hope we've paid our dues—that's why we have to *act.*

Next to me, things are lining up in Key. She has her head

bowed, her focus entirely on the holes in her and what she can do about them. Her conclusions are the same. If the Fleet's going to Alpha 37, it sure as hell won't be doing it under Yasmin. Key's done with being a figurehead, a prop, a tool in someone else's hands. She's going to be a revolutionary.

You're with me? Key asks.

You're in my head. You already know, I reply, and both of us bare our teeth, Scela-wide.

Murmurs from the other end of the ship shift in tone. Our exos snap our cameras around, narrowing our focus onto the humans. They're restless, wary, their eyes on us. Of course they are. Yasmin made sure to pit them against us, made sure they think that we're to blame. But they don't know that we're the four Scela who were on the ship before any others.

Not until one of the dyeworks kids points a little red finger at me and whispers something in her mother's ear.

Wooj's panic is the first to hit the system. He fears if something goes wrong, he won't be able to control his exo. He might cause even more irreparable damage. He shrinks back against the ship's hullmetal, folding his arms against himself.

My audio flares, trying to pick up the whispers and accusations that pass between the humans. A burst of horrified amusement comes from Praava as she counts just how many of them there are. All these people we saved. All of them starting to turn on us.

Key's mind whirls with calculations. Her cameras flick to the windows, to the sight of the *Reliant*'s husk growing smaller in the shuttle's wake. Then to the airlock doors.

Oh, don't you dare. Don't you even dare, I think, turning my head to face the crowd. They're just humans. We're Scela. What could they possibly do to us?

The snap of a couple stunsticks firing up answers that.

The four of us are out of our harnesses in a blink. Praava and I pull up our combat protocols, setting our bodies into defensive stances, but before we can even raise our fists, Key's made her decision. *Airlock, now!* she blasts into our heads, her will blazing down our spines, nearly as hullmetal as the marshal's.

Wooj jams the button and the four of us fling ourselves into the compressed space. The airlock snaps shut just as two humans throw themselves against the doors. They strike with a muted thud, then drift back, their stunsticks held aloft and terror sparking through their eyes. Key's fingers fly over the controls, and I know exactly what's running through the humans' heads.

They think we vented the *Reliant*. And now, with the airlock controls in our grasp and our breach suits protecting us, we're going to vent this shuttle too. I shake my head, wave my hands—as if that's going to tell them anything. Alerts wail through the airlock as Key brings up the protocol to open the spaceward doors.

I press my hand against hullmetal and pray for peace in the hearts of the kids inside who, for the second time tonight, think they're about to die.

Key pops the airlock open, and the void rushes in. The magnets in our breach suits instinctively go live as the four of us vault out into the vacuum. There's a moment of breathless flailing before the magnetism catches, but then we land securely on the shuttle's hull.

Our relief doesn't last long. The pilots have gotten wise, and a moment later, the shuttle lurches, our grips straining as the force of the twist tosses us outward.

Try to snag a Seventh District ship. Regroup when we're all secure, Key thinks. We withdraw into our own bodies—my exo walls away the system, demanding my focus. I let the warming sensation of the machine taking over roll through me as my muscles align and my targeting picks a hull.

Just as the shuttle lurches again, I launch myself out into the void's cradle.

CHAPTER 28

KEY

Fuck.

I miscalculated. The last-minute roll of the shuttle threw off my trajectory, and now I'm sailing through space without a target. I pull up my harpoon and twist it into a spin, my cameras searching for something to latch on to. My momentum has me flying through a gap between the Seventh District starships, but if I can toss my line just right, I might be able to catch one of them.

The exo triangulates distances, my HUD whirling with the math of it. One ship is farther away but easier to hit. The other is a larger risk but a closer target. My exo can't pick for me.

I choose the closer ship.

I choose wrong. My harpoon shoots several meters wide. I yank desperately, trying to get it back in my hands before it's too late, but my exo forces me to face the truth. I don't have enough time to spin it up and throw it again. Horror sinks in the pit of my stomach as I sail clear of the Seventh District tier. Only the *Panacea* and the distant stars lie ahead of me. Only the inevitable.

Which is what my exo is trying to keep me from comprehending when a weight slams into my back. A Scela-strong arm wraps around my midsection as we jerk forward, hurtling even faster toward the stars. Then there's a jolt that does its best to crush the air out of me as behind us, a harpoon line snaps taut.

Gotcha, Aisha thinks.

Though it violates every instinct in me, I go limp with relief. Aisha's hold is tight and sure, and with a jerk of her wrist, we go sailing back toward the ship hull her harpoon is anchored on.

Thank you. Thank you. Thank you. I think it over and over, but it will never be enough. I have no idea how she reacted so fast—she must have made her next jump and thrown her harpoon the instant she landed.

She seems a little stunned too. When her feet magnetize and lock on to hullmetal, I feel it hit her in a rush—first the sheer, overwhelming thought of what she just did, and then the *why,* the reason she threw herself into the void without a second thought. Usually it takes family to get that kind of knee-jerk sacrifice out of her. She's a little stunned to find that Key Tanaka can do it too. But Aisha Un-Haad has lost enough today. Of course she'd do anything just to make sure she didn't lose more. As I get my footing next to her, I clap one hand on her shoulder, both for stability and because it's the only other way I can think of to show her how grateful I am.

That is, until Aisha lunges and wraps me in a hug that would crush a human. *Don't you dare leave me,* the entire system sings.

You're gonna rip my breach suit, I groan, but I hug her back anyway. The holes in me barely matter in the face of how this feels. Even if caring about shit fucks us over in the end, I'm starting to think it's worth it.

But it can't last forever—not with the Fractionist revolt stirring and the data we delivered bound for the *Pantheon.* We pull back simultaneously, our thoughts in parallel agreement. It's time to get to work.

Aisha and I regroup with Woojin and Praava on the hull of a Sixth District ship. Both of them are holding back their amusement, along with a healthy dose of embarrassment because they did basically the same thing when they were reunited. Our exosystem prickles with unease. Broadcasts are flying across the Fleet as more and more people respond to Yasmin's call to arms. The *Dread* is already mobilizing, every Scela deployed as hotspots of chaos flare up.

We resist the urging of our exos to go charging where we're needed most. The orders in our skulls aren't aware of where we're needed most. We're the only ones who've seen Yasmin's true treachery. We're the only ones who can stop it. This time, no order is going to be enough to override our will.

So we leap into the void, flying between the districts like we've been doing it our entire lives. The terror of our first jumps is long gone, overwritten by urgency that leaves no room for doubt. Even Woojin has his movements under control, and by the time we hit Third District, I've stopped worrying every time he drifts close to me.

It's exhilarating. I feel like this is what I was born to do, or better yet, what I was made for. True purpose courses through my blood, purpose that's *mine* and mine alone. No more Fractionists pulling my strings. No more General Body hacking loyalty into my head. I didn't choose any of the things that happened to me, but I'm choosing what's happening now, and it's making me come alive.

My enhancements weave fluidly through my muscles with every push and pull. I almost forget that I have eyes when my HUD flares with input from my cameras. It sinks into my bones all at once how *incredible* my Scela body is. There's no tragedy in losing the Archangel or losing my humanity when I can leap between starships in a single bound.

When we hit the Second District tier, I spot the distant, shining curve of the *Pantheon*'s hull. The Fleet's head is almost a district to itself, positioned in front of the rest of the ships that make up First District. It's our guiding light, our beacon, the Fleet embodied.

I launch myself at it, borrowing a little from Aisha's quiet rage.

I've made mistakes today. Done things ranging from stupid to downright malicious to cowardly. If I make it through this, a day won't go by in my life where I don't regret the actions I took in the past hours. But I'll never make those mistakes again—or at least, I'll try my hardest not to.

I thought I could be the Archangel. I thought I could do what was expected of me, what everyone wanted to fill those missing pieces. But the Archangel was just a prop in Fractionist hands. I don't think they ever really saw her as a person. She was a tool they used to get what they wanted, a pretty face who could speak well and throw money at their cause. She was an empty thing long before the General Body got its hands on her mind.

I'm not the Archangel, and I never will be.

Not with this body that's been forced on me, not with what I've been through in the time since the metal was woven into my flesh. I've been focusing so much on the holes in me, trying to make myself fit the past that I lost. But they're just holes. The rest of me is enough. And it's time for Key Tanaka, the Scela, from the starship *Dread*, First District, to move past what she was and what people made her. Time for her to become what she *is*.

I crush into the hull of the *Pantheon* with a now-familiar *whump*, all my bones creaking as the remnants of my human biology squeal in complaint. Three similar experiences press into the edge of my consciousness as Aisha, Praava, and Woojin land behind me. I tilt my head back for a moment, my cameras zeroing in on the *Dread*'s hull farther along the First District tier. The intership decks swarm with activity as the *Dread* belches its shuttles into the void. They stream for different parts of the Fleet, weaving through the hulls. With no sound in the vacuum, the activity seems even more distant, even more insignificant. But the entire Scela force is mobilizing. The Fleet is falling into anarchy.

I find myself hoping that Zaire's all right. Praava and Woojin let out quiet bursts of amusement, but Aisha crouches against the *Pantheon,* presses one slightly magnetized hand against the hullmetal, and prays for him. I don't share her religion—I don't really share any religion—but for the first time I appreciate the sincerity of the sentiment pouring out of her. The little nudge of her genuine will is better than anything her God could give me. I push my gratitude into her, and feel her smile the other, rarer sort of Scela smile, soft and barely there.

When we jumped for the *Reliant,* we had prepared. Marshal Jesuit gave us a specific airlock to target, chosen from Lopez's intel. With the *Pantheon,* we're flying blind. None of us has been aboard. We have no sense of the ship's layout, and it takes several minutes of the four of us crawling across the ship's hull in different directions to find an access point. Praava's the one who discovers it on the underside of the ship's anterior. The rest of us rush across the hull to meet her, avoiding windows just in case. We don't want anyone on the interior to see Scela skulking along the hull and panic.

We pop the exterior door with no resistance from the ship, pack into the tiny space—which was meant more for one human and less for four jacked-up Scela—and a moment later we're greeted by the blissful, gentle return of sound as air hisses in through the interior door. Once the chamber is equalized, the door slides open, and we spill into a service corridor in a bulky heap.

I push off Woojin and stagger to my feet. Even though the void jumping was starting to feel more natural, the return to a ship's gravity feels about the same as it did the first time. Even Aisha, who's burning to go after her aunt, has to take a moment and sag against the corridor wall, focusing only on her heartbeat until it's slowed to a reasonable rate.

But once she's set, she takes off, dragging the rest of us behind her.

We keep to the service corridors and the access tunnels like the ones that played host to the Fractionist gathering within the *Reliant*'s walls. The longer the ship goes without knowing we're here, the better. The *Pantheon*'s eerily quiet, the smooth hum of its mechanics barely noticeable, and every noise we make feels blasphemous.

Our instinct for ship design agrees that the bridge, where the Fleet direction is set, is somewhere on the upper levels of the ship's fore. Praava swears that she saw a cast about it once, and when she spots something familiar, Aisha picks up the trail. We climb up a narrow ladder—one at a time, because it was clearly designed for human weight—and spill out onto a causeway that runs along the highest deck of the ship. The whole structure rattles in a worrisome way with every step we take, and I spider my hands from support to support just in case.

Up ahead, Woojin thinks, his cameras zooming. *Service door. Probably leads right to the bridge.* Of all of us, he's the one with the most experience sneaking around the inner walls of starships, so we trust his word.

The door is locked, and the ship's management software doesn't budge when we try to force it open. But hullmetal has nothing on four Scela on a mission. We rip it from its mounts in a matter of seconds and charge through.

We're greeted by the crack of stunsticks firing up throughout the bridge as dozens of Fractionist eyes turn on us. My HUD doesn't have time to parse the situation—all I see are targets. Sixteen targets, all armed, all running straight at us.

Time to put those combat protocols to use.

My exo is thrilled. For once our intentions line up with the orders that have been pouring into it. We've dived into the heart of the Fractionist threat, and the machine on my back is desperate to eliminate it.

My consciousness twines with the others, myself forgotten. We're a single unit, meeting our attackers head on. I give my muscles over to the system and let it do the rest for me, my body moving instinctively into a dance my human remnants could never follow. Somehow there's a stunstick in my hand. Somehow there's a man on the ground who used to be holding it. Our system knows its weaknesses—Praava sweeps around Woojin, making sure that no one lays a blow on our weak link, who's managed to grab a pair of stunsticks for himself.

Our attackers fall back, scrambling over the rows of control panels as they group with their fellows against the massive windows that show the distant stars. Several humans remain sitting at computer stations. These must be the workers who guide the Fleet—not Fractionists, just people who were here doing their jobs when the revolt took over.

As the combat protocols wash out of our system, I take in the rest of the room. The cluster of Fractionists has one notable exception in their number. The elegant Chancellor Vel is in the middle of their knot, her arms wrenched behind her back by the people holding her. Of course—to set Fleet direction, they need the Chancellor's approval, the Chancellor's biometric.

My focus locks on her, but beside me, Aisha only has eyes for the woman at her right. Yasmin's eyes bulge when she realizes exactly which Scela have just burst in on her coup.

Then Aisha lunges, her rage paralyzing the exosystem.

CHAPTER 29

AISHA

She's nothing in my hands. She's a flimsy rag doll. A dyeworks child in a vacuum. Yasmin struggles and scrabbles to get away from me, but she'd have to break bone to get loose. She doesn't have that kind of strength in her, much less that sort of self-sacrifice, and for a moment I just let her flounder, squirming uselessly.

I tighten my grip, and she lets out a low groan. The Fractionists back away, dragging the Chancellor with them. None of them look like they're about to try anything, but I keep my stunstick on and charged just in case.

"Aisha, please—" Yasmin begs.

It only takes a flick of my wrist to shatter hers.

Yasmin screams, and I let her go. She collapses back against one of the control panels, cradling her arm to her chest as tears form in her eyes. Something horrible and human rises up in me at the sight of them. Envy. I'm jealous that she can weep when that's been stolen from me.

"You killed Malikah," I snarl. I snap back my headpiece so she can look me in the eyes, so she can see every wicked thought written across my face.

"It was an accident, Aisha. A trigger misfired, and the charges blew early. I never meant to—"

"But you *did*."

"For all humanity, for the good of the Fleet—"

"I don't give a damn about the good of the Fleet," I thunder, and I swear the windows rattle from the force of my voice. "My sister is dead. I have only two family members left in this forsaken universe—one who's wasting away on that plague ship and one who's sniveling in front of me, trying to justify mass murder. All I ever wanted to do was keep my siblings safe, and turns out the person I should have protected them from was *you*."

A hint of nervousness curls into the exosystem. The other three are trying to decide if they should stop me. Wondering if they *can*.

"It's bigger than that, Aisha," Yasmin says.

"No. It isn't," I snap back. I don't care about the Fractionists, the General Body, the habitable world within our grasp. I barely care about the injustices of the districting system that drove Yasmin to the Fractionists in the first place. Those things have never mattered as much to me as family. I'm not a savior of the human race, a person with a say in this fight. I'm just an older sister, giving up everything I have for my siblings.

And it wasn't enough.

My rage builds like an avalanche on an Old Earth cast. The exo encourages it. It wants my power unleashed, my revenge to be total. It wants me to rip and destroy, to crush, to take everything from the woman who's taken almost everything from me. She can't keep getting away with this. The exo wants me to tear her in half, and I want it too. I want it so badly that my whole body, metal and flesh, sings with the thought of slaughtering Yasmin.

She can't keep getting away with it.

This isn't justice, Key whispers in the back of my mind. I can feel her intention pulling against me, humming weakly at my neck. She knows she can't stop me by force. My will's hardened to hull-metal, and my squadmates are frozen in my thrall. She can only ask. Plead. Beg.

I take a step forward.

You're better than this. Better than her.

I lift my arms, my hands curling into fists.

Look at where we are.

That actually does stop me, mostly because I have to process what she means. My cameras whirl, taking in the bridge of the *Pantheon,* the point of control of our entire Fleet. I breathe in, absorbing the way the power rests in the room. It's not in the hands of the Chancellor, who's still straining against the Fractionists holding her. It's not in the hands of Yasmin, who can barely use one of hers, nor any of her fellow revolutionaries. And it's not in the hands of the workers crouching underneath their control panels.

No, the power in the room rests firmly in the hands of us. The Scela. The enhanced warriors meant to be living weapons—tools to be wielded, not independent beings in their own right. The four of us, here on the bridge of the *Pantheon,* are the most powerful people in the entire Fleet. No one in all humanity stands above us at this moment.

I look down at Yasmin. She's bowed her head, like she's accepted what I'm about to do. Like she knows she deserves it.

But if this is how I wield power when there's nothing that can stop me, I don't deserve any of the strength coursing through my enhanced muscles. I don't deserve this body that I sacrificed myself for.

I take a step back, and Key's relief nearly knocks me over.

Yasmin glances up when she hears my footfall. "Aisha, I swear—"

I hold up a fist and she falls silent. "This Fleet will go to Alpha 37. To the world we've been promised. But we will *never* do it with you at our helm." I spin to face the Fractionists cowering against the windows with the Chancellor in their midst. "A group that would vent a ship for the sake of the people's sympathy has no place leading humanity."

Behind me, Yasmin's staggered to her feet, clutching her broken wrist. Her skin is ashen, her eyelids heavy. She looks utterly defeated, and satisfaction prickles through me.

"Your rebellion is over," I snarl. "Release the Chancellor."

They follow the order like I broadcast it right into their heads. Chancellor Vel staggers forward as the Fractionists around her hold up their hands. She draws herself up, setting her shoulders as she shakes her robe out. For a moment, I worry we're about to be overtaken again, but the eerie buzz of Vel's hanging orders is nowhere to be felt. Now that I have a moment to think, I realize that the rebels must have dragged her out of bed to get her in the bridge at this hour—she must not have her cuff. "Well done, Aisha," she says, giving me a curt nod.

I let my muscles relax, lowering the stunstick.

"Now, if you four would be so kind." Chancellor Vel wears a wicked, human look. "Kill them all."

Our exosystem goes live with rejection, all four of us balking at the words. The Fractionists in the room let out gasps, some of them sliding farther along the wall in an effort to put more distance between them and us. Footsteps approach behind me as Key, Praava, and Wooj flock to my side. There's an agreement flowing in the space between our minds. We won't follow the Chancellor's order. And she can't force us.

As one, our fingers open, and our stunsticks clatter to the ground.

Chancellor Vel's wrist twitches. I spot the bangle under the sleeve of her robe, and fear curdles through me. *Was it just not active? Why hasn't she used it, if she's had it this whole time?* My body locks up, bracing for the burn, as if tension in every single one of my muscles will keep me from doing her bidding.

But the sensation doesn't come. My body remains my own. I nudge into the other three's exos, and I'm met with the same confusion. We're all disobeying the Chancellor. And yet she hasn't used her trump, her bangle, the thing that will force us into obeying her every wish. We can't even feel it.

She must read our confusion, even behind the breach suit masks and headpieces that hide our faces. Chancellor Vel lifts her arm, exposing the bangle. "I'll have to have a word with Isaac and his technicians about the makeup of the blockers they wrote into your heads."

In our system, puzzle pieces snap into place. Why our treasonous, order-defying trip to the *Reliant* was possible in the first place. Why we haven't been compelled to follow the orders broadcast for all the Scela forces tonight. They installed blockers in our heads to keep us isolated from everyone except the marshal.

The side effect being that we're also blocked from receiving orders from the Chancellor herself.

Before the relief can settle, the Chancellor opens her mouth again. "Strange—nothing's working right tonight. Scela should have been deployed to the *Pantheon* the moment the Fractionists announced their intent. For some reason, none of them seem to have made it off the *Dread*."

Some reason, I strongly suspect, that has to do with "malfunctioning" launch tubes and a crafty man in the Master Control Room.

"But if you continue this pointless defiance, I have other Scela at my command. Ones who could be headed to the *Orpheus*."

Wooj stiffens.

"To the *Lancelot*."

Sheer, numbing fear pours out of Praava.

"To the *Panacea*."

I should rip out her throat. Right here, right now. Key's hand comes down on my shoulder, grounding me.

"What happened to your loyalty?" Chancellor Vel asks, her eyes narrowing. "You promised me that, didn't you?" Key goes stiff as the Chancellor's gaze fixes on her. "I had such high hopes for you especially, Key Tanaka. We went through such trouble to have you on our side, you know."

"I know," she growls, squaring her shoulders.

Across the room, some of the Fractionists start to relax as they realize their lives are no longer in danger. They have us to stand between them and the Chancellor, the strength of four Scela as their shield.

But Chancellor Vel lifts her chin. She won't let go easily. "These people are *mass murderers*. They've forfeited their right to live by violating the safety and stability of the Fleet—the safety *we've* fought so hard to maintain. You came to stop the rebellion, and yet you won't see this through? You freed me, you seek to restore order, and yet you won't do what's necessary?"

"We came to stop the rebellion," Praava says, pulling her words from all our thoughts. "But a woman who chooses to vent an innocent ship has no place leading the human race. And that goes for you too."

Chancellor Vel scoffs. "Don't tell me you believe that nonsense propaganda cast."

"I was *there*," Praava thunders. "I felt the air rush out of my birthship, and through my squad's eyes, I watched as people died." Her end of the exosystem is charged with her own purpose—purely hers, no longer reliant on her sister's genius. "And we saw the First District camera crews picking through the wreckage, suited up and prepared. It wasn't the Fractionists who vented my home, and no one else in this room believes that. Except for, well ..." She gestures vaguely over her shoulder at the technicians. "Maybe them. But the rest of you *know*."

Something about the Chancellor's posture is unsettling the exo. She should be cowering like the Fractionists and technicians, but instead she stands tall, unblinking. She can't control us directly, and we could snap her neck in an instant. Her fearlessness before was impressive. Now it seems stupid and unfounded. She should be quaking before us. Why isn't she?

"The *Aeschylus* vent was a necessary measure," the Chancellor admits. "You saw tonight the lengths to which Fractionists are willing to go to put people on their side. You'll notice that we only vented the necessary sector, the one the protest was centered on, whereas these monsters"—she points emphatically at Yasmin—"made sure to take out an entire starship."

"Being not quite as monstrous as them doesn't make you any less monstrous," Wooj mumbles. His legs are starting to weaken, and he leans slightly against Praava as the adrenaline fades from his body.

"But who would you rather have leading this Fleet?" the Chancellor counters. "Those who take necessary measures, or those who take excessive ones?"

We shouldn't have to make a choice like that, Key grumbles inside the exosystem, but she doesn't dare put that thought into words. Like me, she's stuck on the issue of the Chancellor's confidence. Wooj shares the sentiment. He's run enough cons to spot when someone has a card up their sleeve.

"It seems like reason won't work on you four," Chancellor Vel says, lifting that useless cuff again. "Fortunately, I don't need that."

Panic snaps through the exos as they realize her gambit. She was stalling. She isn't anymore. Something's changed. The Chancellor makes a beckoning motion, and the doors of the bridge fly open.

Lopez must have been keeping the other Scela from shipping to the *Pantheon.* But there's one he knows is working for his side. One he'd allow to fly out, thinking she'd help the Fractionists.

Marshal Jesuit steps through.

My autonomy dissolves as she reaches into our exosystem, my body locking in place. The buzz of an invasive will runs up my neck, but it's far too kind to be the Chancellor's. When we had the blockers installed, Marshal Jesuit became our conduit, the nexus through whom our orders were supposed to flow. The only way to get to us is through her. And the Chancellor, with her gauntlet, is doing just that.

The marshal doesn't want this. I feel her in our heads, whispering an apology over and over. *The Chancellor summoned me the instant she realized you were here. I tried to resist. I'm sorry. I'm so sorry.*

But no amount of "sorry" can make up for the fact that Chancellor Vel has her hands on the marshal's strings, and the marshal wields absolute control over us.

"Now, before we begin, I know I made some promises," the Chancellor says. "The others can be dealt with later, but one of them can be taken care of right away." She runs a hand over her cuff, and I will everything in me to rush forward and tackle her, rip the device away before we're forced into doing something we can never take back.

It's not enough. My will may be hullmetal, but the marshal has fifteen years in Scela metal, and she bends our minds like it's nothing. There's no escape.

The Chancellor flips a switch, and in the exosystem, I feel something *shift*. Something horrible and dreaded rips through all four of us, but my focus instantly sharpens on Key, on the holes inside her that suddenly aren't holes anymore.

Key Tanaka falls to her knees and screams.

CHAPTER 30
THE ARCHANGEL

I'm nothing but white-hot pain and the strange metal around me, the abomination woven into my flesh. Death would be better than this. Better than being this beast, this weapon, this tool in the hands of the people I devoted myself to fighting. Every twitch and movement of my enhanced muscles is a reminder of what they did—

What they did—

They beat me before they wrestled me into the chair. Said I was a worthless bitch, a waste of First District airspace. Then they ripped my clothes off, tied me down in that saddle, and lowered that *thing* onto my back as I screamed and pleaded.

My teeth shattered when the exo took hold of me.

They doped me up for the rest of it, but the agony was still there even if the sensation wasn't. I watched them peel back my muscles, run reinforcements along the lines of my skeleton, jam new ceramic molars in where the old ones had been. They wove their own strength into what was left of me, and then they sealed me back up.

The worst part came after, the part where they dragged my limp, surgery-weak body to a room with computers and jacks that burned like the surface of a star when they plugged them into the back of my neck. They pulled and tugged at my mind until I was full of holes.

It feels like moments ago. The moment I lost myself.

Now the holes are gone. Now I remember everything.

Now I want to die.

Human, human, human, my blood screams, twisting through a Scela body, looking for an escape.

There's a month and a half of a new person's experiences crowding my head—the Key Tanaka who started when I ended. I can't tell if I *am* her, if we can ever coexist. All I know is it *hurts.*

I'm vaguely aware of what's going on around me, of the situation I left behind when I became myself. Of the Scela bending down and picking up the stunsticks they dropped. Of the crackle of lethal levels of electricity—so familiar, but from another life, one *I* didn't fully live. Of my Fractionists running, hugging the walls of the bridge. Of the doors sliding shut.

The Chancellor doesn't seem to mind that I'm not following her orders. She's content to leave me crumpled on the ground, suffering under the weight of Scela metal. She doesn't need me for her plans—her only plan where I'm concerned is to make me pay for who I am and what I've done. To make me relive the hell I've earned over and over again.

The exo, the *thing* they've strapped to my back, writhes against me like it did at the moment of integration. I feel my spine bending, my neck stretching as the machine flexes against it. My muscles are shredding in its hands. *You are Scela,* it insists—like a voice in the back of my head, like the whisper of a General Body agent against my ear as I struggle in her headlock. It slams that lie into my head over and over.

But I'm not Scela. I'm a human being trapped in the metal they made me wear. I never consented to any of this, never believed in it, never dreamed that the General Body would go so far. I'm not Scela. I'm the Archangel, the girl who started screaming and fighting when they threw me in a shuttle and shipped me to the *Dread*.

I'm the girl who never stopped.

My rage is perfect. Pure. Overwhelming. And as I turn it on the exo at my back, glee like no other rushes through me. Because it recoils. It doesn't know what to make of me. It's built for brains that are already a little bit Scela to begin with. Brains that consent, that embrace the metal with purpose. It helps shape them into perfect hosts. It got used to me being one of those perfect hosts.

But consent under duress isn't consent at all. Even if I let the exo in when they strapped it to my back, I never chose this machine suckered onto my brainstem. They wiped the part of me that fought it.

Now she's back.

And the exo doesn't know what to make of the girl who's suddenly appeared in its grasp.

Pleas for mercy fill my ears, and I grapple with my control of the machine's cameras. The girl I was thirty seconds ago knew how to manage this body, but she was truly Scela, and I'm a human in Scela metal. Every extra second is a painful reminder of what they turned me into, but it's also not a second I can afford when my people are on the line.

Time to show them I'm not just a Fractionist mouthpiece. Time to show them I'm not just a General Body weapon. Time to show them I came to fight. The hum on my neck fades.

I drive one fist into the floor next to the stunstick I dropped. The metal warps where my knuckles strike, and a shattering crunch judders up my arm. Bracing against it, I pull my feet under myself and rise.

My vision's still swirling, disorienting me, but I manage to pick out the two women who aren't running. One is the Chancellor, whose concentration is fixed on the Scela she commands. The other is Yasmin, who's clutching her broken wrist and slumped against one of the control panels. Fury whites out my pain at the thought of what she's done for the Fractionist cause. She's every flaw I saw in the movement embodied. I never should have committed so much to the Fractionists with people like her calling the shots.

Yasmin must feel my stare, even with the headgear and cameras standing between my eyes and hers. Her gaze snaps to me, her eyes bulging wide. And maybe it's just my silly human brain making things up, but I think she can tell exactly who's looking back at her. Not the Scela girl with holes. The Archangel she knew. The herald of her cause.

I'm on unsteady legs, their length utterly foreign to me, but I think I can use my voice. The Scela machinery clamps down tight around me, but I manage to croak, "The cuff."

Yasmin's eyes widen. She hesitates. Of course she does—she's used to giving the orders. Letting other people do the dirty work.

I don't have time for that. I force my legs up, one foot in front of the other, teetering into a run. I point myself right at the Chancellor, my anger swatting back the exo as it tries to wrestle control away from me. If I can just get the device, I can stop all this.

But before I get there, the Chancellor turns and stops me. It takes just a flip of her wrist to bring me under her command, the uncomfortable hum settling back into my neck. In the strange, foreign system that weaves through my thoughts, I feel the Scela go still, then stagger back from what they're doing. One of them, Woojin, has the sense to throw the stunstick he's holding clear across the room.

But if Chancellor Vel cares that her extermination order got stopped in its tracks, she doesn't show it. Her sole focus is on me, on how I managed to get five feet away from her before she noticed I had my legs under me.

None of the Fractionists on the other end of the room are moving. They're trapped either way, no matter what happens next. I feel the horror of the Scela as they take in the bodies they've already felled.

"Impressive," Chancellor Vel breathes. "You're tough as hull-metal if you're standing after that."

Two more steps and I'd have been close enough. Two more steps and I could have crushed the manacle and her wrist along with it. I seethe. I burn. The longer she holds me still, the more the agony of this body etches itself into me. I think she sees what's happening. Her smile grows wider. She must know how much I want to die.

She also probably sees how much I'd love to take her with me.

The machine on my spine forces me to my knees again. My hands twist behind my back as it presses me down, tilts my head back, bares my throat. "Your rebellion is over," Vel says.

"Not while I'm still breathing," Yasmin hisses from behind her, and brings my discarded stunstick down.

The Chancellor drops, crumpling on the floor as her intention evaporates. The will holding me in place dissolves, and my limbs go limp. I slump, my cheek pressing into the cool floor just two feet from where Chancellor Vel's head rests. Across the bridge, I hear cries of relief and grief, as well as the approach of heavy footsteps.

I don't care. All I can focus on is the metal forced into my body, the machine on my back, and the way I'll never be free from any of it. My eyes burn, but no tears come. My mind wasn't made for this. I never *chose* this. I can't last in this mess of a body with my mess of a brain.

My gaze rolls, the cameras flashing confusingly. There has to be a stunstick somewhere within reach. Something I can turn on myself. Something that can make all this stop.

A shadow falls over me. *Not on your life,* Aisha Un-Haad says. She crouches at my side, winding her hands in my shoulder pieces and hauling me to my feet. I sway, but she props my body up against hers. *We'll set it right. She flipped a switch to take away your holes. There's got to be a switch we can flip to get them back.*

Her gaze roves from me to her aunt. Yasmin cowers, the stunstick in one hand, her other dangling at an uncanny angle at her side. "I didn't make it lethal. I didn't kill her," she stammers, pointing the stunstick's end at the Chancellor. As an afterthought, she lets the metal baton tumble from her fingers, laying her palm open for us to see. A moment later, she slams that same hand over her mouth as she bends over her stomach.

Now she gets nauseous. *Now* she grasps what it feels like to get your hands dirty.

Aisha shakes her head. She can't find it in her to be furious anymore—she's too exhausted. For now, her aunt's shattered wrist is enough to satiate that burning rage that eats away at her heart with each beat. There's no doubt in her mind that Yasmin will answer for her crimes in full. Just not with violence. Not with hurt. And not until we get the rest of this madness sorted out.

Her eyes flicker between her aunt and the Chancellor. One of them broken, the other a boneless heap on the floor. A bubble of mirth rises in her, the only logical reaction to seeing the woman who's ruled us for a decade, that fearless, powerful leader, the untouchable Chancellor Vel, unconscious and slack-jawed.

I turn back across the bridge to my people. The Fractionist cause that used me up and got me welded into this metal suit. Praava and Woojin crouch among them, consoling the living and attending to the people they felled. The rebellion's methods—or the methods they went along with—were horrific, but their cause was right. I know that in my bones. Humanity can't live under the General Body's rule. This confinement, this Fleet, isn't sustainable. We need room to spread, to flourish, to have our differences and work through them without resorting to destruction.

We need a planet. Not the promise of one and a future uncertain. We need dirt under our feet and a sky above our heads. A place to start building and growing, rather than somewhere to survive. I remember dreaming of it. The one thing a pampered life in First District could never give me. The thing a Fractionist victory might.

I want real air, real dirt, real sky. I want a world.

It won't bring me peace in this body. I don't know if anything ever could. But it makes it worth hanging on just a little bit longer if I can see this through to the end.

If I can take us home.

"Yasmin, the data jack," I groan. Aisha has to take a little more of my weight. I can't seem to focus on both the task at hand and keeping this monstrous body upright at the same time.

Yasmin holds up the little device with our entire future written into it. She doesn't have to ask what I want done with it—she passes it off to one of the technicians climbing out from under a desk, who takes it and plugs it into the machines. "We'll be needing the Chancellor's handprint and retinal scan to authorize," the technician says, glancing nervously up at us.

"Shouldn't be a problem," Marshal Jesuit replies. She crouches and picks up Vel's unconscious body. The Chancellor looks so small and fragile in her massive arms, and for a moment I'm filled with envy for the human body I'll never have again. The marshal carries her around to the instrumentation panel. A second later there's a chime, and a smooth voice announces, "Authorization confirmed. Fleet redirection in progress."

A distant rumble starts up as the ship's engines roar to life. It will take minutes to spin them up before the FTL drives can fire. Across the Fleet, alarms are blaring for citizens to prepare. Shuttles are landing. Families are bracing. Decks are shutting down.

A slight tug pushes at me as the ship starts to accelerate, and Aisha tightens her grip to keep me from toppling over. It barely seems worth it to keep me upright when my mind's control over my body is all but lost. My thoughts flick to Kellan, to the cell aboard the *Lancelot*. No one ever explained how I got caught in the first place, but there's a wisp of memory—rootless and strange, from the parts of me that weren't *me*—of him apologizing, and I think I know. There's not enough fight left in me to hate him for it. I was spineless, soft, First District, just like him. I probably would have done the same, for a chance to avoid the *Endymion*. All the same, I'm glad he can't see me like this. I hope he never does.

I'm not Scela. I never will be—not as long as my memories are whole and my humanity's intact. Complete with my history, I can never survive in this body. I can barely even move it, and every twitch of my muscles brings a fresh wave of pain. The only way out is forward. *Promise me,* I think, trying my best to point my words at the Scela girl holding me up. *Promise me you'll put me right again. Flip that switch, make me the Key who can handle this. Otherwise . . .*

I'll do it, Aisha says with a nod. *I've got you.*

Relief rushes through me, mitigating some of the pain. I push my thoughts toward the window, and Aisha understands what I want. She steers me around so we're both facing the stars. Even with the press of the ship's acceleration, the distant sparks of light don't seem to be getting any closer. The *Pantheon* starts a slow turn, pointing its nose toward our heading, and I know that behind us, the rest of the Fleet is orienting itself to match.

The acceleration doubles, then triples. The machine on my back shivers with excitement. I do my best to ignore it, leaning against Aisha. She grins, Scela-wide, and I share it.

We trip over the light-speed barrier, and the stars blur past us.

AISHA

One month after we land, my little brother takes his first steps on the planet's surface.

I crouch next to Amar in the hard-packed dirt, keeping one hand outstretched for him to hold as he totters on legs made unsteady both by illness and by the unfamiliar pull of the planet's gravity. His skin bears the scars of the disease, red lines etched where the purple tracks once ran down his face, but his body is on the mend. The nurses have reassured me several times over that he's beaten the wasting fever completely. Still, I keep my headpiece down and all my cameras fixed on him as he traces wobbly circles around me, pausing occasionally to kick a rock.

The wind tugs gently at the loose ends of my headscarf. It took some adjustments to make it lie comfortably under the headpiece, but those compromises were worth the comfort it gives me to properly mourn Malikah.

I let my eyes slide closed, sinking more comfortably onto my haunches. Moments like this have been few and far between in the tumult of the past weeks. The logistics of settling a new world don't allow for much downtime, no matter what your place in it is. The General Body's control dissolved when the Fleet did. With each starship uncoupled from the *Pantheon*'s direction and free to choose its own landing site, the human race has fractured from a nation among the stars to a scattering of loosely allied city-states on the ground. There's enough cooperation still that supply lines have been established for our most critical resources, and ships that once floundered as underappreciated, overstuffed manufacturing cores now have the room they need to expand, finding themselves the jewels of our new infrastructure.

Which, granted, has not been a widely accepted transition. Nothing about the new order of things goes down smoothly, and more often than not, we Scela find ourselves standing between arguing factions, hoping it doesn't get ugly.

So far, we haven't even agreed on a name for our new planet.

But maybe that's not such a bad thing. For every dispute, there's a resolution that makes us even stronger. Slowly but surely, we're piecing together what this new world is going to be. It would be stranger if it *weren't* a complicated thing.

"How tall are you now?" Amar asks, his focus still on putting one foot in front of the other. He sways a little, and I adjust my grip on his hand so he can brace against me.

"Taller than you'll ever be," I reply, and he scowls. It's actually a terrible thing to say—the illness will likely stunt his growth. In the exosystem, I feel the others start laughing at me. *Quiet,* I grumble.

Some Scela wanted to break from the system and live in their own heads. Others wanted to stay a part of the big group they'd grown used to having with them at all times. One of the easiest things for humanity to agree on so far has been this: no one should be able to control the Scela anymore. Our autonomous rights have been restored, and the choice lies in our hands. And our choice was to stick together.

I squint across the plain toward the massive bulk of the starship *Orpheus,* which has made its berth near the *Panacea.* At this distance, I can't see Wooj and Praava, but I can feel them through the exosystem—their sweat, their exhaustion, and a little of their resentment that I'm on a break and they're not. It's slow, grueling work, peeling back the hullmetal from the habitat domes, but as far as applications of Scela strength go, it's one of my favorites. We're coaxing the starships into bloom, letting starlight touch the cities for the first time in three hundred years.

Across the plain, Wooj tips a little salute my way. *Enjoy it while it lasts, Un-Haad,* he thinks, grinning.

I scoff. "Hey, Amar, you ready to go back in?"

"No!" my brother shouts, then pulls out of my grip and takes off across the rocky plain. His knobby legs somehow *fly,* and I start after him at an easy jog, my enhanced strides closing the distance between us in seconds. I scoop him up, my touch feather-light. He shrieks and flails in my grip as I toss him over my shoulder and turn toward the *Panacea.*

"Not today," I tell him, and one of my cameras picks up the edge of his pout. "When you're stronger. There's a whole world out there, and it's not going anywhere."

As I approach the medical ship, I summon a nurse and pass my little brother off. He's still being kept in his ward there until they're absolutely sure he's in the clear. At least today he hasn't asked when he has to go back to Yasmin, so I don't have to explain again that she's in a jail tank for a good long while. I'm still not entirely sure how I'll take care of him when he clears the ward, but I'll figure something out. As the nurse walks him up the ramp and through the massive door, they pass two humans and one Scela making their way down.

He's looking better, Key remarks when she reaches the end of the ramp. Her headpiece is cocked back, revealing the thick, spiky hair that's grown in around her exo. Isaac hangs slightly behind her, keying information into his datapad as his eyes follow Key's movements.

You are too, I tell her earnestly. The toll the Archangel took on her body was frightening. Her muscles essentially shredded themselves from the stress, and as soon as the memory blockers were reestablished in her head, Isaac swept her away for reconstruction. This time, they had to cut her open to stitch her back together, and her recovery's been slow. But today she walks out onto the plain with barely any stiffness in her limbs.

Mostly she's just showing off for Zaire, who trots alongside her. His hovering has been constant and his attempts to be casual about it have been the subject of numerous mental gossip sessions in the exosystem. But Key doesn't mind it—doesn't even discourage it.

They make a strange pair. He barely comes up to her chest when she's in her full rig, but she doesn't see him as anything but an equal. They're deep in conversation as they approach, but I block it out to give them their privacy, waiting for the moment I'm invited in.

"Hey, Aisha," Zaire finally says with a wave. "You guys really going for it today?"

"Depends on Key," I reply, baring my teeth.

"Oh, I'm ready." She rolls her shoulders, stretching the fabric of her jumpsuit. We decided on no full rigs. No metal to weigh us down or risk tearing Key's still-healing musculature.

This afternoon is the first time she'll see her parents after the night she was dragged from their apartment and turned into a weapon. They've been reluctant to meet with her ever since she started reaching out, no doubt filled with resentment over the dissolution of the General Body and their daughter's role in it, but they finally agreed to a reunion. She's scheduled to depart on a shuttle for the coastline where the *Antilles* has settled in just a few hours. There'll be hell to pay if Key has to miss it for an injury.

Her mind is abuzz with the thought of seeing them for the first time since her conversion, and the rest of us have spent the whole morning reassuring her with our own experiences. But first Key has to vent all the pent-up nervous energy out of her system, and there's nothing better for it than running the open plains around these landing sites. Already I can feel her muscles shuddering, ready to launch herself forward.

Isaac looks up sharply from his datapad. "Don't you dare undo all my hard work just for a little fun, Tanaka," he warns. "I'm getting tired of stitching you back together."

"If she collapses, I'll drag her back by her ankles," I promise.

Zaire rolls his eyes and offers an arm to the medic. "They can take care of themselves, Isaac," he says. Then he passes a wink over his shoulder and mouths *To be continued* at Key.

The humans head back up the ramp into the ship, leaving us on the dusty plain with nothing but the curdled embarrassment and delight running through Key's thoughts.

We set off at a jog through the settlement. I shorten my strides to make it easier on Key, and she pushes hers longer and longer until warnings ping through her body. We weave around the massive forms of the starships scattered across the plain, the first stages of humanity's rebirth. New structures have cropped up in their shadows, assembled out of star-baked bricks, and the routes between them are halfway to becoming roads.

It will be long and hard and complicated. It may take our entire lifetimes or more to figure out exactly how our civilization will manage. But after everything we've been through, I think we know one thing for certain between the four of us.

It's just a matter of time until we find our balance.

We round the last hull, and our cameras fill with nothing but open plain. A Scela-wide smile spreads over Key's face, and our systems slip into perfect alignment. We break into a sprint, tearing toward the horizon, with nothing but the stars above and the future ahead.

ACKNOWLEDGMENTS

This was a hard book for me. But the nice thing about that is it's so clear how much I owe to other people for the fact that you're sitting here reading it.

First of all, this book would not exist without Thao Le, my outstanding agent. Thank you, Thao, for putting this story on track, for sticking with it through thick and thin, and above all, for loving it before I'd learned how.

This book would also not exist without my massive privilege of being my parents' daughter. Thanks, Mom and Dad, for being patient with me in the long months after college when I did nothing but write this book and fail to get a job. Sorry it took so long for either of those tracks to pan out, but I'm forever grateful that I had you to support me before I took the leap. Sarah, study hard and don't be like me. Ivy, be good.

Thanks to my wonderful editor, Monica Jean, for asking all the right questions, and to the whole team at Delacorte—including Barbara Marcus, Beverly Horowitz, Colleen Fellingham, Tamar Schwartz, Natalia Dextre, Regina Flath, Stephanie Moss, Dominique Cimina, Elena Meuse, John Adamo, Kim Lauber, Kate Keating, Adrienne Waintraub, Lisa Nadel, and Kristin Schulz—for investing in my angry cyborg girls. Thank you, Larry Rostant, for the badasses on the cover. And an additional thank-you to Tiff Liao, whose notes were invaluable to this story's development.

Thanks to Tara Sim, for being there through all of it. To Jessica Cluess, who tells me I'm good, and to Traci Chee, who makes me better. To Cobbler Club—Gretchen Schreiber, Alexa Donne, and Alyssa Colman—for every needed vent session. To the Sweet Six-teens, #TeamThao rock stars, and all the other authors in my net-work who make this gig easy to love.

Thank you to the booksellers and bloggers, the reviewers and other cheerleaders who've supported my work through the years. I owe my career to their enthusiasm.

And of course, thanks to you, the reader, the one who's seen this story through. Thank you so much for picking it up. Sorry about the body horror.

ABOUT THE AUTHOR

EMILY SKRUTSKIE was born in Massachusetts, raised in Virginia, and forged in the mountains above Boulder, Colorado. She attended Cornell University and now lives and works in Los Angeles. Emily is the author of *Hullmetal Girls, The Abyss Surrounds Us,* and *The Edge of the Abyss.* To learn more about her and her books, go to skrutskie.com or follow @skrutskie on Twitter and Instagram.